"I've Never Lied to You!" Valerie Cried.

"No, certainly not. You simply neglected to tell me that you were married. What do you call that, if it isn't lying?"

"I don't know! I didn't mean to hurt you. I didn't expect it to happen." She moved away, her voice dropping. *"I'm aware that you hate me. And after the other night, I swore I'd never turn to you again. But I need help—badly, and for the record, I'm a widow."* She turned, her eyes wide and soft in the dim light. *"I'm sorry. What I did was wrong. Do you think we could call it even and start over?"*

Ashe gazed at her, and his eyes darkened with a passion he couldn't control.

The fabulous *Sky* series, begun in *The Golden Sky* and continued in *The Sapphire Sky* and *Summer Sky*, concludes with the story of Ashe Harlan and a love that blazes under *The Amber Sky*.

Dear Reader:

Silhouette has always tried to give you exactly what you want. When you asked for increased realism, deeper characterization and greater length, we brought you Silhouette Special Editions. When you asked for increased sensuality, we brought you Silhouette Desire. Now you ask for books with the length and depth of Special Editions, the sensuality of Desire, but with something else besides, something that no one else offers. Now we bring you SILHOUETTE INTIMATE MOMENTS, true romance novels, longer than the usual, with all the depth that length requires. More sensuous than the usual, with characters whose maturity matches that sensuality. Books with the ingredient no one else has tapped: excitement.

There is an electricity between two people in love that makes everything they do magic, larger than life—and this is what we bring you in SILHOUETTE INTIMATE MOMENTS. Look for them wherever you buy books.

These books are for the woman who wants more than she has ever had before. These books are for you. As always, we look forward to your comments and suggestions. You can write to me at the address below:

Karen Solem
Editor-in-Chief
Silhouette Books
P.O. Box 769
New York, N.Y. 10019

The Amber Sky

Kristin James

Silhouette Intimate Moments

Published by Silhouette Books New York

America's Publisher of Contemporary Romance

Other Silhouette Books by Kristin James

Dreams of Evening

 SILHOUETTE BOOKS, a Division of Simon & Schuster, Inc.
1230 Avenue of the Americas, New York, N.Y. 10020

Copyright © 1983 by Kristin James

Distributed by Pocket Books

ISBN: 0-671-46851-0

First Silhouette Books printing September, 1983

10 9 8 7 6 5 4 3 2 1

America's Publisher of Contemporary Romance

Printed in the U.S.A.

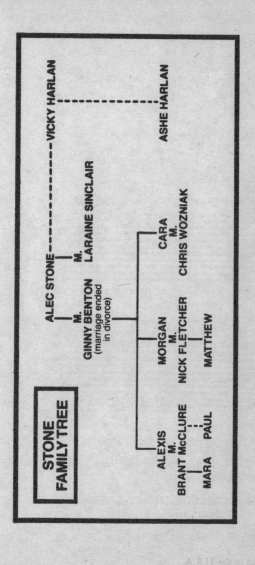

Chapter 1

VALERIE SAT BEFORE THE ORNATE MIRROR IN HER PLUSH Dallas hotel suite, brushing her hair. Funny, she thought, once she had paid little attention to her looks or her clothes, feeling so dimmed by her mother that she had believed herself past help. But over the years, through sheer boredom, makeup, hair and clothes had become an important ritual in her life. They were the only things a genteel woman of San Cristóbal could turn to, to occupy her time. Valerie couldn't begin to count the hours spent shopping for elegant clothes, testing perfume, or trying out eye shadows, lipsticks and rouges, always accompanied by a female relative or a well-bred friend, with her husky chauffeur-cum-bodyguard loitering behind, his eyes watchful and face determinedly blank. Such activities made the days pass and provided a change from reading, or watching the old American movies and television series annoyingly dubbed into Spanish for the San Cristóbal audience.

Three years of such activity and the tutelage of her husband Felipe, a man used to charm and elegance, had turned the gawky girl who had been the despair of her stunning mother into a woman of streamlined, sophisticated beauty. She had learned to create a lovely image, but to her it was all artifice and art, something she had learned to *do*, not something she *was*. In her mind she was still the teenager with flyaway, poorly cut hair, and clothes that overshadowed her delicate coloring and features.

Valerie subtly applied eye shadow, lipstick and rouge, and arranged her hair—so pale a blond that it was almost white—into a smooth coil at the nape of her neck. She was satisfied that the image was what she wished to convey: a woman older than twenty-four years, ladylike, elegant and assured. It was a role she had created both to please her husband and to sustain her faltering courage in a country which would always be foreign to her.

"Ah, my dear, how beautiful you look—as ever." Felipe de la Portilla stepped into the small dressing room. In a dove gray suit, with silver cuff links and tie tack set with discreet rubies, he was the picture of a Latin gentleman. His skin was dark, his eyes a warm, liquid brown, and his hair black as coal except for the wings of white at his temples. Forty-seven years old and twenty-three years Valerie's senior, he was still a figure who turned women's heads whenever he entered a room. Few noticed that he no longer took the stairs when there was an elevator available, and fewer still saw the bluish tinge to his fingernails. And since he had a lovely, much younger wife, it went largely unremarked that he had given up many of his former strenuous activities for quiet evenings at home.

Valerie smiled up at her husband, her eyes concerned. She was afraid that this trip was taxing him severely. When Felipe had first mentioned flying from San Cristóbal to Dallas to negotiate an oil lease with Stone Oil, Valerie had eagerly agreed to accompany him. Not only would it give her an opportunity to be in the United States again, but she could also visit her mother's cousin, Laraine, who was married to the president of Stone Oil, Alec Stone. Laraine had no children of her own and had always been close to Valerie. But now, even though Valerie had enjoyed seeing Laraine again, she wished they hadn't come.

High-level oil negotiations were too much of a strain on
Felipe. He looked tired. Valerie frowned. "Are you
leaving already?"

"Yes, it's almost time, and you know these Texans—
vulgarly addicted to punctuality."

Valerie grinned in response. "Now, now, Felipe,
don't talk about my relatives."

"Not relatives," he corrected teasingly. "In-laws.
That most dreaded word."

"Well, Alec Stone is as much my relative as my
cousin Laraine." Her eyes warmed as she thought of
her cousin's husband. Laraine had married Alec Stone
when Valerie was an adolescent. It was the second
marriage for both of them. During her teenage years,
Valerie often visited them in the summer, for her
mother, Pamela, had been eager to get rid of an
embarrassingly old daughter. Valerie had quickly developed a massive crush on the handsome, charming
Alec Stone. Although the crush had died with the
passage of years, she remained very fond of Alec.

"I know. There is a warmth between the two of
you . . . which I have not hesitated to exploit, in my
own quiet way."

"The day someone can exploit Alec Stone, I'd like to
be there to see it."

Felipe laughed, his dark eyes twinkling. "You're
right. He's a hard man, that one. But very appealing to
women, I think. No?"

"Yes."

"Well, enough of Alec Stone and business. Tell me,
what do you plan to do all day while I am involved in
my so-boring business talks?"

"Oh, maybe shop a little, visit Laraine—nothing
exciting."

"But the kind of thing you miss," he added perceptively.

"Yes," she admitted reluctantly, "the kind of thing I
miss."

He smiled down at her fondly, one hand stretching

out to touch her hair. "Poor Valerie, so far from home and family. Are you too unhappy?"

"No. I enjoy my life with you."

"Thank you. I suspect you are lying, little one, but I appreciate it." He kissed her lightly on top of her head. "Are you going to shop with one of the lovely Stone sisters?" He mentioned Alec's three daughters by his first marriage.

"No!" Valerie blurted out, and Felipe shot her a startled glance. Valerie sighed and explained, "I've never gotten along well with them. They didn't like Laraine. Besides, I feel so inadequate around them."

"Inadequate? But why?"

"Because they're intimidating, that's why. They're beautiful and competent and full of personality."

"Is there something wrong with that?" He smiled.

"No, of course not, but the combination makes me feel inferior."

"You are never inferior."

"Thank you. *You* are *always* courteous. But I still feel like Cinderella, before her fairy godmother showed up, around the Stones. I mean, Alexis is superintelligent—a lawyer, no less—while Morgan is so beautiful she'd put most models to shame, and Cara's warm, vivacious and sickeningly efficient."

Felipe chuckled and shook his head in mock despair. "Americans! I take it that you feel it isn't enough to be a lovely, kind, genteel lady with a wicked sense of humor and a smile that would brighten a night sky?"

"Is that supposed to be a description of me?" Valerie joked and made a move as if to look in the mirror to find such qualities.

"Goose. All right, then, if you won't go with one of the Stone girls—none of whom outshines you in the least—who will you take shopping?"

"Myself."

His brows drew together in a worried expression. "But, my dear . . ."

"Now, Felipe, don't go chauvinistic on me. This is

Dallas, Texas. I don't need a bodyguard to protect me or a chauffeur to drive me, and my reputation won't be ruined if I appear in public without either my husband or a *dueña*."

"All right, all right." He raised his hands in surrender. "I won't make a fuss, I promise. But are you sure you can handle a car in this traffic?"

"Positive. The one we should be worrying about is you." Valerie touched his cheek lightly with one hand, her eyes steady and beseeching. "Are you sure you're up to all this negotiating?"

"Of course. Didn't my doctor say I had several more years if I took care of myself properly?"

"Well, I don't think bargaining with Alec Stone over oil rights to your land is exactly taking care of yourself properly."

"Please! I've cut out cigarettes and sex, limited myself to one brandy each evening, and given up cholesterol entirely. I do not hurry or walk up stairs or worry. Am I to be denied even the pleasure of haggling?"

"You make me feel like a monster," Valerie teased, but worry lurked in her silver-green eyes. "Okay, I promise I won't bother you anymore about your work. Only, please, Felipe, you will be careful, won't you?"

"Of course. Aren't I always?" Again he gave her an affectionate peck on the forehead, then strode quickly through their luxurious suite, grabbing his briefcase as he went. The door to the hallway closed hollowly behind him, and Valerie sank into her chair. Chewing her underlip, she stared at the array of expensive beauty products spread out before her. But instead of the jars of creams and lotions, she saw the gray tone of Felipe's skin when they had returned to the hotel the day before and the way he had almost fallen onto the bed, letting her remove his shoes and jacket for him as he fell into a shallow sleep.

Felipe was sicker than he wanted her to believe,

probably more than he wanted to admit to himself. How serious was it? Two years ago she had discovered that he had a serious heart defect, but he would never reveal to her the full extent of the danger. She knew only that any strenuous exertion, either physical or emotional, could tax his weak heart past its strength. Valerie closed her eyes against the terrible image her thoughts summoned up. Felipe could not die, not now, not yet. He was too young, only forty-seven. That wasn't so very old, was it?

She sighed and leaned her forehead on her crossed arms. Oh, Felipe, she thought tearfully, what would I do without you? She loved him dearly, as he loved her, though their relationship had never been passionate. He had married her out of fondness, pity and a need for an American wife through whom to funnel de la Portilla family funds to safety in United States banks— a practice strictly forbidden by the military regime that ruled his country. Valerie, a shy, awkward girl of twenty-one, had been embittered by an engagement that had failed when she discovered that her fiancé was far more interested in Darryl Stanton's wealth than in Valerie Stanton's charms, and she had married Felipe on the rebound.

She was very fond of Felipe de la Portilla, whom she had known for several years as one of her mother's innumerable male friends. He had been at her home frequently through the years, and she had often run into him at this resort or that art gallery opening. He had always been kind to the ugly-duckling daughter trailing in the glamorous wake of Pamela Rutherby Stanton Ferrar McKenzie, lonely and eclipsed by her mother's charm and beauty. Felipe talked to her when they met instead of staring straight through her as so many of her mother's friends did. He was friendly and understanding, assuring her that he had often wished he had a daughter instead of only one son. Valerie did not idolize him as she did Alec Stone, but she liked and respected Felipe. Deeply hurt by her fiancé's deceit,

she had convinced herself that the gentle, steady feeling
she and Felipe shared was far better and more substantial than the excitement of romantic love. She was
happy to help Felipe by providing him with an American wife and even more happy to find a haven for her
wounded emotions.

After almost a year of infrequent and tepid sex,
Felipe had been forced by his weak heart to abandon
her bed. More than ever, he assumed the role of doting
father to Valerie, rather than husband. But the arrangement suited her. A father was something she had
always wanted desperately, since Darryl Stanton had
never attempted to fill that position. Felipe, with his
innate good taste and kindness, had subtly shaped her
style and taste and encouraged her to dress in clothes
and colors that suited her. With Felipe's encouragement Valerie had matured and blossomed during the
few years of their marriage. Although her ingrained
self-doubt still pricked at her, at least now she was able
to cover it with a cool mask of disinterest. She could
hold her own at a party instead of stammering through
nervous, disjointed conversations.

She was light-years ahead of what she had been and
she knew that she owed most of it to Felipe. Whenever
she thought of him, she was filled with gratitude and
gentle love. She worried about the ill health which
plagued him and which she could not combat—and
most of all she worried about the uneasy, restless
feelings she had been experiencing lately. She longed to
escape the stifling social atmosphere of San Cristóbal,
where women were treated in accordance with ancient
Spanish custom. She wanted to get away from the
constant fear and danger of living in a country continu-
ously on the edge of revolution. Whereas at first she
had been struck by the beauty of the graceful capital
city, La Luz, now she saw the dirt and poverty and was
disgusted. Once the de la Portilla banana plantation
and the sluggish Rio Miedo which flowed beside it had
appeared exotic, but now they seemed merely hot, slow

and mired in outmoded custom. Valerie wanted to be free.

And she wanted the full love that should exist between an adult man and woman. As she had gradually emerged from the cocoon of anger and pain caused by her failed engagement, she had realized that what she had with Felipe was only a pale imitation of what married love should be. She wanted more: love, passion, laughter, closeness, a melding of mind and spirit. She recognized her marriage as a refuge, not a partnership. But even the thought seemed disloyal to the man who had been much more of a father to her than her own.

Sighing, Valerie shook her head and rose. She had to stop thinking this way. She would never leave Felipe, who had been so good to her, and that meant she could not escape San Cristóbal. It was her home, just as the de la Portillas were her family—although neither welcomed her. Valerie strode to the closet and pulled out the light jacket that matched her trim pants suit. The jacket and trousers were a pale powder pink, and the severe blouse beneath it a coordinated hot pink. She glanced in the mirror to check her clothes and face, and was satisfied with what she saw. The tailored suit fit perfectly, neither clinging nor loose, and the coil of hair had not a wisp out of place. The only jewelry she wore was silver studs in her ears and the ornately carved silver antique wedding ring that had been Felipe's grandmother's, which was so different from the conventional gold band that few people recognized it for what it was.

She looked calm and mature, even remote. She fit the mold of a de la Portilla wife and Felipe was very proud of her, she knew. Valerie straightened her shoulders and forced a smile onto her face. After all, today at least she could be an American woman again. She could go where she pleased and do what she wanted. That idea changed her false smile into a reality, and she left the room in an almost jaunty mood.

Three hours later, exhausted, footsore and laden with purchases, Valerie turned the dark Mercedes sedan loaned to Felipe by Stone Oil in the direction of Alec Stone's palatial Highland Park home. The sunny spring afternoon was too warm for a jacket, and she shrugged hers off. At the first stop light she rolled up her long sleeves and unbuttoned the top button of her blouse. Glancing at her image in the rearview mirror, she grimaced. When she had tried on dresses in the stores, strands of hair had come loose and now straggled around her face. She'd have to redo it when she reached Laraine's house. Sometimes Valerie hated the trouble of wearing her long hair up, but Felipe preferred it that way. It made her appear older and more in keeping with the image he felt his wife should project.

The light changed and she stepped lightly on the accelerator. The powerful car surged forward. Valerie smiled. It was fun to drive again instead of having a chauffeur, just as it had been a lark to be alone in the vast shopping mall. For once she had escaped her restrictions. On an impulse she reached up with one hand and pulled loose the pins binding her hair. The long mane tumbled free in a shining cascade, and she ran her fingers through it, enjoying being released from the tight prison of hair pins. She turned into a side street and stopped to dig a brush out of her purse and run it through her hair. Felipe wasn't around to see, and neither was anyone he knew. It didn't matter if she looked more like his daughter than his wife, nor did it matter if she was thought improper or less than elegant. This was Dallas, and there were no spying old ladies to report her conduct to the de la Portillas, no brother-in-law or stepson to harangue her about the proper behavior of a lady.

Still smiling, Valerie started the car again and drove to the stately white Colonial mansion where Laraine lived. The front lawn of the Stone house was a vast sweep of green even this early in the spring, and yellow

jonquils bloomed brightly along the edge of the porch.
Valerie turned into the long, narrow driveway and
stopped beside the covered porte cochere. She noticed
a battered pickup truck parked farther down the driveway, directly in front of the detached garage. Its tires
were caked with mud, and the sides were liberally
splotched with the same substance. Various strange
tools poked up from the bed of the truck. The vehicle
was in startling contrast to the immaculate mansion and
grounds, and Valerie assumed that it belonged to the
gardener who kept the grounds. Valerie smiled to
herself, thinking how aghast Laraine must be at having
that heap parked beside her house.

Valerie stepped out of her car and walked around the
outer wall of the porte cochere toward the side door of
the house. A pale green Mercedes station wagon was
parked beneath the white brick carport, its hood raised,
and long, lean legs clad in faded denim were all that
could be seen of the man bending over the engine. The
legs shifted suddenly and a resounding thud sounded
beneath the hood, followed by a loud, short expletive
that Valerie hadn't heard in three years. She couldn't
stifle a giggle. It was even fun to hear a thoroughly
male, thoroughly American curse word!

Immediately the rest of the body swiveled out and up
and the man turned to face her accusingly. "What the
hell's so funny?" he demanded, hands on hips and pale
blue eyes blazing. He was tall and slim, with a lean,
youthful build that was powerfully muscled without
being heavy. His brown-blond hair was streaked with
bright gold, and his skin was darkly tanned, making the
pale blue of his eyes even more arresting. Squint lines
ran out from those eyes, marking him as a man who had
spent most of his life outdoors and making it impossible
to guess his age. His slender patrician nose was saved
from elegance by the small bump at the bridge, which
indicated a long-ago break. Above the jeans he wore an
equally faded flannel shirt of an indeterminate blue
plaid. Because of the sudden spring heat of the after-

noon, the shirt hung outside his jeans and was unbuttoned down the front. The cuffs were rolled up to his elbows, revealing corded brown arms. His hands were calloused and dirty, and grease marked both his shirt and his cheek. The fierce glare he directed at Valerie had been known to make seasoned oil rig roughnecks back away, but his frown, combined with the pratfall comedy of hitting his head on the car hood and the long streak of grease on his face, merely made Valerie giggle again, even louder.

"I'm sure it's—it's painful," she gasped, forcing down another laugh by clamping one hand over her mouth.

"Oh, hell!" he exclaimed and emitted a rueful laugh. They glanced sideways at each other, sharp blue eyes meeting soft silver-green ones in an unexpected harmony of humor. Suddenly both of them were chuckling, then laughing outright.

"I—I'm sorry," Valerie finally managed to get out, her giggles calming. "I know how much that hurts, but it just looks so—so—"

"Funny," the man finished for her with mock disgust, leaning back against the brick wall. "I know." He stared at the car, then raised one booted foot and poked at the front tire of the offending vehicle. "Dumb German machine. How am I supposed to fix the blasted thing? I told her I didn't know up from down on German cars, never had one in my life. I'm not even used to metric tools. But try to tell Laraine Stone anything."

Valerie smiled and leaned against the back end of the car. It was fun to talk to an American man again, to hear the soft slur of Texas speech, the blunt words and undisguised opinions, the sturdy disregard for wealth or status. "I've tried to do it a few times," she agreed, aware that she wanted to prolong the conversation. Talking to a man alone would have made her nervous at home, sure that someone would see her and immediately affix a blot to the precious de la Portilla name. But here it was acceptable, ordinary, common. He wouldn't think her brazen or strange.

"Oh, I'm sorry. Did you come to see Laraine?" he asked.

"Yeah."

"Well, she's not at home. She went to Morgan's house for a few minutes."

"That means at least an hour, if I know Laraine." Laraine had told Valerie the night before that Alexis, Alec's oldest daughter, was in town with her baby. If possible, Laraine was even more enamored of Mara, the only granddaughter in the family, than she was of Matthew, Morgan's boy. Since both Mara and Matthew were now at Morgan's house, Laraine would have difficulty tearing herself away.

The blond man gave a grunt, which Valerie interpreted as amused assent, and raked a hand through his tousled hair, then fumbled in his shirt pocket for a cigarette and lit it, inhaling the smoke slowly as he tilted his head back against the wall. "I don't suppose you know anything about Mercedeses."

"No, 'fraid not." It didn't surprise Valerie that she could talk so easily to him. She had always been able to get along with the people who worked for her, a result, she guessed, of having been raised largely by her mother's servants. It was only around the laughing, careless, wealthy young men of her own age and upbringing that she was reduced to tongue-tied silence. They had an arrogance about them that withered her self-esteem and made her every utterance seem witless and contemptible.

He extended the cigarette pack to her. "Cigarette?" She shook her head in silent refusal. He took a long drag, eyes narrowing, as he observed her. Without haste his gaze drifted down, missing nothing from the top of her white-blond hair to the slender-strapped sandals adorning her feet. His look wasn't hot and smoldering, as was too often the case with some of Felipe's acquaintances, who were sure a much-younger wife was on the lookout for a little extramarital romance. Rather, his glance was cool, almost appraising, an impersonal assessment. Yet there was something in the blue eyes that set up a quick throbbing in her veins. Without knowing why she felt it so strongly, she was sure that there was nothing casual about this man's relationships with women.

Valerie straightened unconsciously, suddenly very aware of her hair spreading loose around her shoulders. Why had she taken it down? It looked much better up. And her blouse was wrinkled and bunching around her waist. It needed to be tucked in. Firmly she resisted the impulse to do so and tore her eyes away from his, glancing at the side door. She ought to go inside to wait for Laraine instead of standing around talking to a stranger.

Valerie hesitated a moment more, and the blond man rose to his feet, dropping the cigarette onto the pavement and crushing it with one booted toe. "One more time," he vowed grimly, looking at the engine with evident dislike, "and then our friend Mrs. Stone is going to have to take it to the Mercedes dealer." He turned toward Valerie. "Are you planning to wait for Laraine?"

"Yes, I guess so." Now was the time to walk away and go inside. She didn't move.

"Would you mind helping me here? I promise I won't get you dirty. I just need someone to hold this." He unhooked a small hanging light from the inside of the hood and extended it toward her. "I need you to shine it directly on what I'm fixing."

"Sure." She moved to the front of the car and took hold of the black metal casing by the large hook on top.

He leaned over the engine once more, directing her to aim the light on a certain spot, and she stepped closer, leaning over the engine as he did, careless of her expensive pants suit. He was silent as his hands worked quickly and efficiently, loosening a nut, then replacing a small metal plate with another that looked exactly like it. "There!" he exclaimed with satisfaction as he tightened the nut with a wrench. "Hop in the front seat and turn it on. We'll see whether I've fixed it or broken it."

She did as he requested, sliding into the leather seat and turning the ignition key. The engine hesitated for a moment, then purred to life. That fact earned her a quick grin from the blond man. "Sounds like you fixed it," Valerie commented.

"Maybe. Let's take it for a spin and find out whether it dies on us."

"Okay," Valerie agreed readily, surprising herself.

"I need to get this junk off my hands before I touch that wheel." He held up blackened hands, then walked with lanky strides across the drive and opened the side door to the kitchen, taking the two shallow stairs up to the house in one lithe step. Valerie slid across the seat to the opposite side and waited for him, wondering what had possessed her to agree to go. She knew nothing about him except that he was working on Laraine's car. Normally she was reserved even around people she knew, yet here she was going off with a stranger without even a qualm.

Moments later the man emerged from the house and slid into the driver's seat. The grease was gone from his fingers and face, and the faded shirt was buttoned and tucked into his jeans. He started the car and backed out, laying one arm along the back of the seat and twisting backward to watch his progress. His long, work-roughened fingers almost touched Valerie's shoulder. If she moved even a fraction of an inch, she would make contact with him, she knew. Carefully she refrained from making such a move.

"Oh, sorry," he remarked as he put the car into drive and started down the street. "I forgot to introduce myself. My name is Ashe." He lowered his arm to shake her hand.

"Valerie," she replied, placing her small hand in his toughened one. He held it for a long moment before he released it and replaced his arm on the back of the seat.

Valerie stared out the side window, seeing none of the scenery they passed, aware only of the remembered touch of his rough skin. She wondered how it would feel floating across the tender skin of her breasts and stomach. She flushed and cast a sideways glance at Ashe. He was staring straight ahead. Thank heavens he hadn't witnessed her blush or he might have guessed her thoughts.

The car nosed onto a busy street. A few blocks later Ashe turned onto an even more heavily traveled thoroughfare lined with fast-food restaurants. Without warning he slowed the car as he approached one of them and swung into the parking lot.

"You hungry?" he asked. "I'm starving. How about a hamburger?" With those words, he was out of the car. Valerie hesitated, more and more sure that this was a situation she should not be in. After all, hopping into a car with a man she didn't know and then going to a restaurant with him were not things a married woman commonly did, even in the U.S. Especially when that man was blond and handsome—and she felt such a quivering response in her stomach when he shook her hand. However, she was hungry, and he was already coming around the car to open her door. How could she refuse without looking foolish and conceited enough to think he was after her body? As she had so many times in the past, Valerie reminded herself that she just wasn't the sort of woman to turn any man into a lust-crazed demon. It wouldn't hurt to eat lunch with him. No one would know about it, and nothing would come of it.

Chapter 2

ASHE ESCORTED HER INTO THE MODERN BUILDING, ONE
hand spread lightly over the small of her back. The spot
he touched was suddenly hot and alive with nerves. No,
Valerie thought, "escort" was much too tame a word
for the way Ashe strolled beside her, his body so close
that she could feel his heat, the hand on her back
possessive. There was a primitive quality to it, a sense
of the male protecting his property, that made her
realize that there was something elemental and raw in
this man. The thought was surprisingly stirring. Valerie
tried to ignore her reaction and regain her usual calm.
But it remained lost to her, abandoned somewhere
back at Laraine's house when she had agreed to leave
with Ashe.

Valerie bit her lip and glanced up at her companion.
His pale blue eyes were on her, still cool, but so intent
that she caught her breath and had to glance away.
Inside the restaurant Ashe turned politely to wait for
her to decide what she wanted. She opted for a
cheeseburger and pulled out her billfold to pay for it,
but he pressed his hand against hers, forcing the wallet
back into her purse, his blue eyes amused. "I think I
can handle it."

Valerie swallowed hard, her hand tingling from the
contact with his. Her knees went watery, and to hide

that fact she walked away and sat down at the nearest table. Ashe joined her moments later, sliding into the opposite side of the booth as he handed her the tray containing her meal. They ate their unexceptional food and talked about ordinary things, chuckling now and then over a wry observation or humorous statement. Valerie thought that Ashe wasn't a man who laughed often. The lines on his face betokened a certain grimness, at best a serious approach to life. Yet now, as they talked, his eyes were bright with amusement, almost dancing, and his teeth flashed in a grin that was dazzling against his tan face.

"You from Dallas?" he asked.

Valerie's breath stopped for a moment. "No," she responded slowly, not sure why she hesitated. "Actually, I was raised in the East. New York and Connecticut, mostly." There was no reason to get into a lengthy explanation of San Cristóbal and her marriage, was there? Yet she was aware of a faint feeling of guilt when she didn't reveal her present circumstances.

"I didn't think you sounded like you were from around here."

"Where are you from?" Valerie quickly shifted the focus away from her own life.

"Originally? Tulsa, Oklahoma. Since then, though, I've lived lots of different places. Canada, Texas, Louisiana, California, even Scotland once."

"Scotland? Why?"

He shrugged. "I was on an oil crew. It seemed like a terrific opportunity at the time. I made good money, I'll admit that." He grinned suddenly, his eyes crinkling up. "Nearly froze to death, though. When I got back, one of my friends wanted me to go to Alaska with him to work on the pipeline. No way. I spent the next few months in South Texas."

"So you're an oil field worker?"

"Roughneck. Yeah, for a long time. Then I was a tool pusher for a couple of years."

"I see. Do you work for Alec?"

"Yeah. I work for him." His eyes turned suddenly opaque and he glanced away. Valerie was certain she had struck a sensitive spot, but she didn't know what it was.

She went on gingerly, "I've known Alec for years. He's—I really like him."

The hidden look vanished from his eyes, replaced by a glint of humor. "He seems to have that effect on a lot of women."

Valerie chuckled and wrinkled her brow in an exaggerated pose of puzzlement. "Now, why do I keep hearing that statement? And always from men. . . ."

He shot her a piercing look, then had to grin. "Careful, you're very close to threatening the fragile male ego."

"I wouldn't think you'd have anything to worry about in that regard."

"Meaning my ego's too big to be hurt?" he bantered.

Valerie grimaced. "You know that's not what I meant. Stop fishing for compliments." Had she stopped to think about it, she would have been shocked at her easy, joking manner with a man she didn't know. But she was far too wrapped up in her enjoyment to spoil it by examination. Whatever worries or observations pricked at the edges of her consciousness, she quickly locked them away. He grinned and made no comment, merely leaned back in the booth and watched her, his cool gaze missing nothing. Valerie shifted, uncomfortably aware of the warmth rising in her. "Why are you looking at me like that?"

"Like what?"

"I don't know—just sort of staring. Is something the matter with me?"

The smile began in his eyes, darkening and warming them, then spread to his mouth. "No," he responded slowly. "There's not a thing wrong with you." His intimation floated between them, and Valerie blushed, wishing she hadn't spoken. A more sophisticated woman wouldn't have mentioned it, would have assumed that this look was admiring. "Now you're the one fishing for compliments."

"I'm not!" she protested heatedly, then stopped as she realized he was teasing her. "Oh, you! I'm leaving." She rose with a haughty air, which seemed to impress him not at all.

"Can't take it, huh?" He slid out of the booth and followed her, once again opening the door for her and guiding her out with a large hand on her back. Valerie was guiltily aware of how much she liked having his hand there. The world was suddenly alive and exciting —dangerous, but in a wonderful way. She knew it wasn't the way she should feel at all, but again she ignored the prickings of doubt.

When they were both seated in the Mercedes and the engine had started without hesitation, Ashe said almost reluctantly, "Well, apparently I fixed it."

"Yeah." Disappointment surged through Valerie. Now they would have to go home. She would say good-bye and that would be the end of it. It was crazy that the idea should hurt.

They wound slowly through the curving streets of the residential area, both suddenly silent. All too soon they reached the white Colonial mansion where the Stones lived, and Ashe pulled to a stop behind Valerie's car. There was a silver Cadillac parked beneath the cover of the porte cochere, indicating that Laraine had returned home. Ashe opened his door, and Valerie hastened to open hers before he could, then stepped out of the car.

"Thank you for the hamburger," she said lamely.

"You're welcome. Thanks for the help."

"It wasn't anything." Every word she uttered was stupid, she thought. Yet there was nothing momentous to say. Their meeting had been brief and casual, and she would never see him again. There was really nothing to it, and certainly no reason for the heavy lump developing in the region of her stomach.

"I guess I'll be getting along." He hesitated for a moment. "Are you doing anything tonight? I have to go to a party and I hoped you might come with me."

Valerie's throat went dry as dust. She would give anything to be able to say yes. "I—I'm sorry. I already have a commitment tonight." She bit her tongue to keep from adding that she'd love to see him the next day instead.

"Sure. I was afraid you would. Well, I'll be seeing you."

"Yeah." The word was almost inaudible. He waved one hand in farewell, and Valerie called after him, "Good-bye."

Ashe spun around, and for a moment she thought he was about to return, but he merely nodded and said, "Bye." He jumped into the muddy pickup and backed out of the wide driveway, skirting Valerie's Mercedes. Valerie realized that she was staring and with an inward shake turned to enter the house.

"Valerie!" Laraine exclaimed, opening the door for her. "Where have you been?" She embraced Valerie lightly and kissed her cheek. Laraine wasn't an effusive or emotional woman—except about Alec's beloved grandchildren—and her calm, almost indifferent greeting didn't indicate a lack of liking, or did Valerie interpret it as such. She and Laraine came from the same family, and Valerie was no more used to displays of emotion than Laraine was. She was well aware of the affection between them.

Laraine, as immaculate and attractive as ever in an ice blue slacks set, directed Valerie into the breakfast room, where a woman sat, a baby standing at her knees. Both woman and child turned at their entrance, and the woman rose, briskly extending her hand to shake Valerie's. "Hello, Valerie. Nice to see you again."

"Hello, Alexis." Valerie smiled faintly. The woman was Alexis Stone McClure, Alec's oldest daughter. She had always been the friendliest of Alec's daughters, since she had the best relationship with Laraine, but her confident manner and quick, often acidic tongue made Valerie almost as frightened of her as she was of Morgan. Tall and assured, with red-blond hair and dark blue eyes, Alexis was attractive as well as competent. She was an attorney in a small town in the Texas Panhandle and before her marriage had worked in the legal department of Stone Oil. Then she had met Brant McClure, a rancher who had opposed Alec Stone on an oil deal, and they had fallen helplessly in love. There had been many struggles between the equally iron-willed husband and wife, but it was evident from the serenity in Alexis's face that she had truly found happiness.

"This is Mara," Laraine announced proudly, and scooped up the baby. Mara favored her with a smile and grabbed a handful of Laraine's elegantly coiffured blond hair. Laraine merely beamed at the child's attack on her hairdo. "Isn't she a doll? She has her mother's hair. And her eyes are amber, like Brant's. The combination is dynamite. She'll be the biggest heartbreaker this family's ever seen."

Alexis chuckled. "I think you may be a wee bit prejudiced."

"Nonsense," Laraine responded with a twinkle in her eye.

Valerie laughed. "You are the epitome of a doting grandmother."

"I have to admit it." Reluctantly Laraine set down the now-squirming Mara. "Oh, guess what! The nicest thing. Cara and Chris flew in from D.C. today, so they'll be at the party tonight, too. And she's pregnant!"

"Cara!"

Alexis laughed. "Yes. The Stone family's become a baby factory. Cara's the craziest about kids of all three of us."

"And Chris is ecstatic," Laraine inserted. "His first

wife never had any children, and I think that was one of their problems. Have you met Chris?"

"No. He was married before?"

"Yes, and he was involved in the messiest divorce case." The three women settled down for a good gossip, and Laraine poured a cup of coffee for Valerie as she talked. "Well, that's his ex-wife for you. She couldn't stand to let him go, even though the two of them had been at each other's throats for years. Of course, Cara was right in the middle of it, but thank heavens she's such a level-headed girl. She managed to ignore it all, even though Monica went so far as to phone her and say all sorts of nasty things. Monica even had a detective follow Cara—not that it did her any good. Chris wasn't about to let Cara get pulled into the case. They hardly saw each other until it was all over. But now they're married and very happy."

Alexis glanced out the window. "Uh-oh. Time to go. Brant's pulling into the driveway." She turned to Valerie. "I just wanted to drop by and say hi. Brant's picking me up on his way home from the zoo. That's where he and Paul have spent the day."

The next few minutes were a flurry of greetings and departures, with Alexis scurrying around gathering up Mara's things while Laraine introduced Valerie to Alexis's husband, Brant. He was a tall man, rather stern-featured, with the same sort of weathered face Ashe had. His eyes were arresting, absurdly long-lashed and an unusual golden brown hue. Brant's son, Paul, was a smiling, talkative child whose Oriental features bespoke his mother's heritage. Valerie had heard that Alexis had fallen for Paul the moment she met him, and Valerie could readily understand why.

The McClure family left, waving, and Laraine closed the back door with a sigh. Valerie smiled at her fondly. "Things have really changed between you and Alec's children, haven't they?"

Laraine nodded. "It's amazing how grandchildren can cure emotional splits. Even Morgan and I get along now. She's really a sweet girl." For a moment Laraine seemed lost in reverie. Then she shook her head a little, as though waking up, and reached out to take Valerie's hand. "But not as sweet as you. Did you know how fond I was of you when you were a child?"

"No. I liked you because you let me hang around, but I was never sure how you really felt about me," Valerie answered as they strolled back to the breakfast room.

"I was crazy about you. I wanted a child, but when John was alive we weren't able to have one, and after I married Alec I was too old. But I was thrilled when Pamela would let you stay with me. Oh, I envied her for being your mother. It seemed horridly unfair that she should have a child when I wanted one so badly and couldn't."

"And she didn't want one at all," Valerie finished sadly.

"I'm sorry," Laraine said quickly. "I didn't mean . . ."

"Don't be sorry. That's exactly what you meant, because it's the truth. Mother didn't want me or any child. As I grew up I became an embarrassment to her. I showed how old she was, you see, and I wasn't pretty."

Laraine made a disgusted sound. "Don't be silly. You *were* pretty. Just ask Alec. He always called you my 'lovely little cousin.'"

"Did he?" Valerie stared.

"Of course. I wouldn't lie to you. *That* was why Pamela couldn't bear to have you around. She's a vain woman, always has been. And you were competition when you became a teenager. I don't think Pam's wicked. She can be sweet and very amusing, a lot of fun to be with."

"I know. I can remember going shopping with her and things like that when I was a kid. She made everything fun."

"But she can't take competition. When we were

growing up, she always had to be the prettiest, the most popular. So when you started turning into a beauty, she was afraid everyone would notice you instead of her." Laraine sighed. "Do you ever see Pamela?"

Valerie shook her head. "Not often. She came to San Cristóbal a couple of years ago at Christmas, but she was bored and left after three days. But I accept our relationship now. I'm grown and have a husband, a life of my own. Mother and I will never be close."

Laraine gazed at Valerie through narrowed eyes for a moment, then forced a smile and changed the subject. "Well, I see you met Ashe. When I saw your car in the driveway and you weren't here, I assumed you'd gone with him, but it surprised me. I hope he didn't upset you."

"Why, no, I thought he was nice," Valerie answered casually.

"I'm glad. I'm very fond of the boy myself, but sometimes he can be absolutely rude. He has a lot of resentment against wealthy people, you see."

"Well, he was quite polite to me." Valerie searched her mind for something to divert the conversation from its present topic. The last thing she wanted to discuss, even with her favorite relative, was the man who had induced such strange and guilt-provoking feelings in her.

But everywhere her mind turned it seemed to run into Ashe again, so she was grateful when Laraine herself moved to a new subject. "Valerie, I hope you won't think I'm prying, but are you and Felipe all right?"

"Fine," Valerie responded, surprised. "Why do you ask?"

Laraine paused, then said carefully, "Well, Felipe seemed . . . thinner than when I met him at your wedding."

Valerie glanced at Laraine, tears springing into her eyes. "Yes, he is. Oh, Laraine! He's dying!"

Laraine reached out to cover one of Valerie's hands

with hers. "I was afraid of that. He looked so tired and frail. What's the matter?"

"He has a heart condition. I don't understand it. I didn't even know about it when I married him. When I pressed him about his health last year, he admitted his doctors had said his heart was weak and he wouldn't live many years."

Laraine sighed, keeping her eyes on the coffee she kept stirring aimlessly. "But I don't think his death will bring you happiness."

"No," Valerie agreed softly. "I'm sure most people wonder about our marriage. They think we don't suit each other. And they're right in a way. Ours is a different marriage. But I love him. Maybe not the same way you love Alec or his daughters love their husbands. But, still, I love him. That's why I've felt so guilty recently."

"What do you mean? Have you . . ." The older woman paused delicately.

The thought of a darkly tanned, lean, blond man sprang unbidden to her mind, but Valerie sternly banished it. "No, I haven't taken a lover. I've never been unfaithful to Felipe. But lately I've been restless. I've felt bored and hemmed in. I hate my life there!"

"I suppose his relatives are a problem," Laraine suggested shrewdly.

"How did you know?"

"My dear, if there's one thing I'm familiar with, it's marriages and all the complications of families. Any new member of a family is tested, and when there are stepchildren involved it's much worse. An older man marries a younger girl, and immediately everyone in the family starts worrying about his having more children or leaving all his money to his wife. She's a conniving gold digger in their eyes before they even meet her."

"It's worse when she's from a different culture. I've never fit in with the de la Portillas. Not that I'd want to. Except for Felipe, they're thoroughly unlikable. Felipe had only one child, Esteban. He's very cold and disagreeable. His wife, Inés, is worse. Alfonso, Felipe's brother, is something of a rounder, although he's very censorious about me. Alfonso had four excessively dull, proud daughters and a son, Carlos, who's an absolute brute. Then there are hundreds of aunts, uncles and cousins, all of whom seem to spend their time spying on each other, but mostly on me! They've resented me from the first, and everything I do seems to make it worse. I'm far too American for them—as if I could be anything else! They deplore my boldness, my dress, my speech, my actions."

"Your boldness?" Laraine repeated, amused.

"Yes, can you imagine? The girl Mother always called a 'brown mouse'? But to them I'm bold—not because I'm aggressive or flirtatious, which you can find in their family aplenty, but because I say what I think. It's unfeminine not to flutter my eyelashes and refuse to give an opinion. I'm not subtle, secretive, manipulative, which is what they admire in a woman," Valerie said bitterly, then heaved a sigh. "I'm sure I didn't try hard enough. I knew I didn't have to get along with them because I wasn't dependent on Felipe. I can return to the U.S. any time I want, and I have more money than they do—at least until this oil deal goes through. So they can't control me, which aggravates them terribly and makes me rather insensitive to their demands."

"And well you should be. I've never been a women's libber, but I think a woman ought to be independent. A husband shouldn't control her because he has all the money."

"Oh, Felipe doesn't control me. I try to fit in with the customs of his family and San Cristóbal only because I'm fond of him. He doesn't demand it. He's always been the kindest, most generous man. That's why I feel guilty about being bored and restless. But I'm suffocating! A few months ago some American archaeologists began a dig not far from the de la Portilla plantation, where Felipe and I live most of the year. Felipe is very interested in archaeology and his country's past and treasures, so he and I went to welcome the team. And you know what? I was fascinated! It's so interesting. I read Felipe's books on archaeology and the Mayan culture, and then I began going to the dig to watch. Before long Dr. Robertson asked if I'd like to help. For the past two months I've worked at the dig and I've loved it."

"Why, that's marvelous, Valerie. You have an interest now, a hobby. It ought to relieve your boredom."

"It relieves my boredom, all right. My problem is every evening when I go home. I see the contrast so clearly. On the dig I'm excited, alive. At home I have nothing to do, and I'm constantly under pressure from the de la Portillas to act properly. When this expedition's over the archaeologists will go home, and I'll have nothing but my old life to return to. Except now it will be worse, because I'll have something to miss. What I really want is to make a career of archaeology."

"Then why don't you?"

"I'd have to go back to school for several years, first making up undergraduate courses in archaeology, then earning a graduate degree. I can't leave Felipe for that long, especially not with him being so ill. He would be hurt by my absence, and lonely. I couldn't humiliate him in front of his friends and family. Besides, he needs me now more than ever. No one else would make him take his pills and watch his diet. He'd get sicker, and I can't repay him like that. He's been so good to me, so kind."

"It's a tough situation," Laraine agreed. "I wish I had the answer for you."

Valerie smiled wryly. "So do I. But I'm afraid there isn't any. I'm caught. Stuck. There's so much I want that I know I can't have. I want to accomplish something instead of wasting my whole life." Her voice dropped to a whisper. "I want to love and be loved."

* * *

The Stone mansion was ablaze with lights when Felipe and Valerie stopped in front of it. Laraine had seized the opportunity to have a party in honor of Valerie and Alec's new business associate, Felipe. With Cara and Alexis both in town also, it had seemed the perfect time for a big to-do. Cadillacs, Mercedeses and Continentals were parked along both sides of the street, and laughter sounded from the rear, where guests had spilled over onto the terrace in the warm spring evening. It was obviously a large party and in full swing. Valerie drew a deep breath as she stepped out of the car and straightened her long evening dress. She wore a one-shouldered toga-styled dress, which softly followed the contours of her slender body without clinging. A wide diagonal swath of fabric with two metallic silver stripes separated by a narrow, deep purple band slanted down from the covered shoulder to wrap around under the opposite arm. At her hip an identical band slanted across her body in the other direction, ending just above her knee. Between the two bands, the torso was a deep shade of purple frosted with silver beading. Below the lower band the same purple material, thinly striped with silver beading, fell softly to her ankles. It was an elegant dress, simple, yet bold in concept. With Valerie's delicate coloring, and accented by a fragile necklace of tiny diamonds and amethysts, the dress was enticingly cool and aristocratic.

A servant opened the door and ushered them inside, and Laraine rushed forward to greet them, catching Valerie's hands and offering her a cool peck on the cheek, then doing the same to Felipe. Laraine was as fashionably and richly clothed as always, wearing a strapless black sheath with a full rust-colored overskirt which was cut away to reveal the black fabric beneath. She led the couple into the coolly formal living room and introduced them to a business associate of Alec's. "Now, where is Alec?" she mused, glancing around. "I know he'll want to see you."

She wandered away, looking for her husband, while Valerie smiled at the man to whom she had been introduced and wished she were somewhere else. She disliked social occasions. There was a burst of laughter in the hall, and Valerie glanced out to see Morgan Fletcher, Alec's middle daughter. She stood beside Nick, her darkly handsome husband, as she chatted vivaciously to a bland brown-haired man. Morgan wore a dress that only someone as beautiful and clothes-wise as she could carry off: a short cocktail dress of ivory silk, Fortuny pleated and sassily turned back into ribbon-edged ruffles across the strapless top and hem, and diagonally across the hips and thighs. An ivory satin ribbon sashed Morgan's tiny waist. She wore no ornamentation on her bared shoulders and chest. Her auburn hair was pulled up into a tight, high knot that emphasized her excellent facial bones. She managed to look stunning, outrageous and utterly stylish. Valerie knew she herself would have looked merely foolish in such a dress.

Morgan glanced into the living room and saw Valerie. Amazement flitted across her face before she politely schooled it into pleasant interest. Murmuring something to Nick, she led him over to Valerie and Felipe. Valerie stiffened at her approach. There was no one in the world, except perhaps her mother, who made Valerie feel as inferior as Morgan Stone Fletcher did. Valerie had first met Morgan when she was a gawky girl of fourteen and Morgan was already an acknowledged beauty. Morgan had been graceful, alluring, at ease with men and perfectly adept in any social situation, precisely the opposite of Valerie. Ever since, Valerie had felt gauche and plain around Morgan.

"Hello, Valerie, I almost didn't recognize you. You've changed so," Morgan began in her warm voice, extending a hand to shake Valerie's.

Valerie froze, her smile wooden and forced. "There

was a lot of room for improvement," she remarked stiffly.

Morgan blinked, taken aback by Valerie's blunt, almost antagonistic remark, and Valerie immediately wished she could call back her words. "I wouldn't say that exactly," Morgan demurred.

"Only because you're too polite." Now why had that popped out? Morgan wasn't trying to be nasty. It was she herself who kept up the icy atmosphere.

"Valerie, my dear, you're too hard on yourself, as usual," Felipe interjected smoothly. He nodded to Morgan, exuding Latin charm. "I am Felipe de la Portilla, Valerie's husband."

"I'm sorry . . . I didn't introduce you," Valerie said. "Morgan, Felipe. Felipe, this is Morgan Fletcher, Alec's daughter, and her husband, Nick."

"How do you do?" Felipe shook Nick's hand and kissed Morgan's with Continental grace.

"I wasn't sure whether you knew Nick," Morgan began again.

"Oh, yes, I met him once before when I was visiting here." Valerie smiled at Nick, feeling as though her face were cracking from the forced smiles. "Alexis and you came over—" She stopped, realizing that once again she had made matters worse. It was well known that Morgan's husband had been in love with her older sister for years before he married Morgan. Valerie flushed with embarrassment.

Nick laughed, his dark eyes dancing. Valerie didn't dare look at Morgan, too embarrassed at having managed to be both cold and offensive in the space of a few minutes. "That's all right," Nick assured her in a mock aside. "It doesn't hurt to keep Morgan on her toes."

Morgan shot her husband a look that was at once amused, indignant and laced with love. The cold knot in Valerie's stomach grew. She wouldn't want a man like Nick Fletcher. He was too handsome, too assured, the sort of wealthy playboy whose sophistication made her feel as awkward as did his wife's beauty. But the evident love between the two of them made Valerie yearn for the same feeling, for a man who could inspire it in her and return it in kind. Valerie glanced away, afraid that her thoughts would show in her face. Felipe continued to talk to Morgan and Nick, but Valerie stayed out of the conversation, resolved not to utter any more faux pas. Soon the Fletchers murmured a polite good-bye and drifted away. Felipe turned to Valerie, his face stamped with surprise.

"My dearest, I've never seen you be so rude before. And to Alec's daughter! I thought you admired him."

"I do, but not his daughters," Valerie snapped, irritated with herself and with him for reproving her. "Oh, I'm sorry, Felipe, I don't know what's the matter with me. I promise, I'll be good the rest of the evening."

"No doubt you are tired." He patted her hand soothingly. "Why don't we find you a seat, and I'll bring you a glass of wine. All right?"

"All right."

They strolled onto the terrace, and Valerie sat down on a black wrought-iron patio chair while Felipe went in search of a drink. She caught sight of Alexis in a conversational knot at the edge of the terrace, but she was careful not to catch her eye. Facing Morgan was enough for the moment. She couldn't take Alexis as well, at least not yet. Valerie casually watched the door, wondering how long she would have to stay before she could politely leave.

A man stepped out of the open door and glanced idly around the terrace. He was dressed in an expensive charcoal gray suit that darkened his eyes to a midnight blue, and his thick blond hair was combed ruthlessly into order. The well-cut suit displayed his trim figure but concealed the hard muscles beneath. He was the picture of a sleek, shrewd businessman, far different from the jeans-clad mechanic Valerie had met earlier that afternoon. But he was the same man!

Chapter 3

VALERIE STARED AT ASHE IN AMAZEMENT. WHAT WAS Laraine's mechanic doing at her party? She turned to a group of three women who stood chatting just behind her and touched the closest one's arm. "Excuse me, but do you know who that man is?"

The woman looked at her in surprise. "What man?"

"The one standing in the doorway."

The woman glanced at Ashe, and a faint smile touched her face. "Oh, that's Ashe Harlan. He's one of the top executives at Stone Oil."

Valerie turned away, too stunned to thank the woman for the information. An executive at Stone Oil! And she had thought he was a mechanic, then decided he was an oil field roughneck. She brought her ice-cold hands up to her flushed cheeks. How humiliating! She had made a fool of herself. No doubt Ashe had been laughing at her inside.

As Valerie stood watching him, frozen with embarrassment, Ashe Harlan caught sight of her. He straightened and strode toward her. "Valerie? Your commitment was this party? And I thought you were just giving me the brush-off."

Valerie looked up into pale blue eyes warmed by some indefinable emotion. Valerie hoped it wasn't laughter. "Oh, Mr. Harlan!"

"Mr. Harlan?" he repeated in amazement. "When did I become that? This afternoon it was Ashe."

"Ashe. I'm sorry. Oh, heavens! You must think me a perfect idiot. This afternoon I had no idea who you were."

He chuckled. "Oh? Am I somebody?"

"Someone told me that you're an executive at Stone Oil. When I saw you repairing Laraine's car I thought you were a mechanic, and then when you said you had been a roughneck I assumed you still were."

"That's perfectly reasonable. I look more like a mechanic than an executive. I should have explained who I was."

Valerie smiled, then glanced away nervously. So Ashe was one of those bright, ambitious young men to whom she normally found it difficult to talk. Yet it had been so easy that afternoon. Even now, embarrassed by her mistake, she wasn't as ill at ease with him as she had been with Nick Fletcher. There was an earthy quality to Ashe and none of the brittle sophistication which generally surrounded a prep school/fraternity product. But perhaps that wasn't his background. He could be a self-made man, a poor boy who had pulled himself up to the heights of the business world. That would account for the way he spoke and moved, the work-hardened palms and firm muscles.

"What are you doing out here all alone?" Ashe continued.

Valerie faltered. "Uh, someone's getting me a drink." How could she tell him that she had a husband after not revealing the fact that afternoon when Ashe had asked her for a date? What a mess. Why hadn't she told him the truth to begin with? It was crazy to not want Ashe to know she was married. Frantically she searched for a way out, knowing that the longer she delayed telling him, the worse she would look, yet still reluctant to let him know.

Before she could come up with anything adequate to say Ashe put his hand under her arm familiarly and guided her toward the edge of the terrace. "Have you seen the backyard yet? Come on, I'll show you."

Guiltily Valerie let him lead her off the patio and down the terraced sidewalk to the swimming pool. The pool area was softly lighted, and a few people sat around it in lounge chairs, conversing in low tones. Ashe strolled past the pool, his hand sliding down Valerie's arm to clasp her hand. Valerie's fingers trembled in his, but she made no move to remove them. It was so pleasant, and a tiny voice whispered inside her head that it couldn't hurt—not for only a little while.

Beyond the pool the enormous yard sloped gradually downward, and two pebbled cement sidewalks ran in opposite diagonal paths toward the far corners of the estate. Each walk was lined with ankle-high shaded lights which were spaced farther and farther apart until the pathway faded in gentle darkness. Beyond the lights, bushes delineated beds of flowers, and in the center of the lawn a small fountain tinkled delicately. Ashe turned from the cement path and led Valerie through the gardens to the huge oak at the rear. Shadowed by the spreading limbs of the tree, a low stone bench half circled the trunk. They sat down on the bench, hidden by the tree and the quiet darkness.

"Here you have a view of the whole place." Ashe indicated the spread of yard and house before them. It seemed to Valerie as if the two of them were observers of a play or movie, sitting concealed in darkness while the others postured and spoke on the brightly lit stage before them.

"It's beautiful," Valerie commented, for it was a lovely scene, perfectly planned by Laraine to create that effect.

"Yes," Ashe agreed, then fell silent. Valerie turned inquiringly and found him watching her, his pale eyes shadowed and unreadable. Her heart began to pound. She couldn't look away. "Was it only your commitment to this party that made you turn me down this afternoon," he asked softly, "or were you saying you didn't want to see me?"

Valerie swallowed. "No, I—it wasn't that I didn't want to see you."

"I wasn't sure what to think. Any other woman that I liked as well as you, I'd have gotten her number from Laraine and pursued her, even though she'd turned me down. But you're different. I don't know much about women like you. I was afraid I was too rough or something. Maybe I'd offended you."

"Women like me? What do you mean?"

"Oh, you know. Society types. The kind who grew up in a house like this."

"You didn't?"

He gave a short laugh. "No. I grew up on the wrong side of the tracks."

Valerie smiled. "I knew you couldn't be a preppie. I've never been able to say two words to a man who went to Choate."

Ashe laughed again, with more merriment this time. "Hell, lady, you're talking to a guy who doesn't even know what Choate is."

Valerie joined in his laughter. "Good!"

He raised his hand to her face, one callused finger tracing the line of her cheek, sliding down to the soft underside of her jaw and onto her neck. Valerie shivered as his finger trailed over her flesh, rasping yet gentle, and a sudden flame licked along her veins. "I don't want to rush you." His voice was low, almost hoarse. "Tell me if I come on too strong. See, looking at you turns me inside out. As soon as I saw you this afternoon I wanted you. What I'd like to do right now is take you home, pour some wine, talk a little, touch a little . . . and then take you to my bed. But I don't want to scare you. I know you're probably used to more subtle men. Suaver."

Valerie's mouth was so dry that her tongue stuck to the roof of her mouth and her lips were glued together.

She had to tell him she was married. She couldn't let it go any further. But still she stared at Ashe without speaking, her eyes locked with his. More than anything in her whole life, she wanted to feel his mouth against hers. Ashe leaned closer and his hand cupped her face. The pulse in her throat throbbed furiously as blood rushed to her head. Ashe's face loomed nearer, his eyes glittering and his tan skin colorless in the cold moonlight. Valerie could smell the faint tangy scent of his skin mingled with cologne. His breath brushed her face with heat. Then his lips were on hers, firm and warm.

Valerie quivered all over at his touch, and Ashe drew in his breath sharply. He wrapped his arms around her, pressing her into him. Her breasts were crushed against the hard muscle of his chest, and Valerie felt her nipples tighten at the pressure. He shifted and the movement rubbed the material of her dress across her breasts. Though the friction was brief, it stirred her. She linked her arms around his neck, sliding her fingers into his thick coarse hair. His lips widened on hers, and she responded, opening her mouth. His tongue delved into the sweet, warm cave, slipping wetly over every surface, then retreated as he took her lower lip between his teeth and worried it gently. He entered her mouth again, and this time the hot flickering tongue was delightfully familiar. Eagerly her own came forth to meet his, twining and lashing in a battle of desire.

Ashe groaned deep in his throat, the sound dying in their joined mouths. Valerie twisted a little, unconsciously pressing her legs together to soothe the pulsing ache that started there. Ashe's hands began to roam her body, gliding down her back and onto her thighs, then up between their locked bodies, moving quickly, eagerly, as though he wished to touch all of her at once. But their tight embrace impeded his movement, and finally, with a muttered exclamation of impatience, he wrenched away and pulled Valerie onto his lap. He settled her against his chest, one arm going around her back to support her. This time, with easy access to her breasts, his hand explored freely as he kissed her again.

He cupped the lush softness of one breast through her dress, his thumb circling the tight, eager bud of the nipple, causing it to pucker even more and strain against the material. Ashe's breath was ragged and harsh as he went to the other breast, his large hand covering it and rubbing gently across the peak until it, too, turned into a hard button of desire. His lips left her mouth to nuzzle her neck, scorching the soft flesh, and his hand slid lower to caress her abdomen and thighs. "Come home with me," he murmured into her neck. "Please. Come home."

His words ripped away the veil of pleasure surrounding her. If he had pulled her to the ground and taken her then and there, she no doubt would have given herself to him gladly, so lost was she in the tingling delight of his kisses and caresses. But when he spoke of going to his home to continue their lovemaking reality intruded. She would have to leave the party, escape from all the people she knew—including her husband. That shattered the spell, and Valerie realized with horror what she had been about to do. She had almost betrayed her husband and her marriage vows, almost repaid Felipe's kindness and trust with treachery. Shocked, she twisted out of Ashe's embrace.

"Valerie?" Ashe stared at her in amazement.

"Oh, Ashe! I—this is wrong."

"What do you mean?" He jumped up and grabbed her wrist, his brows drawing together grimly.

"Let me go!" She jerked free, appalled at the way her body trembled at his mere touch. Was she so weak? So unable to control her passions?

Confused and seething with frustrated longing, Ashe snapped, "What the hell is the matter with you?"

Valerie froze. She couldn't tell him the truth and face his disgust and anger. She just couldn't. Unconsciously she retreated behind the cool mask she had learned to use. Her eyebrows rose and her mouth thinned. "I can't, that's all." She whirled and struck out across the grass to the walkway. Without looking back to see if Ashe followed, she fled toward the house, slowing down to a fast walk when she reached the periphery of the party. She smoothed her hair with shaking fingers, thinking with a sick sinking in her stomach that her lipstick must be smeared and her lips swollen, her whole face stamped with passion. Keeping her head lowered, Valerie hurried through the crowd on the terrace and through a back hall to Alec's study. Surely it would be blessedly quiet and empty.

The door to the study was closed, and she opened it tentatively. Reassured by the darkness inside, Valerie stepped in and closed the door behind her, flipping on the light switch as she shut the door. She gasped, one hand flying to her mouth. She was not alone, as she had thought. A couple stood in the center of the room wrapped in a tight embrace. They whirled at her abrupt entrance. The man was handsome in a tough sort of way, the woman dark-haired and very pregnant. For a moment the three of them stared at each other in amazement. Then the pregnant woman burst out laughing at the same instant as Valerie recognized her. "Cara! Oh, my goodness, I'm sorry."

"That's okay. I'm rather proud to be discovered in a compromising situation, considering the size of my stomach." She jokingly patted her protruding abdomen. "Valerie, this is my husband, Chris Wozniak. Chris, this is Laraine's cousin, or rather, second cousin, I guess. Anyway, this is Valerie— Oh, Lord, I'm sorry. I never can remember your husband's last name."

"De la Portilla," Valerie supplied, and reached out to shake Chris's hand. His clasp was firm and warm, and he seemed as unembarrassed by the situation as Cara did. Valerie, however, wished she had a convenient hole in the ground into which she could disappear. "I—I'm very sorry. I was—uh, looking for the powder room and I must have opened the wrong door."

"It's the next door—back up the hall." Cara gestured.

"Thank you." Valerie quickly retreated into the hall and ducked into the vacant guest bathroom. She studied her image in the mirror. Her face was flushed and her careful hairdo was marred by a few stray wisps. But her lipstick was completely gone, thank heavens, not smeared; and if her eyes were brighter and more silvery than usual, surely no one would notice a thing like that. Hopefully Chris and Cara would have no suspicions. Of course, she had acted strangely, but it was an embarrassing situation, and they probably put her nervousness down to embarrassment at barging in on them while they were locked in a passionate kiss.

Remembering the scene, Valerie smiled faintly. It really would have been amusing if she hadn't been so upset. Imagine catching a couple kissing secretively in a dark study and then discovering that it was a husband and wife—with the wife enormously pregnant, to boot. Valerie mused wistfully that that must betoken love, and for an instant the question of whether Ashe Harlan would want to kiss her if she were pregnant flashed across her mind. Heaving a deep sigh, she leaned against the closed door.

What had possessed her out there? Never in her life had she responded so quickly or so passionately. Not even David, the fiancé whom she had thought she loved madly, had caused such a surge of pleasure inside her. In fact, her lukewarm response to his lovemaking had been one of the reasons why she had so readily accepted the sexual void of her marriage. But with Ashe she had been lost to everything else in the world except him and the delightful sensations he aroused. It wasn't like her at all, but she had been acting like a stranger to herself from the moment she met him. It was as if the man brought out all the deep yearnings from the center of her soul and revealed the romantic, sensuous woman hidden beneath the shy teenager and the cool-as-ice Señora de la Portilla.

He had introduced Valerie to the world of real adult desire, and it frightened her as much as it stirred her. Valerie glanced into the mirror again. Her cheeks had resumed their normal color and her eyes no longer sparkled. She looked perfectly normal again. But inside she was a mass of confused emotions and thoughts, and she didn't know how she could remain at the party feeling as she did. What if she had to face Ashe again—in public! She couldn't bear to think of it. She must find Felipe and tell him that she wanted to leave, make up some excuse like a headache or weariness from jet lag. He would be very understanding and kind and whisk her away.

Valerie wet her lips, opened the door and started down the hallway. Felipe stood at the end of the hall, a drink in each hand, chatting with Cara and Chris. Valerie's heart sank. She couldn't whisper to Felipe that she wanted to leave with Cara there. Her husband turned and, seeing her, smiled. "Ah, there you are, my dear. When I returned to the terrace you were gone, so I have been searching for you all over the house. I was beginning to feel like Diogenes searching for his honest man. Or was it Demosthenes?"

Valerie forced a smile and answered smoothly, "Diogenes." It was amazing how calm and natural she sounded, Valerie thought. There must be more of her mother in her than she realized. She went on brightly, "I'm sorry. I decided to take a look at Laraine's garden. It's really beautiful. You should see it."

"Why, yes, you shall have to show me. Cara was kind enough to tell me where you were, so I have been having a pleasant chat with them. You know her husband, Chris?"

"Oh, yes, we met earlier." A smile tugged at the corners of her mouth. It *was* funny. She detected an answering amusement in Cara's eyes. "Sorry. I must have acted like an idiot. I was startled."

"Don't worry. I'd probably have jumped three feet if I'd walked in on a scene like that. Oh, look, there's Nick's grandmother, Mrs. Armstrong. Have you ever met her?"

"No," Valerie admitted reluctantly.

"Oh, you have to. She's something else." Cara took Valerie's arm and propelled her across the room, skirting the band and the few dancing couples. They came to a halt beside a white-haired woman who was fashionably dressed and perfectly made up. She looked at Valerie with shrewd, sparkling dark eyes and smiled. "Feeling overwhelmed by all these Stones?" she asked perceptively.

"I guess so." Valerie couldn't help but like her. Regal and spirited, Mrs. Armstrong made effortless, amusing conversation, towing everyone in the group along after her. Cara shot Valerie a glance as if to say, "Didn't I tell you?"

Cara glanced past Valerie and her face brightened. "There you are! I was wondering if you came to the party. I want you to meet someone. Valerie . . ." Valerie turned obediently to be introduced and froze. She was staring into the bright blue gaze of Ashe Harlan.

"We've met." Ashe placed a firm hand on her wrist. "Would you care to dance, Valerie?"

Cara was taken aback by his abruptness, but Ashe ignored her, whirling Valerie onto the dance floor and into his arms before she could gather her thoughts enough to utter a polite refusal. "Ashe, really," she protested weakly.

"I'm going to talk to you. After that I'll leave you alone, if that's what you want. Okay?"

"But—"

"I want an explanation. Is that too much to ask?"

"No, of course not," Valerie replied in a muffled

voice, keeping her face down so that he couldn't see her expression.

"Valerie, for God's sake, what's wrong?" Ashe rasped. "One minute you're in my arms, eager to make love, and the next you're running to the house like I'm a mad rapist. What's the deal?"

"Ashe, please, I can't. Don't ask me to explain." She raised her face to him, her clear silver-green eyes sparkling with unshed tears, so beautiful and at the same time so vulnerable that it took his breath away.

"What do you expect of me? I'm not made of steel."

"I know. I shouldn't have let things go so far." She lowered her head, unable to meet his eyes, embarrassed and ashamed. His arms were hard, enclosing Valerie in a private world with him. Still shaken from their earlier encounter, Valerie could feel herself succumbing again to the lure of his masculinity. It was too comfortable, too right, too warm in his arms. She couldn't think, and it was too easy to forget her obligations and principles.

"Why?" His voice was almost frenzied. "Look, if you're worried that this is going to be a one-night stand, don't be. I want only one woman at a time, and I know I'll want you for a long, long while." His hot breath ruffled the wisps of hair above her ear, sending shivers down her spine.

"That's just the problem. *I'm* the one who can't make a commitment!"

"Why not?"

"Because I—" The words stuck in her throat, and then it was too late, for suddenly Felipe appeared behind Ashe.

"Excuse me." Felipe tapped Ashe on the shoulder, and Ashe turned, frowning at the interruption. "Would it be too gauche for a husband to cut in? I'm afraid I haven't had a chance to dance with my lovely wife all evening."

"What?" Ashe stared at him like a man still half-asleep.

"I—I'm sorry," Valerie stammered. "Felipe, this is Ashe Harlan. He's a—an executive at Stone Oil. Ashe, this is my husband, Felipe de la Portilla."

Ashe swung back to Valerie, realization dawning on his face, and his hands fell away from her as if they had touched something hot. "Your husband?" Hurt and accusation blazed from his eyes. He turned to Felipe. "Of course," he said stiffly, answering Felipe's original question. Then he strode away, his parting remark barely audible. "You can have her."

"How very peculiar," Felipe commented idly. "A rather rude young man."

Valerie watched Ashe's quick strides carry him out of her sight. Her chest felt pierced, and she wanted to run after him, crying that she hadn't meant to hurt him, hadn't intended to lead him on. Oh, God, he had looked at her with such disgust and contempt. He had spoken of commitment, and now he must think she was the one looking for a cheap one-night stand. But what was the point of explaining it to him? She could never have anything with Ashe. It was better to let it die, even if he despised her.

"Americans," Felipe sighed. "I'm sorry, my dear, but sometimes I wonder if I'll ever understand your countrymen. So abrupt, so quick."

"Felipe, could we go home?"

"What? Why? Is something the matter?" he asked, all concern for her, increasing her queasy guilt.

"No, I mean—I have a little headache, I guess. I'd like to lie down if you don't mind."

"But of course, my dear. Let's find Alec and tell him we're leaving." Felipe guided her from the dance floor into the living room. Valerie spotted Ashe at the front door, opening it to leave, and she glanced hastily away.

"Valerie, there's my beautiful girl!" Alec Stone exclaimed, striding forward to envelop her in a hug. Out of the corner of her eye Valerie saw Ashe throw her a last cold look and walk out the front door. She

returned Alec's embrace with a good deal less enthusi-
asm than she normally felt.

"Hello, Alec."

He stepped back, holding her away from him to look
at her. Valerie gazed back, wishing again that he was
her father and that she could take her problems to him.
Alec Stone was still a handsome man, his coldly perfect
face brought to life by startling blue eyes. He was trim
and flat-stomached, and although his jet black hair was
now liberally streaked with white, he looked younger
than his age and a good deal more handsome than any
hard-driven executive had a right to be. Vibrant, forceful, handsome—Valerie had no trouble understanding
her youthful adoration of him. He was the kind of man
who appealed to any woman of any age.

One arm around her shoulders, Alec chatted with
Valerie and Felipe for a few moments before Felipe
offered a polite good-bye. It took another five minutes
of reassurances and thank-yous before they were able
to retrieve Valerie's light wrap and leave the house.
Gratefully Valerie sank into the plush seat of the
Mercedes and leaned her head back, sighing. Felipe
patted her arm. "Feeling worse?"

"No." Valerie shook her head. "I'm okay. I just hate
crowds." Felipe nodded and was silent, concentrating
on finding his way back to their hotel. Tears formed in
Valerie's eyes, and she turned away so that he wouldn't
see them. Felipe was too kind, too good. He must not
suspect her passion for Ashe Harlan. She couldn't hurt
him that way. She had to suppress it. No, more than
that—she had to conquer it. She had no right to
anything with Ashe; she had to let him leave her life
completely. She must make no attempt to find him and
explain.

Chapter 4

ASHE HARLAN PARKED HIS CAR IN THE UNDERGROUND parking lot of the Stone Oil Building and strode to the elevators, his footsteps echoing in the vast room. He punched the button and waited for the elevator, contemplating how little he felt like going to his office that morning. Saturday night, after the party, he'd gone out to a honky-tonk, an old bare-bones bar with a couple of pool tables, red vinyl booths, and customers and waitresses who bantered back and forth with long familiarity. It was the kind of place you could always find somewhere near an oil rig, and it didn't matter that now and then a fight erupted between a couple of patrons too far gone in drink. You either picked up your beer and moved out of the path or joined in if you felt like it. Ashe was never afraid in his own milieu. What made him wary and unsure was Alec Stone's wealthy world . . . and wealthy women.

He closed his eyes at that thought. No use rubbing it in. He'd drunk too much and had a devil of a hangover on Sunday. Today there were still a few remnants of it left, although yesterday had been sober—far too sober, really. He'd had too much time to think. What he needed today was to get outside and work it out in hard physical labor, not sit behind a desk and think some more. He'd taken this job only because its trouble-shooting nature would allow him to travel and visit rigs. He hadn't wanted to be tied down to one place or to be banished from the outdoors. Ashe had spent his whole life in the sun, and he hated to be shut away from its brightness for days at a time. He enjoyed his job and had found he enjoyed dealing with other executives, but he missed the opportunity to work out his bad feelings in hard, sweaty labor out in the oil fields. He needed it to clear his head. Particularly to clear it of women like Valerie de la Portilla.

The elevator doors slid open and Ashe stepped in, thinking grimly that there she was again. He couldn't seem to get rid of the thought of her. No wonder he had taken to her so quickly, found her easy to talk to. She was no society girl brought up in wealth and luxury, used to cars and clothes and polite young men who conducted themselves according to her own set of rules. No. She had probably grown up as hard and tough as he himself had. What other reason could she have had for marrying a man twice her age except for the money and status?

In some ways he couldn't blame her. He knew what it was to want and not have, to be poor and envy the rich. Over the last couple of years, since he had met Cara and Alec, he had shed a lot of his hatred for the wealthy in general and the Stones in particular. He could look at their life in a more realistic way and see that it wasn't always a bed of roses. The Stone sisters had suffered from their parent's divorce and had resented their father's all-consuming interest in his business and his lack of time for them. Alec, though married to a loving woman, still yearned for his first wife, Ginny. Yet he had been driven by some need to be a philanderer, always picking up pretty young women on his business trips, women like Ashe's mother. He had wanted a son with all his heart and hadn't known for all those years that he had one. Ginny, the woman Ashe's mother had tried to protect with her silence, had suffered Alec's infidelities until finally her love for Alec had died. And Laraine, poor Laraine, loving Alec with all her heart, had never had his complete love. That was the life of the wealthy, too: heartbreaks and sorrows, just like anyone else. He knew that now.

But once he had not. Once he had seen only the glitter and vowed that somehow, someday, he would have it. He was certain that Valerie had done the same thing. She was a gold digger, a beautiful young woman who had traded her face and body to an old man for his money. And though it made Ashe almost physically ill to think of her in bed with de la Portilla, his old hands caressing her vital young flesh, he could accept and forgive the motive that had made her do it. What he couldn't forgive was her deception. She hadn't told him that she was married. She had led him on, flirting and responding to his lovemaking. If it hadn't been for the difficulty of leaving the party without anyone suspecting, he felt sure she would have gone to bed with him. Obviously Valerie de la Portilla was in the habit of cheating on her husband. And lying to her lovers. She would have callously let Ashe fall deeper and deeper in love with her in order to satisfy her sexual itch.

When the elevator opened on the top floor, Ashe walked blindly down the hall to his office, his mind consumed with thoughts of Valerie. What a beauty she was. The instant he had seen her, he had felt like he'd been hit in the gut. Her body in the trim suit had been enticing, dainty but well-formed, with full, pointing breasts and softly rounded hips. Yet there was an endearingly innocent quality to her, too, that made Ashe dream of awakening her body.

That was a laugh, Ashe thought derisively as he strode into his office, ignoring his secretary, who popped up from her desk at his approach. Valerie was about as innocent as a black widow spider. She had bartered her body for money, then taken lovers behind her husband's back. Her little fling with him had not been the first, Ashe was sure. No matter how shy she had seemed at first, she had been too passionate to be content with an old man's lovemaking. What a fool he must have appeared when he earnestly assured her that he wasn't the type for one-night stands. A one-night stand was exactly what she was searching for! After all, she had immediately informed him that she didn't want any commitment.

The intercom on his desk buzzed and Ashe grimaced. Much as he hated to, he had to get to work. It wouldn't be as good as sweating in the fields, but it might help clear his mind of Valerie. All he could hope to have with her was a furtive, unsatisfying affair. Considering the way he had spent yesterday trying to shake the memory of her soft lips and clinging body, he was lucky it had been nipped in the bud. He wasn't sure he could have gotten over her if they had actually made love.

Shaking the thought from his mind, Ashe pressed the intercom button. "Yes?"

"Mr. Stone wants to see you in the conference room right away."

"Okay." Ashe suppressed a sigh. Alec never asked; he ordered. At first his commands had made Ashe seethe, but after a few weeks of working with his father and a conversation with Alexis, he had realized Alec knew no other way to speak. He neither minced words nor wasted them. And his summonses were never frivolous.

Ashe left his office for the plush conference room at the end of the hall, excitement growing in him. Maybe Alec had a job for him, something to take him far away and help him forget he had ever seen Valerie de la Portilla or her husband. He pushed open the heavy door of the conference room and found three men seated at the wide oval table. Alec sat at the head, and on one side of him was Wesley Chalmers, the chief of Stone Oil's legal department. On the other side of the table sat a polished middle-aged gentleman whom Ashe recognized immediately as Felipe de la Portilla. Ashe paused fractionally before he entered the room, and

Alec glanced up from the document he was reading. "Ashe. Good, I'm glad you're here. You know Wesley. This is Felipe de la Portilla. Did you meet him the other night at the party?"

"Yes, briefly."

Felipe added smoothly, "I'm afraid I kidnapped my beautiful wife from him. Isn't that so, Mr. Harlan?"

The Latin American's smile was charming and inscrutable. A twinge of uneasiness ran through Ashe. How much had de la Portilla guessed about him and Valerie? What had she told him? "Yes, I was dancing with Mrs. de la Portilla." Ashe kept his tone carefully noncommittal.

Alec smiled. "Ah, Valerie. She's even more beautiful, Felipe, than when I knew her. Lovely girl."

"Thank you. *I* think so."

Ashe remembered the affectionate hug Alec had given Valerie and how he had called her his "beautiful girl." The suspicion that had started then now grew in his mind. Had Valerie once been one of Alec's women? And had she left the wealthier man for one who could offer the safer status of marriage? No. The thought revolted him. Surely Alec and Felipe couldn't meet this casually if that were so. . . . Unless, of course, the husband knew nothing about it?

"Now," Alec went on, signaling that they were about to get down to business. He took off his reading glasses and tossed them on top of the documents. "Sit down, Ashe. The reason I called you is that we've signed a deal with Felipe. We'll be drilling on the de la Portilla plantation before long if everything goes right."

"Congratulations."

"You're going to be dealing with Felipe from now on."

"I don't understand. I thought you said the deal was completed."

"You're a good troubleshooter, which I expected you to be, but I've also discovered that you have a hidden talent for diplomacy."

Ashe had to grin. "I wouldn't have guessed it."

"Well, maybe it's not diplomacy. I don't know what you say to them, but you've persuaded some rather resistant people to do what we want. You always solve the problem. Here we have a problem before we start. Felipe's government is a strict dictatorship, and they insist on approving any business arrangements with companies outside their borders." He made a dismissive gesture with one hand. "It's a device to get a little graft out of the deals."

"However," Felipe picked up smoothly, "I'm afraid my government is not especially fond of the de la Portilla family. In the past we have supported their opposition, and the junta both fears and dislikes us. I am not positive that the money they receive from this will insure their approval. I have explained to Mr. Stone that I feel a representative from Stone Oil would receive fairer treatment at their hands than I would."

"Besides," Alec cut in, "I'm interested in offshore drilling on the coast of San Cristóbal. I'd like to work out a deal with the government itself to drill offshore."

"I see." Ashe could think of little to say. The last thing in the world he wanted was to visit the tiny, troubled country of San Cristóbal and work with Valerie's husband. It wasn't de la Portilla's fault that his wife deceived him, but Ashe knew he couldn't be around the man without experiencing the sharp thrust of jealousy. If he went to San Cristóbal Felipe would politely invite him to the de la Portilla home, where he would have to face Valerie and talk casually to her as if nothing had ever happened between them. Nothing was less appealing to Ashe at the moment. But how could he refuse? Alec would resent it and Felipe would be insulted. Ashe scraped up a smile. "Well. Good. I'm sure I'll enjoy working with you, Mr. de la Portilla."

"Felipe, please."

"Felipe."

The talk continued for some time, with Alec and Chalmers explaining the terms of the contract to Ashe while Felipe listened gravely. Thirty minutes later Chalmers excused himself to attend another conference. Alec pulled a decanter of whiskey from the low credenza and poured a round of short celebratory drinks. Ashe noticed that Felipe sipped his drink sparingly. Personally, Ashe felt like downing his in one gulp. The more he thought about working with Felipe, the worse it seemed. Perhaps he could ease out of it after Felipe and Valerie returned to San Cristóbal. He could explain the awkward situation to Alec— No, how could he, if Alec had been involved with Valerie, too? He sighed.

"Well, gentlemen, I'm afraid I have to leave," Alec announced cheerfully after he finished his drink. He shook hands with Felipe. "When are you and Valerie flying back?"

"Thursday. I promised Valerie a little vacation here. She misses the States badly."

"I'm sure I'll see you before you leave." Alec turned to his son. "Ashe, I need to speak to you this afternoon on the Rawlins matter."

"Sure. I'll be there. Say, two o'clock?"

"Better make it two-thirty."

Alec walked out the door and Ashe was left alone with Felipe. He rose and began awkwardly, "It's nice to have met you. I—uh, have some work in my office that I need to get back to—"

"Just a moment, Ashe." Felipe held up a thin hand. There was a slight tremor to it, and the flesh clung to the bones. Ashe did not see the illness in him, only the age, and again he was repulsed by the thought of that hand on Valerie's firm young body. "My wife and I have a pleasant relationship," Felipe began, choosing his words carefully. "It is a great comfort to me. However, it is not the usual relationship of husband and wife."

Ashe stared, disconcerted by his words. What was the man getting at?

Felipe paused for a moment and placed the palms of

his hands together, seemingly studying them for inspiration. "I watched you the other night after I so
clumsily cut in on you and Valerie. I saw the way you
looked at her, the way she looked at you. I have
witnessed her unhappiness since the night of the party,
although of course she does not speak to me about it."

"I don't know what you're talking about," Ashe cut
in roughly.

"Don't you?" Felipe gave him a tired, thin smile. "I
think you do. I think you are—how do you say it?—
enamored of my wife?"

"I never—"

"No, no, no. I do not suggest anything illicit or
wrong between the two of you. But you are both young
and you desire each other. Valerie has little enough
pleasure, I'm afraid. As I said, ours is not a normal
marriage. I would not be averse to your 'interest' in my
wife. I am not so selfish as to deny her what her heart
longs for."

Ashe struggled to collect his stunned wits, rage
bubbling up inside him, flooding his throat and tinting
his face a ruddy hue. "Do you think . . . do you
actually think I would accept something like that?" he
spat out when he was able to speak coherently. "Good
God, man, do you pimp for your wife? Can't she find
enough men on her own? Look, I don't know what
your perverted pleasures are, and, frankly, I don't
care. You can arrange affairs for her and enjoy them
vicariously or whatever thrill you get out of it. And she
can hop into bed with any man she wants, collect hearts
like trophies to show you. I don't give a damn. But get
this straight: I won't be a part of any of it. I wouldn't
touch your wife. You may not have any scruples, but I
do." Ashe whirled and strode to the door, flinging it
open with a loud crash. He paused and turned. "And I
can assure you, I won't be seeing you in San Cristóbal.
Alec can get another man for the job."

Felipe jumped to his feet, his brow contracting and
his eyes shooting sparks of dangerous light. But Ashe

was already gone, and the door slammed behind him. Felipe's enraged expression changed to a grimace and he placed one hand on his chest. He sank into his chair and breathed slowly, carefully, waiting for the moment to pass. The seconds clicked by, and the pain didn't burst like a grenade in his chest. It faded, leaving a dull ache in his left arm. Felipe let out a long, shuddering sigh and relaxed. His face was pasty and dotted with sweat.

Ashe thundered down the hall, his face so set and grim that Mrs. Jenkins, Alec's secretary, who happened to step out of Alec's suite at that moment, took a quick step backward. He reached the elevator just as the doors slid quietly open and Valerie stepped out. She was dressed in a simply styled black dress of polished cotton splashed with vibrant pink roses and edged at the neck and hem with a band of the same hot pink. The black was a startling contrast to her white skin, and the pink lent color to her cheeks. Her long moonlight-tinted hair was artfully twisted into a knot atop the crown of her head, and the severity of the style emphasized the delicate lines of her face.

They halted and stared, equally surprised and dismayed. Finally Valerie extended her hand in a tentative gesture. "Ashe, about the other night. I wanted to explain."

He flinched away as if her hand would burn him. "Don't bother," he growled. "I've been having a nice chat with your husband."

"What?" Cold fear stabbed through Valerie's stomach. Had he told Felipe what had occurred between them? Oh, no! Felipe's heart—he couldn't stand it. What would he think? What would he say? "You didn't tell him—"

"No." His voice was frigid with contempt. "I didn't reveal your almost-infidelity. I didn't have to. Felipe is quite anxious for me to fill your bed. Does it take the pressure off him? Is that the only way he can keep you? Or is it a private amusement you share?"

"I don't know what you're talking about. Did Felipe say he knew that I . . . that we . . . ?"

He laughed humorlessly. "Too modest to say it? That you crawled all over me, wanted me to take you in Laraine's flower garden? I don't know how detailed his knowledge is. He encouraged me to satisfy you, and I declined. Believe me, lady, I don't want any part of you."

Ashe stormed past her and slammed through the door leading to the stairs. Valerie stared after him, stunned by his revelation and hurt beyond tears by his low opinion of her. Did Felipe suspect that she was filled with desire for Ashe, had been from the moment she met him? Had he offered to look the other way if Ashe took her to his bed? If so, she knew that Felipe had done it out of an unselfish desire to make her happy, even though it meant hurt and shame for him. Tears swam in her eyes. Again he was kind and generous, while she—it seemed as if she were as selfish as he was not.

Valerie drew a deep breath and walked on to Alec's office, where she had agreed to meet Felipe. Alec's secretary explained that Mr. de la Portilla was in the conference room across the hall. When Valerie opened the door to the meeting room she saw Felipe seated in one of the chairs, his eyes closed. His face was gray-tinged and drawn, and he looked exceedingly tired. Valerie's heart sank in her chest. Whatever Felipe had said to Ashe, it had cost him a great deal. It was time she started thinking of him instead of herself.

Felipe opened his eyes at her entrance and smiled faintly. "Valerie, my love. Are you early?"

"Yes, a little." She decided not to tell him about her original plan of asking him to shop with her before lunch. Instead she said brightly, "I've been thinking. Would you like to go back to San Cristóbal ahead of time?"

"Well, of course, but I thought you wanted to spend a few more days at home."

Valerie shrugged and lied smoothly, "No, actually I've been missing San Cristóbal. Why don't we fly out tomorrow, or, even better, this afternoon? San Cristóbal is my home now, you know."

His face lightened. "We could leave early. My bargaining is over." He paused, then smiled again. "I think you are a liar, little one—but a very pretty liar. And I am an old, tired man. Yes, let's take the first flight back to La Luz."

They landed in La Luz late in the afternoon of the following day. The flight from Dallas to Mexico City had been smooth and uneventful, the first-class seats comfortable, but the trip from Mexico's capital city to San Cristóbal's was cramped and rocky. The government no longer permitted any airline except the approved locally owned one to fly into the airport, a nationalistic gesture which had resulted in huge losses for the San Cristóbal resorts. The planes were small and old and invariably produced a bumpy ride.

Felipe dozed fitfully on the long flight home, and Valerie occupied herself by alternately worrying about her husband's health and firming her resolve to be a good, unselfish wife. It was ridiculous, she told herself, to be so attracted to Ashe Harlan. She hardly knew the man—and if his tirade against her the day before had been any indication of his temper, she doubted she would like him if she knew him better.

Yet from the instant she met Ashe, she had been very aware of him as a man. He assaulted her every sense, and her body had sizzled with an electric excitement. Because of her physical desire she had let him believe she wasn't married, had encouraged him to make love to her, and then had cut him off without an explanation. It had been a cowardly, despicable thing to do, and it wasn't surprising that Ashe despised her, especially after Felipe sanctioned an affair between them. Felipe had merely been trying to make up for tying her to a sick, rapidly aging man, but Ashe had no way of knowing that. He saw the worst, and while it hurt her that Ashe regarded her with such contempt, she couldn't blame him. Miserable, she reflected that she had hurt everyone, including herself. But from now on it was going to be different. She swore it.

She would work to fit in with Felipe's family and country. She wouldn't rail against their customs and strictures. Instead she would obey them quietly, calmly. She would be pleasant to Felipe's son, Esteban, who disapproved of her, and even try to tolerate Esteban's wife, Inés. And that was something which ought to entitle a person to sainthood!

After the plane had landed safely and taxied to the small airport building, Felipe and Valerie gratefully left it and went to the customs desk. Because of the de la Portilla wealth and influence, they were passed through quickly. However, a nearby guard insolently appraised Valerie as they waited, his expression barely short of a leer. Fear gripped her stomach. Such rudeness was an indication of Felipe's progressive fall from what favor he had known with the junta. That was the way things were here. Casual remarks, the way people looked at you on the street—these were the barometers by which the life of the country was measured. If one knew the signs and watched carefully, one would know that the government was tottering or a revolt was brewing or his neighbor was likely to be thrown into prison on some trumped-up charge.

Their chauffeur met them on the other side of customs, bowing and ceremoniously ushering them into the back of the long black sedan before he retrieved their luggage. When the chauffeur returned he stowed the bags in the trunk, then hopped into the front seat and pulled away from the curb. He turned into the mainstream of traffic with little regard for life and limb, but Valerie didn't even flinch. She had long ago become used to the La Luz style of driving. Their huge limousine nearly always won any argument of honor in heavy traffic.

Valerie noticed that there were few people on the streets. A still, deserted atmosphere hung over the city. More soldiers than usual lounged on the street corners. A gray and blue van of the Policía Nacional whizzed past, sirens blaring in a chilling singsong. Valerie shivered and glanced at her husband. She wished she could ask Felipe if he, too, felt the tension in the air. But she couldn't, for there was always the chance that the chauffeur was a government spy. There were only one or two old family servants whom Felipe really trusted, but even so, he would not endanger them by saying anything politically significant in front of them.

In the few days they had spent in Dallas, Valerie had grown accustomed to not living in a police state. It was hard to face it again—the fear, the tension, the suspicion. Would the revolution come? And if so, what would they do? If the government won, the de la Portillas might be killed for not having been strong supporters. But the leftist guerrillas weren't likely to treat them kindly either. Only if an army faction opposing the regime came to power would the de la Portillas be able to feel relatively safe. Valerie was certain that Felipe would protect her and spirit her out of the country as soon as any danger developed—if he could. But would he know in time? And how could she leave him alone? He wouldn't leave his country. He had too much old-fashioned pride and honor. Valerie swallowed the lump of fear in her throat, but she couldn't quiet the voice inside, which asked how she could hope to carry out her vow to accept San Cristóbal when this was the way it was.

Chapter 5

THE DE LA PORTILLA HOME IN LA LUZ WAS SMALLER than the plantation house but far more formal. It stood behind a high stone fence, the short driveway barred by black wrought-iron gates. On the outside it resembled a stately ivory-colored box decorated with black wrought-iron bars over the windows. Three shallow steps led up to the imposing carved door guarded on either side by stone lions. Inside, the mansion was equally grand, filled with massive, ornately carved furniture crammed into narrow rooms. It had been decorated by Felipe's grandmother, and none of the succeeding generations had had the daring to change it. Valerie preferred the plantation house, which was open, airy and decorated with light cane and wicker furniture.

The limousine pulled to a stop in front of the iron gates, and the chauffeur jumped out to open them, then drove through to the house. As Felipe and Valerie emerged from the car the front door opened and their butler, Bernardo, stepped out as quickly as his dignity allowed. Felipe returned Bernardo's greeting gravely and they moved inside, crossing the cool marble hallway to the large family room. Felipe's brother, Alfonso, sat beside the French doors leading onto the patio.

When he saw Felipe, he rushed to greet him. The two men embraced emotionally while Valerie stood back, waiting for a chance to say hello to Alfonso before she slipped away.

Finally Alfonso pulled away from his brother and turned to Valerie. "Ah, my lovely little sister." He held out his arms to her, and instinctively Valerie's hands went up to ward him off. Quickly she changed the gesture by putting her hands on Alfonso's arms as she leaned forward to place her cheek against his for an instant. Alfonso was younger, heavier and shorter than his brother, and he lacked Felipe's spontaneous charm.

Valerie had never dared to intrude on Felipe's quiet reserve by asking how he felt about his brother. She suspected that Felipe put up with a great deal from Alfonso because he felt guilty for receiving the majority of the family's gifts: charm, looks, intelligence and money sense. Alfonso was extravagant in his personal life, keeping house for his mistress as well as collecting expensive automobiles. From a chance word now and then Valerie had surmised that Alfonso had also been foolish in his business affairs. Valerie had never been able to like him, for he seemed to her a sly, oily sort. Moreover, he disapproved of her and upbraided her in private for her loose American ways. Valerie had been careful not to tell Felipe about those lectures, just as she had not complained of his son's hostility. She refused to add to his burden by making him defend her to his family.

"It's good to be home," Valerie lied valiantly, and Alfonso cast her a curious glance. "Now, if you gentlemen will excuse me, I'm sure you have business to discuss, and I would like to wash away the dirt of travel."

"Of course, my dear." Felipe smiled at her, and she hurried from the room and up the stairs, hoping she could make it to her bedroom before anyone intercepted her. But she was not to be so lucky. As she topped

the magnificent winding marble staircase Alfonso's
wife, Pilar, left her room at the end of the hall.

"Valerie!" Pilar flung wide her arms and rushed to
Valerie. "I'm so happy you're home. I saw the car
outside and I hoped you and Felipe had returned
early."

Valerie returned the greeting affectionately, although she dreaded facing Pilar's chatter. Her sister-in-
law was the only one in the family who liked her or
tried to make her feel welcome. Pilar, a meek middle-
aged woman herself, admired Valerie's independence
and comparatively daring ways. Pilar was completely
under her husband's thumb, hardly able to purchase a
dress without his approval. Though Valerie liked her,
she was careful never to reveal any secrets, for she was
sure that Pilar told Alfonso everything she heard.

Valerie patiently endured a long hour of conversation with Pilar, who was anxious to hear about her trip
and her beautiful cousin, Laraine. Pilar had been
intrigued by Laraine ever since she had seen her picture
in Valerie's wedding album. It amazed her that a
woman older than herself could appear so thin, attractive and self-assured. Valerie recounted their dinner
with the Stones as well as the large party Laraine had
thrown for them, although she carefully avoided any
mention of Ashe Harlan. Though not the brightest of
women, Pilar had an innate feminine perception which
could cut straight to the truth when romance was
involved.

When Pilar left Valerie was able to take the bath she
had been longing for all afternoon, although Pilar's
visit had made it impossible for her to soak as long as
she wished. She soon had to leave the tub and dress for
dinner, which at the de la Portilla town house was a
formal occasion. Valerie redid her hair and makeup
and zipped herself into an eggshell-colored dress. The
outfit was unadorned except for a high quilted collar
and matching quilted strip along the top of the shoul-

ders. A plain belt cinched her slim waist. Glancing in the mirror, she decided that she looked satisfactorily elegant, although for some reason she seemed far too pale. She appeared every inch a lady, but the woman inside yearned for something else, a bright spot of color, perhaps, to bring a flame to her cheeks.

Valerie whirled away and hurried down the stairs to the small sitting area beside the dining room. Felipe and Alfonso had not arrived yet, presumably delayed by their business discussion, but Pilar was there, along with Esteban and Inés, who had driven over from their home on the newer, fashionable Avenida de las Palmas. Esteban turned at Valerie's entrance and barely managed to summon up a smile. Obviously he had been hoping she would decide to remain in Dallas.

"Esteban." She inclined her head formally but made no move to shake his hand or give him even a cool embrace.

"Valerie." He was equally abrupt and moved away immediately to pour himself another drink. Physically Esteban was a younger replica of Felipe, though Valerie could detect little of his father's grace and charm in him. She had seen him on a few occasions flash a winning smile or turn an elegant phrase when he was speaking to someone besides her. However, his wit was generally sharp and sarcastic, and his charm a trifle too cold. To Valerie he was hardly even polite. From the moment she had arrived as Felipe's wife it had been obvious that he feared and disliked her. Valerie guessed it was for the reason Laraine had suggested. He was afraid that his father's young wife would produce an heir to displace him in his father's affections . . . and fortune.

Inés was more dissembling than her husband. She swayed forward to peck Valerie's cheek with her thin red lips and give her the same open embrace Valerie had achieved with Alfonso, hands on each other's arms and bodies firmly apart, only their heads meeting.

"Valerie, how well you look. The States seem to have agreed with you."

"Thank you. You look lovely, as always." It was the simple truth. Though she thoroughly disliked her, Valerie wasn't blind enough to deny that Inés was a stunning woman. She was tall and slender, almost flat-chested, but possessing such long, perfect legs that one hardly noticed her small bosom. Her thick black hair was cut in a smooth bob, and a pair of barrettes held it back from her face, highlighting her excellent bone structure. Her skin was a delicate apricot, and expert makeup brought out her dark, heavily lashed eyes. Her eyebrows were thin, curved lines of black. She was dressed in shimmering red, the same shade as her lips and nails. It flashed across Valerie's mind that her nails looked as if they had been dipped in blood, and inwardly she shivered. If Esteban was hostile and resentful, his wife was wicked.

"You are too kind," Inés demurred politely. One eyebrow arching insinuatingly, she continued, "I trust you met many old *friends* while you were home."

"No, actually, I have only relatives in Dallas, not friends," Valerie replied blandly, fully aware of the sexual innuendo in Inés's manner. Valerie had learned long ago to ignore Inés's digs. It was the only way to maintain a modicum of decency in their conversations. "Most of the girls I went to college with live in the East."

Inés smiled. "But girlfriends are so dull."

"I don't think so. I enjoy female company."

"Do you? Well, I suppose there are women like that. Me, I find the men much more exciting." She cast a slanting glance at Esteban and he responded with a burning look. Valerie almost giggled. It was so over-blown. Surely real romantic love didn't need the special effects Inés and Esteban were so fond of. All Ashe had to do was graze her arm or smile— Now why in the world was she thinking of him? That wasn't love, merely brief passion, which she hoped would go away after a few days' absence from him.

Valerie sat down on the sofa beside Pilar and engaged her in conversation, while Esteban glowered and drank, and Inés stared idly out the window. Finally Alfonso and Felipe entered the room, and they could go into the dining room to eat. The family sat at a formal table far too long for their number, while a maid served them. Alfonso and Pilar kept the conversation going, carefully steering clear of dangerous topics. They touched on the weather, the repairs needed on the plantation house, the coming theater season and the latest party given by the Riveras. Valerie struggled to keep her eyes open. The food was heavy and cool from its long journey from the kitchen. Valerie toyed with it but ate little. It was a relief when at last she could leave.

She retired early, pleading travel weariness. Her good resolutions on the plane were unraveling right before her eyes. Because of her guilt about Ashe, she had blamed herself for not getting along with Felipe's relatives, but now she was struck anew by their obnoxious behavior. She wondered how she could change the relationship when the others obviously had no interest in improving it. Esteban and Inés would hate her no matter what she did. Perhaps she could please Alfonso by adopting a meek attitude and behaving like a good San Cristobalian wife, but everything inside her railed against it.

Sighing, she sat down at her vanity table to brush out her hair, then undressed and slipped into an ivory satin nightgown. Valerie loved luxurious lingerie: soft, clinging gowns, seductive lace panties, and slips in delicate hues, all as expensive as they were sensuous. It seemed strange that, being so cool and restrained on the outside, she would indulge in sexually alluring garments next to her skin.

Valerie climbed into the high bed, too tired even to

think about the heavy, claustrophobic canopy above her head, as she usually did. As soon as her head touched the pillow she was asleep.

She was strolling in a garden, surrounded by flowers of bright and varied colors, but as she walked her pleasure in the plants diminished. She realized that she was lost. She speeded up her steps, glancing from side to side, her fear growing with every passing moment. Then she looked back and understood her fear. Inés followed her at a distance, her face a cold mask of hatred, and in one hand she carried a machete dripping blood as red as her fingernails. Valerie began to run, her heart pounding, but she couldn't find a way out. Instead the surrounding plants kept getting higher and higher and changing from flowers into bushes, until she could see nothing but the leafy green walls around her. All the while Inés came closer. *She* never seemed to tire.

Valerie stumbled and fell heavily to the ground. Frantically she struggled to rise, but she could not. Something weighed her down. In frozen terror she awaited the fall of the machete. But suddenly she was pulled to her feet. Inés vanished as Valerie gazed at her rescuer. Ashe Harlan. He had on the open work shirt and faded jeans he had worn when she met him. She leaned against his bare chest, and his warmth passed into her. She was no longer cold, no longer scared.

His hands began to move lazily over her back, and Valerie snuggled closer. The caresses began to cover more and more of her body. He touched her hips, her thighs, her arms, and finally her yearning, thrusting breasts, thumbs teasing the peaks. She ached for him to undress her and he did, sliding off her blouse, then her skirt. She found to her surprise that she wore nothing underneath and was embarrassed at the omission, but he didn't seem to mind. He smiled and studied her. The sun glinted off his hair, turning it bright gold, but his face was shadowed. His eyes never leaving her face,

Ashe grasped the sides of his shirt and pulled it down his shoulders and arms, then tossed it casually on the ground. Valerie stared at him, mesmerized. Slowly his fingers unsnapped the waistband of his trousers, and she waited for him to continue, her breath caught in her throat.

She heard feet running toward them, and she remembered that Ashe was forbidden to her. She whirled, looking for the runner. Who was it? "Alfonso?" she called out, certain it was he. There was more noise, more running. Someone began to pound on the garden gate. Valerie had to open it, but she didn't know where it was. She recalled that she was naked and alone with Ashe Harlan. Oh, dear God, she was caught. Caught! She spun around, seeking a way out.

Valerie sat up with a jolt, sweat beading on her forehead and running down her sides, dampening her gown. For a moment she was disoriented, the dream so real that she could still feel the throb of passion in her veins and the dry fear in her mouth. Where was she?

There was another loud knock on the door. "Señora!" The voice was urgent, and she recognized it as that of Beatricz, Pilar's personal maid. Valerie glanced down to make sure she wasn't naked, as she had dreamed, before she called, "Come in." Why on earth was Beatricz pounding on her door in the middle of the night? She glanced at the small clock on her night table. It read twelve-thirty. "What is it? What's the matter?"

"Oh, señora, come quickly!" Beatricz exclaimed as she burst in, her Spanish so rapid that Valerie could hardly understand her. "It is the señor. Señora Pilar, she sent me to get you. He is sick, very sick."

Felipe! Fear seized Valerie and she ran across the room, jerking open the door to the large bathroom which connected her room to Felipe's. She burst into his bedroom and stopped in the doorway, immobilized by the scene before her.

Felipe lay stretched out on the floor beside his dresser, and Alfonso knelt beside him, holding one of his hands. Alfonso glanced up distractedly at Valerie's entrance. His eyes were filled with tears. "Felipe," he said, his tone wondering, almost childlike. "He's—I think he's dead."

Ashe Harlan strode down the hall to Alec's office, his bootheels noiseless on the thick carpet. He had just flown in from a well in West Texas and was dressed in the same clothes he had worn there, his boots covered with dust. As soon as he had entered his office, his secretary had hustled him out the door, saying that Alec had called several times to see if he was in yet. That meant something important was up.

Ashe pushed open the glass door leading into Alec's luxurious suite. Alec's secretary glanced up and nodded toward the closed door of the inner office.

"Go on in. He's waiting for you."

It sounded like another emergency. Well, that was okay. He welcomed them these days. It had been almost two weeks since Valerie and Felipe had left, and during that time he had worked like a driven man. It was the only way to keep his mind off Valerie. Dreams of her haunted his sleep unless he was dog tired, and during the day he found himself remembering their short time together, recalling her gestures and smiles, her changeable silver-green eyes, her vulnerable mouth that could widen into a smile so bright it dazzled him. Over and over he asked himself why he let her affect him so, just as he questioned why she had married Felipe de la Portilla. He knew the answers. He simply didn't want to face them, and the easiest way to avoid doing so was to work constantly.

Ashe stepped inside Alec's office. Alec was on the phone and waved him to a chair as he finished the conversation. When the older man hung up he raked one hand through his thick, silver-streaked hair and sighed. "What a day. Well, how was it?"

"Everything's under control, I think. The sinkhole

finally stopped growing. We've lost a lot of equipment, of course, but I think it's over."

"Good. I need you to fly to San Cristóbal."

"Now?" Ashe's eyebrows shot up. "I thought I was going next week."

"You were, but I've decided to step things up. Besides talking to the government about the offshore well, you have to see the de la Portillas."

Ashe's stomach tightened. Now was the time to explain to Alec that he couldn't do it. He had put it off as long as he could. But did he really not want to go? Not see Valerie? "I got a call this morning from Felipe's son, Esteban," Alec continued. "Felipe died of a heart attack the night he arrived back in San Cristóbal."

"What?" Ashe stared.

"Yeah. Frightening, isn't it? Laraine told me that Valerie said he had a serious heart condition, but I never imagined . . ."

Ashe's heart set up a wild thumping in his chest. Valerie's husband was dead. No, he couldn't start thinking that way. Good God, the woman was newly a widow. He couldn't make plans to get her into his bed when her husband's body was barely cold. Besides, Felipe's death wouldn't change her heart and soul. She was still a conniver, a gold digger, a woman willing to sell herself for money and eager to cuckold her husband. She was "plain no good," as his mother would have said, shaking her head regretfully. If he got involved with Valerie de la Portilla, he would be condemning himself to far worse grief than any he'd known over the past two weeks. She could tear his heart to shreds.

"I don't know why they waited so long to notify me. And who knows what the situation will be now? That's why I want you to leave tomorrow. Talk to the brother and the son, find out who the executor is and how Felipe's death will affect our deal. I have Schaeffer down in the legal department checking out the relevant

San Cristóbal laws. He'll let you know what he finds out before you leave."

Ashe hesitated. It wouldn't be so bad since he wouldn't have to deal with Felipe. And wouldn't it be better to face Valerie? He wasn't one to take the coward's way out. "Okay. Is . . . uh . . . Mrs. de la Portilla involved?"

"Valerie?" Alec's face softened as he said her name, and a slow smile spread across his lips.

Jealousy stabbed through Ashe like a steel-cold knife. Alec's expression indicated intimacy with Valerie, reawakening the suspicion that he and Valerie had been lovers. Maybe she specialized in older men. It made sense. They were the ones with the money, after all. He'd do well to remember that. Though she might go to bed with him, she wouldn't stay. In the end she'd find another rich old man.

Valerie sat beside her window, staring out across the lawn to the street beyond. Two weeks. It had been two weeks since Felipe had died. For the first time since that awful night feeling was beginning to return to her. When she found Felipe's body and heard Alfonso say he was dead she had been stunned. Her shock had continued through the doctor's visit and the priest's. The doctor had confirmed that he was dead, and the priest, too late for the last rites, had prayed for him. Valerie, pale and shaking, had sunk into a chair and continued to stare at her husband's body, now politely covered with a blanket and lifted onto his bed. Felipe couldn't be dead! He simply couldn't!

No one had paid any attention to Valerie until Pilar edged quietly into the room and led Valerie back to her own bedroom. Pilar stayed with her the rest of the night, and Valerie had been glad for her presence, for she hadn't been able to sleep. It had been close to dawn before she closed her eyes. When she awoke she learned that Esteban and Alfonso were taking care of all the funeral preparations. For once Valerie was content with the San Cristóbal custom of the males of the family taking charge. She had as much as she could handle greeting the many friends who paid sympathy calls. Valerie accepted their condolences graciously, earning the respect of many of Felipe's countrymen. In reality she was not so much exercising ladylike containment as she was numb.

The strangely disconnected feeling continued through the funeral mass and the briefer ceremony beside the grave. She dressed in black and wore a shoulder-length black veil, as was customary for a widow in San Cristóbal. Flanked by Esteban and Alfonso, she knelt in the front pew while the priest conducted the long service. Afterward, as the casket was carried from the church, she followed on foot, with the remainder of the family a few steps behind her. The procession wound across the street and through the gates of the iron-fenced cemetery, then along the row of ancient graves to the de la Portilla family tomb.

Afterward there was a long funeral feast. By the time she returned to her bedroom Valerie was exhausted. She spent the next few days there, alternately sleeping and staring out the window. It was unbelievable that Felipe was dead. At times she caught herself wondering when he would return from work or whether he would wish to remain at home that evening. Once she even rose from her chair to ask him a question before she remembered that he was dead. He had been such a large part of her life for three years that now the future loomed emptily.

That morning she had breakfasted alone in her room as she always did. Suddenly, as she was eating her toast, she recalled how Felipe had often joined her for an intimate breakfast instead of partaking of the large meal downstairs with the rest of the family. He would joke and laugh, as if he were as young as she was and unburdened with worries. Tears had sprung into her eyes at the thought and had burst forth hot and gushing as she sobbed.

It was then that she realized deep inside her that Felipe was gone. He would never again open her door and pop his head inside to smile and ask boyishly if he could join her for breakfast. He would no longer be there to help or protect her. She had loved him; perhaps not with the deep love of a wife for a husband, but still she had loved him. And she had depended on him as if he were her father. Now all that was gone. She would be on her own and would have to make her own decisions.

Valerie was filled with a deep sorrow, but her tears washed away the tired numbness. She realized that she had passed from one stage of her life into another. She was no longer Felipe's wife but her own person again. She must decide what she was going to do. Valerie rose and began to pace thoughtfully. Her future had been given back to her. She could go to school, take the necessary undergraduate courses and then obtain her doctorate in archaeology. The idea even brought a smile to her face. She would fly home and apply to several colleges. Why not visit Laraine, who had always been more comforting than her own mother? And Alec, dear Alec was there. And Ashe. No! She wouldn't think about him. He despised her. It was too soon after Felipe's death. Later, much later, when her life and emotions were straightened out, she would let herself think about Ashe.

She would tell the family about her decision that night. They would be more than happy to say good-bye to her. So, for the first time since Felipe's death, she joined the others for dinner that evening. Alfonso, Pilar, Esteban and Inés were already in the small sitting room when she arrived. Alfonso smiled gravely. "Ah, my dear, I'm glad you are well enough to join us. It is a remarkable coincidence. I planned to discuss something with you this evening after the meal."

"I wanted to talk to you, too." Valerie wondered if

they had decided to inform her that she was no longer welcome in this house.

Dinner was the usual formal, stilted affair. Valerie wasn't hungry and was grateful when it finally ended and they were able to retire to the large family room. The doors to the patio stood open to the soft spring breeze, and the curtains rose lazily on the gusts of mild air. Valerie debated letting Alfonso speak first out of politeness but decided that it would be easier all around if she assured them of her intentions first. Then no one would have to tell her to leave, and she wouldn't have to hear it.

"I've decided to go home," she blurted out.

Blank faces stared back at her, and for one wild moment she thought she hadn't spoken out loud. Then Alfonso cleared his throat. "Now, Valerie, you must not act hastily."

"I'm not. It's been two weeks. I—I've accepted Felipe's death and I need to go on. I can't stay in my room forever. Obviously it's logical for me to go home."

"This is your home now," Pilar assured her.

Valerie smiled. "Thank you for saying that, Pilar, but I would be happier back in the U.S., and you would all be happier if I left, too. We all know I don't belong here."

"You're rushing into this without giving it the proper thought," Alfonso stated commandingly. "You should consult us before making such an important decision."

As if I weren't capable of making one without his help, Valerie thought in disgust. She turned to Esteban and Inés. They'd certainly be glad to see her go. "Esteban, don't you agree that I should leave?"

To her amazement he countered smoothly, "No, Valerie. I have to agree with my uncle. This is a family matter. We should discuss it as a family." Valerie stared. What on earth was going on? There was almost hatred in Esteban's eyes when he looked at her, yet he pretended that he wanted her to stay! It didn't make sense. "My uncle and I have been discussing your future," he went on. "You must understand that since my father is dead, your welfare is our concern."

"Yes," Alfonso chimed in like the end man in a minstrel show. "At a time like this you must trust us to do what is best. You are far too grief stricken to think clearly. Say you'll let us help you."

"I'll be glad to let you help, Alfonso," Valerie snapped back. "You may make reservations for me on the plane to Mexico City."

Alfonso's lips tightened. "This is no time for jokes."

"I'm not joking. Look, I don't understand. Why do you want me to stay here? Let's be honest and admit that none of us like each other much—with the exception of Pilar, whom it would be hard to dislike. I'll go back to the States and we'll never have to see each other again."

"No, Valerie, I don't think that's best," Alfonso intoned in his best head-of-the-family manner. "Esteban and I agree that the most suitable arrangement to insure your and the family's welfare"—again he cleared his throat—"is for you to marry my son Carlos."

Chapter 6

VALERIE STARED, TOO AMAZED TO SPEAK. ALFONSO, taking her silence for consent, went on. "Carlos is unmarried, thirty-one and a member of the family. All in all, an excellent match."

He was also bad tempered, bullying and as sly as his father, Valerie thought to herself, but her anger had boiled too high to let her speak coherently. She wanted to scream and stamp in a fit of rage. How dare they think they could decide her life this way? But she forced herself to be calm, remembering that they were Felipe's family and that they were used to different customs. Choosing her words carefully, she began, "Alfonso, it may be the practice here for the deceased's family to arrange a marriage for the widow. However, it is not what I am used to. It seems indecent when Felipe has been dead only two weeks."

"It must be done quickly."

"Why? Why must it be done at all? Let's be honest. None of you like me, and, frankly, I haven't enjoyed living in San Cristóbal. Why don't we just part amicably?"

"Impossible."

His remark was the last straw. Valerie could no longer control her burgeoning anger. She leaped to her feet, eyes snapping dangerously. "It is not impossible!

Your suggestion is impossible. And absurd, as well. I hardly know Carlos. He's been out to the plantation a few times, mostly when Felipe and I were away. But I didn't like what I have seen of him. It's crazy to think I'd marry him. I'm not marrying anyone! If for some insane reason I rushed into marriage the minute my husband died, I certainly wouldn't choose someone from this benighted country. Most particularly not a de la Portilla! Felipe was the only decent one among you!"

Alfonso's mouth thinned into a grim line. "The marriage is a necessity. You must do it for the sake of the family. For Felipe's memory."

"I think it would be a pretty peculiar memorial to my husband, who, by the way, was not fond of Carlos."

"Carlos is a good boy," Pilar protested, and Valerie realized that she had alienated her only friend in the household.

Valerie sighed and turned to Pilar. "I'm sorry. I know he's your son. Maybe I'm prejudiced and being unfair to him, but the fact remains that I barely know Carlos. I wouldn't dream of marrying a man I don't love. Surely you can understand that."

"Don't act like a vapid eighteen-year-old," Inés snapped. "This has nothing to do with love. It's a matter of the family. Surely you don't think we *want* you to continue in the de la Portilla family. It's a necessity."

"You see, Valerie," Alfonso began reasonably, as if his explanation would make her see the light, "we need a channel to the U.S. for our money. We are more in disfavor with the regime every day. When trouble comes we may be right in the middle. We need to have funds in the U.S. in case we have to flee San Cristóbal."

Valerie gaped. "You expect me to marry Carlos so you can get money out of the country?"

"It's why you married Felipe," Inés pointed out.

"I loved Felipe and wanted to help him. But I have no desire to help any of you. Forget it."

Alfonso exploded, "Damn your Yankee impudence!

Don't tell me what you will and will not do. I am head of this family now, and you will do as I say."

Valerie jumped at his tone, but she faced him rebelliously, her hands on her hips and her chin thrust forward. "I will not! You can bluster all you want, but it means nothing to me. I won't be told who I may and may not marry. I make my own decisions. And I'm leaving tomorrow for the United States."

She whirled and stalked out, rigid with fury, so pale that her eyes glittered like green glass. God knows, she had never been especially courageous and independent, but she wasn't so spineless as to allow Alfonso to command her to marry anyone!

After slamming her bedroom door behind her, Valerie flung herself into a chair, then jumped up and began to pace the room. She started to undress for bed several times, but each time she was interrupted by the memory of Alfonso's insulting proposal or by imagining what she should have said instead of what she had. Almost an hour passed before she had changed into her nightgown, robe and slippers. She was too keyed up to sleep, so she stood at the window for a long time, staring out blindly.

Slowly the anger wore itself out, leaving her exhausted. She thought of Alfonso suggesting the arrangement to one of the Stones, Alexis for instance, and the idea made her giggle. Alexis had a tongue like a knife when she wanted, and by the time she got through with Alfonso, he would have felt flayed alive. Well, perhaps she didn't have Alexis's sharp mind and even sharper tongue, but Valerie knew she had made it clear that she wouldn't stand for his proposal. She had asserted herself without hesitation, which was something of a first for her.

Another thing had happened that night. Her fury at his family had burned away most of her grief. She had loved Felipe. He had been good to her and had helped her to mature. She would mourn him as she would a good friend or a close uncle, but the sorrow would no longer numb her. She knew that Felipe had released her with his blessing.

She stretched out on the bed, contemplating the dark canopy high above her, and gradually she drifted to sleep. It was late the next morning before she awoke. She smiled as she blinked and yawned. Today she would cast off the burden of the de la Portilla family and return home. Valerie threw aside her coverlet and hopped out of bed, humming as she showered and dressed. The maid had apparently entered earlier and, finding her sleeping, left the breakfast tray on the low table beside Valerie's reading chair. Valerie was surprised to find herself ravenous. It was the first time she had been hungry in days. She had lost almost five pounds since Felipe's death, giving her an even more fine-boned, delicate look.

After she had eaten she planned her departure. The first thing to do was to go downstairs and call the airline company for a reservation on the afternoon plane to Mexico City. After that, she would return to her room to pack. Valerie strode to the door leading into the hall and turned the old metal knob. The knob twisted in her hand, but the door did not open. She yanked at it another time before she realized what had happened: they had locked her in her room! She whirled and ran into the bathroom to try the door to Felipe's room. It didn't budge. Valerie slammed her fists against the ungiving wood. Alfonso planned to keep her a prisoner until she gave in to him!

That was the last rational thought she had for some time. She stormed to her bedroom door and beat on it with her fists, even kicked it and screamed. Nobody came and she finally wore out her initial blinding fury. Valerie turned away and flopped down in the easy chair. Obviously the de la Portillas would do almost anything to keep her there. However, they couldn't force her to marry Carlos. Surely Alfonso would realize that sooner or later. If she sat tight and steadfastly refused to marry him, eventually her stubbornness would win out. But that reasonable approach didn't appeal to her.

She wanted out now. She had to get out. She couldn't bear to be trapped. Valerie rose and paced for a time before she forced herself to sit down to wait calmly. No doubt Alfonso hoped she would become so upset and stir crazy that she would agree to anything to get out of the room. Resigning herself to boredom, she sat and stared out the window as the day wore on. There were no books or television in her room. The sun slowly crossed the sky and sank. The room turned dark, but Valerie didn't bother to turn on a light. There was nothing to see.

Finally, for lack of anything better to do, she changed into her nightgown and went to bed, but she was unable to sleep. She tossed and turned for hours, troubled by the same thoughts, angers and fears that had plagued her all day. Nothing could shatter her basic American confidence that no one could imprison her for long or prevent her from returning to the United States. But being locked up was scary. The sheer hostility of the action upset her. Dislike or disapproval had always been frightening to her, but the de la Portillas' concerted hatred was far worse. Her sustaining anger began to seep away. And her stomach, empty since breakfast, was beginning to annoy her. She wished with all her heart that she was home. Sniffing back a tear, she fell asleep.

The next morning there was a full tray of food on her table again and Valerie pounced on it. Afterward she went through her almost hourly routine of trying the locks on the doors. It didn't surprise her that neither door would open. She sat down, struggling to maintain her much-tried patience. Panicky rage wouldn't be effective. That would encourage Alfonso to believe she would break sooner or later. She must present a calm front.

Early in the afternoon she heard steps outside her door, and then Alfonso spoke her name. Through the door he asked if she would agree to marry Carlos, and she refused. He argued and threatened, and she replied as confidently and calmly as she was able, thankful he couldn't see her face. It occurred to her after he left that the whole scene had been farcical: hurling dire threats through a door like two children.

Suddenly she snapped upright. She *had* behaved like a child by sitting there waiting for something to happen, for Alfonso to give up, or for Laraine to worry because she couldn't reach Valerie and to send Alec to her rescue. Waiting was better than bursting into tears and begging to be released, but it was a poor substitute for taking action.

Valerie went to the door and knelt to examine the lock. It was an old-fashioned one with a large keyhole. She crossed to the bathroom and grabbed nail files, hairpins and any other object that could conceivably jimmy the lock. For the next couple of hours she wore her patience thin and turned her fingers numb trying to force the lock. Finally she dropped the manicure scissors she had used last and slumped against the door, staring out the window. Obviously she wasn't cut out to be a burglar. For a long time she gazed into space, aware of an idea nagging at the back of her brain. She was forgetting something. What was it?

Suddenly Valerie shot up, spitting out a short, rude exclamation. She'd been gazing out the window half the time she'd been in there, but it hadn't occurred to her until now to escape that way. There were two long windows in her room, both covered by bars. She opened them and tested the bars. They didn't move. The flat iron borders were bolted into the wall. She had no wrenches, and broke two nail files trying to loosen the heavy bolts with them. Sighing heavily, she crossed her arms on the windowsill and laid her head on her arms. It was then that she noticed the narrow ledge below the windows; it ran past the bathroom window, too.

She bounded up and darted into the bathroom. There was a high opaque window above the bathtub, so small that no one had thought it worth protecting with bars. But someone as thin as she was might be able to slip through . . . if she could just get her shoulders past the frame. Valerie climbed onto the rim of the high old tub to open the window, which swung in and up. She stuck her head out and peered around. Below was so sheer a drop that it made her queasy. She could fashion some sort of rope and climb down, she guessed, but she had never climbed. What if she slipped and crashed to the ground two stories below? More immediately, what if she couldn't even get out the window? Valerie stretched on tiptoe, but her shoulders wedged against the window frame.

She was going about this the wrong way, she realized, and pulled her head back in. First she put out one arm, tilted her head, and eased out her head and one shoulder. With a firm push of her feet, she slid out past her shoulders. Twisting, she looked around the wall beside and above her. What she saw above was encouraging: a circular, curlicued wrought-iron decoration bolted into the wall. That would give her something firm to grasp while she pulled the rest of her body out. Smiling, she worked her head and shoulders back in, which seemed even harder than getting them out.

Almost happily Valerie applied herself to her next task—making a rope. She had often read books in which the heroine tied sheets together and slid from a window to the ground below. But how did it work exactly? Sheets would make very bulky knots that might slip apart when a person's weight was suspended from them. There must be a better method of using the sheets. If she cut them into narrow strips and braided the strips together, then braided the braids together, she would have strength as well as a thinner rope, which would tie more easily.

It was slow work, since she first had to use small

manicure scissors to cut the sheets, then tear them the rest of the way and do the braiding. However, she had nothing else to occupy her time, and it made her feel good to do something constructive. She was taking her future into her own hands, depending on no one else.

At about three o'clock that afternoon there was the sound of footsteps in the hall and then the scrape of a key in the lock. Hastily Valerie shoved her materials under the bed and jumped to her feet just as Alfonso entered the room and closed the door behind him.

For a second Valerie considered rushing for the unlocked door, but she realized immediately that it would be a foolhardy thing to do. Alfonso was between her and freedom, and judging by the black look on his face, he would probably relish knocking her away from the door. She remembered the bruises she had seen one day on Pilar.

Valerie linked her hands behind her back and assumed a cool expression. "Yes? Have you come to apologize?"

"Apologize!" Alfonso thundered and spat out several brutal Spanish curse words. "No, I have not come to apologize," he mimicked bitingly. "I have come to tell you to dress for dinner. We will have an American guest who insists on seeing you."

Valerie's heart leaped. It must be someone she knew, since he had asked to see her. She would be able to explain her situation to him, and he would whisk her away from this dreadful house. She disguised her happiness by assuming a haughty air.

But Alfonso was aware of her elation, for he began to threaten her with various painful punishments should she tell "a wild story" to the American. Valerie said nothing, unmoved by his words. Alfonso couldn't keep her from speaking to the guest. She raised one eyebrow disdainfully, waiting for him to finish his threats. Finally, casting a last glare at her, Alfonso backed out the door, locking it behind him. Valerie laughed aloud as she twirled around her room. She glanced at the bed, under which her materials lay, and was unexpectedly disappointed that she wouldn't be freeing herself after all. That was silly. Leaving with the American by the front door would be much easier and safer.

She hummed as she bathed, speculating on the identity of the guest. She applied light makeup and drew her hair back from her face, securing it with combs. She liked the style and was glad she didn't have to put it up in order to appear older. She was no longer Felipe's wife. She was herself now. Crossing to the old-fashioned wardrobe, she selected a white satin pants suit formal enough for evening wear. Alfonso would disapprove, both because it was trousers and because it wasn't black mourning. But her beliefs didn't require wearing black after a loved one died, and she would be issuing Alfonso a challenge by appearing in this outfit.

The trousers were slim-cut, and the jacket had a high, upstanding Mandarin collar and sleeves puffed from shoulder to elbow, then gathered tightly at the wrist. The material was covered with a pattern of tiny white-on-white flowers, adding to the rich sheen of the satin. It was an exquisite outfit, modestly outlining her trim figure, yet emphasizing her delicate good looks. She wore no ornaments except a ruby ring that Felipe had given her and her antique wedding ring. She was ready early and had to cool her heels, waiting to be released. When at last she heard Alfonso's footsteps in the hall she schooled her face to reveal only cool indifference.

He entered the room and she rose without haste. Ignoring his extended arm, she swept past him and started down the winding mahogany-railed staircase. Inside, her heart pounded with excitement. The American guest waited at the bottom of the stairs, his height foreshortened because she stood above him. He was

turned away, but Valerie would have known him
anywhere, from any angle. Ashe Harlan. A shimmering thrill of happiness ran through her. Ashe had come
to rescue her. He swiveled and glanced up at her. His
blond hair was darker than she remembered and his
face even more handsome. But he stared at her with an
expression as cold and hard as rock. He still despised
her.

Valerie made her feet continue down the stairs. She
grasped the banister as if it were a lifeline, her knuckles
whitening under the force of her grip. Ashe hated her.
Her pride compelled her to act as if that didn't matter,
when in fact it turned her heart to lead inside her chest.
Her need to escape was lost beneath the sudden flood
of pain. She could feel nothing but Ashe's rejection,
think about nothing but how to survive the evening
without falling apart. When she reached the last two
steps she forced her frozen lips to move. "Hello,
Ashe."

"Valerie." He gave her a brief, indifferent nod.
"You're looking well. Alec asked me to check on you.
He'll be glad to hear you're doing splendidly."

The barb in his tone implied that she looked better
than a widow should, but what hurt her more was the
fact that Ashe hadn't wanted to see her but had come
only because Alec asked him to. Valerie wished she
could run back to her room. At the moment even a
prison seemed better than Ashe's cold antagonism. But
she stood her ground. "It was kind of Alec to be
concerned. Please thank him for me."

She went down the final step and strolled past Ashe
to the small sitting room where the de la Portillas
gathered before dinner. She didn't see the way Ashe's
gaze followed her, the coldness replaced by an angry
yearning. Inés and Esteban weren't in the sitting room,
and Valerie breathed an inward sigh of relief. At least
she would be spared that ordeal. It was bad enough
facing Ashe under Alfonso's watchful eye without

having the other couple there to witness and enjoy her pain. Valerie faced the door, politely waiting for the men to catch up. Alfonso poured mixed drinks for Ashe and himself, then offered Valerie a glass of dry white wine. She refused it, not wanting to relax her guard even slightly.

"How is Laraine?" she asked conversationally.

"Fine." Ashe's answer was short to the point of rudeness. Even Alfonso stared at him in surprise.

Valerie ignored his tone. "And Cara? Has she had her baby yet?"

"No. Any day now, the doctors say. Alec put the heat on her to have the baby in Dallas, but she flew home to D.C. a couple of days after you left. She wants the same doctor she's been seeing there to deliver it."

"That's understandable."

"To anyone but Alec," Ashe retorted, a trace of humor and warmth entering his voice for the first time. "He wanted Alexis to do the same thing. Of course, it was more reasonable with her, since she lives in the middle of nowhere. It was a thirty-mile trip to reach the hospital. But Alexis and Cara can be as stubborn as the old man. I've even seen Morgan act like a mule with Alec."

"Alec has been kindness itself to me," Valerie commented stiffly, more to place herself at odds with Ashe than from any belief that Alec's daughters were wrong to oppose him. "He never forced me to do anything."

"I'm sure he wouldn't." Ashe's eyes were as cold as a glacier. "Any man would fall all over himself trying to please you." His voice stung bitterly. Valerie glanced away to hide the sudden tears in her eyes. She wished she were anywhere in the world but there.

Pilar bustled into the room, apologizing charmingly for her lateness. She avoided Valerie's eyes. Valerie knew that Pilar felt guilty and unhappy because her husband had imprisoned Valerie in her room, but she wasn't brave enough to oppose Alfonso, nor could her mother's heart accept Valerie's refusal to marry Carlos.

"Quite all right, my love," Alfonso replied automatically. "Ashe, I'd like you to meet my wife, Pilar."

"Ma'am." Ashe shook Pilar's hand firmly.

Pilar giggled. "Señor Harlan. I am so pleased to meet you. Do you know our dear Valerie?" Valerie shot her a chilling glance, which Pilar managed to avoid.

"Yes. We met in Dallas." His tone was flat and noncommittal.

"Has my husband told you the happy news?" Pilar bubbled. "Valerie will soon be our daughter. She and our son Carlos are to be wed."

Ashe stared at Pilar blankly. Valerie's breath froze in her throat at this new betrayal. Oh, God, how could she convince Ashe it wasn't true? She opened her mouth to protest, but Ashe moved first. He swung toward her, his face stamped with contempt, his eyes slivers of ice. "Congratulations, Valerie. You've managed it again. At least this time you chose a younger victim."

Valerie gaped, too hurt to reply. Alfonso cleared his throat ostentatiously and announced that dinner was served. He led the way into the dining room. Ashe whipped after Alfonso as if he couldn't get away from Valerie fast enough. Fury swept her. How dare he! He had condemned her without giving her a chance to defend herself. He assumed that whatever anybody said about her was the truth, no matter how damning it was. Well, if he wished to believe she was a cold-hearted woman who married another man as soon as her husband was in the grave, then let him! She didn't need him to escape. She had it planned and ready. That thought stiffened her courage, and she was able to saunter into the dining room with every appearance of calm.

Valerie was seated at Alfonso's right and Ashe at his left. Valerie had to keep her gaze on her plate to avoid looking at Ashe. Only once did she steal a glance at him. There was a stern set to his jaw which hadn't been there when they met in Dallas. But at least the emotional fury he had exhibited in the hall of the Stone Oil Building was missing. He was firmly in control of himself, though he appeared older and very tired. Valerie wondered if he had been working too hard, then dismissed the thought as idiotic. What did she care about the state of his health or the amount of work he did? He was nothing to her except a terrible mistake she had been fortunate enough to escape.

The meal passed with agonizing slowness. Valerie contributed nothing to the conversation, and Ashe almost as little. The social burden fell on Alfonso and Pilar, and before long both of them had run out of small talk. Everyone was thankful when the dessert and coffee were brought in. Valerie, unable to eat any of the cloying candy, set it aside, drank a little of her coffee, then asked the others to excuse her. "I'm rather tired, I'm afraid," she told Alfonso, ignoring Ashe. "Good night, everyone."

Alfonso jumped up with elaborate courtesy, offering to escort her to her room. Valerie didn't acknowledge him, but left the room with him by her side. "You did very well," he informed her in an undertone as they climbed the stairs. "I take it that you are beginning to see reason."

"I have always been reasonable." Valerie opened her door and stepped inside, closing it in his face. Behind her she could hear the scrape of the key in the lock. Her knees went watery and she stumbled to the bed to sit down. Well, the die was cast now. She had no alternative but her escape plan. Had she played the fool by not explaining the situation to Ashe and asking for his help? What if her attempt didn't work? She would have condemned herself to God-knows-how-much longer locked in her room!

But, no, there had been no other choice. Ashe had

looked at her with such hatred, such contempt. He wouldn't have believed her. And she didn't want his help! She hated his smug prejudice and closed mind. She would rather do it without him. And someday, she thought with childish glee, Ashe would discover the truth and regret his actions bitterly.

Chapter 7

IT DIDN'T TAKE LONG TO FINISH BRAIDING THE STRIPS OF sheets into a sturdy rope. Valerie pulled out the largest purse she could find and stuffed it with her passport, billfold, keys and a few clothes. She hesitated over her jewelry box, but finally left it alone, keeping only her antique wedding ring and the ruby ring she wore. Felipe had given it to her on her birthday a year earlier, and it was the only thing of value she wanted to take from the de la Portilla household. She stowed the evidence of her planned escape under the bed in case Alfonso should take it into his head to come "reason" with her that evening. After changing into her night-gown, she set the alarm for five o'clock the next morning and crawled into bed.

Valerie knew she ought to sleep. She would need all her wits the next day if she hoped to escape Alfonso. However, she tossed and turned, too frightened and excited to sleep. Her mind was plagued with thoughts of Ashe Harlan. She recalled every word he had spoken that night and the way he had looked each time. As if her mind were a camera, her quick glances at him had become permanent mental images, which she now took out and pored over. Dreamily she rewrote the evening, imagining how it would have been if he had transfixed her with a smoldering glance as she came down the stairs and vowed that he meant to make her his now that she was free. After she finally shook the ridiculous dreams from her mind, she began to worry about all the things that could go wrong with her escape plan. Yet she also looked forward to it with eagerness.

She fell asleep at about two, and it seemed only minutes later when her alarm went off shrilly in her ear. Valerie was instantly awake, her heart pounding with mingled dread and anticipation. Quietly she crept out of bed and dressed. She picked dark brown slacks and a golden brown, long-sleeved velvet jacket. The jacket was cinched around her waist by a wide worked-silver belt of Indian design with a large topaz in the center. It was casual, yet obviously expensive, exactly what she needed for the physical activity of climbing out of the window and for the impression of elegance she would need to present later that morning at one of San Cristóbal's oldest, most conservative banking houses. She took the time to make up her face, for she didn't want to appear odd in any way at the bank. She wouldn't put it past them to call her closest male relative if she seemed strange.

When her face was done and her hair twisted into a tight chignon, Valerie heaved the bag onto her shoulder and grabbed the rope. Taking a deep breath, she stepped onto the bathtub and began to wriggle through the window. This time the going was a little easier, and though she had to squeeze, she was able to get her torso out and grab the ironwork above her head. With a pull, her hips came through. Very carefully she stepped out of the window onto the narrow ledge below. For a moment she was immobilized by terror and she clung to the iron fretwork, visualizing the long drop to the ground. Her knees began to tremble. Rationally she knew that the ledge was wide enough to stand on. Had it been two feet above the ground, she would have had no problem. But so high up, it seemed a narrow thing indeed. Eventually she won out over her fear and tied

the makeshift rope around one of the bars of the iron
decoration. She tried to remember the most secure
knot she had learned in that camp Pamela had sent her
to every summer to get rid of her. The material was
difficult to work with, and her icy fingers were clumsy,
but she persisted, working slowly and efficiently even
though her racing heart told her to hurry. When the
rope was fastened she tested it with a good jerk or two.
It stayed securely tied. Valerie leaned her forehead
against the cool stone, unsure whether she was praying,
delaying or psyching herself up for what lay ahead.

She had to act now if she was going to act at all. It
was close to six, and the servants were up fixing
breakfast. One of them might step into the yard. By
six-thirty or seven the gardening crew would be out
working before the full heat of the day set in. Even
Alfonso would soon arise and might hear the noise she
would make. Valerie hesitated, almost too terrified to
move, then gripped the rope tightly and took a sudden
backward step. For a second she panicked at the
nothingness beneath her feet and her hands slipped
down the rope, scraping her palms. But she held on and
stopped her slide, then began to move downward
slowly, her feet feeling for the wall. She had envisioned
bounding down the side like a mountain climber,
pushing away with her feet, but her bare hands couldn't
stand the rubbing and she had difficulty hitting the wall
with her feet. All in all, she came down in a hasty,
ungainly manner and ended up in an ignominious heap
at the bottom. For a moment she lay against the earth,
her cheek pressed into the sweet-smelling grass, ecstatic to feel the ground beneath her once more.

She rose tentatively to her feet, expecting a sprain
somewhere, but she found none. After retrieving one
shoe, which had fallen off and bounced beneath a short
palm tree, she set off rapidly across the drive to the
main gate. Since she had her keys in her purse, she was
able to unlock the gate. She opened it just wide enough
to slip through and relocked it behind her so her escape

wouldn't be obvious. When would the maid bring her breakfast tray and leave it in her room? And what would she do when she saw that Valerie was missing from her bed?

Valerie refrained from running down the street, although it was what she wanted to do. She must not attract any attention. Walking briskly, she soon lost sight of the house. She stopped to brush the grass and leaves and dirt off her elegant suit and straighten it. Then she set off again, coming at last to a bus stop. She sat down to wait, her stomach jumping inside. She kept glancing around, expecting at any moment to see the de la Portillas' heavy black limousine pull into view. The battered blue bus pulled into sight, and she rose eagerly and boarded it as soon as it stopped.

Valerie dropped her coins into the tall metal column beside the driver, hoping she didn't look too ignorant. It was the first bus ride she had taken in San Cristóbal. She endured the jolting ride downtown, so tight with fear that she hardly noticed the bumps. A few blocks before it reached the bank, she left the bus. The bank wasn't open this early, so she went to an open-air cafe for a cup of coffee and a roll as she waited. She was anything but hungry, but ordering and eating would take up time.

Afterward she strolled to a nearby park and sat down on a bench to watch the parade of people on their way to work. Finally, after consulting her watch, Valerie headed briskly toward the bank, excitement beginning to pulse in her. She was almost through with her ordeal. All she had to do was withdraw her money and take a taxi to the airport. She could buy a ticket and wait there until the plane left. Surely Alfonso wouldn't have the audacity to kidnap her in the middle of the airport.

Valerie entered the bank, casting a blazing smile at the security guard, and strode to the desk of the bank official with whom she usually dealt. When the man glanced up and saw her, surprise covered his face. Her stomach tightened with dread. "Señor Lopez," she greeted him breathlessly, her hands keeping a death grip on her bag.

"Señora de la Portilla. Please, sit down. I did not expect to see you. Please accept my condolences on the death of your esteemed husband."

"Thank you. I shall miss Felipe very much. Since he is gone, I've decided to return to the United States. Therefore, I wish to close my account."

He gaped. "What?"

"I want to withdraw my money." She spoke more slowly, hoping it was her poor accent that was causing the problem.

"But, señora, I don't understand. . . ."

"Understand what?" She waited with sick dread for what he was about to say.

"Señor de la Portilla closed that account for you only two days ago."

"He what?" Rage replaced the fear, coursing through her so hard and fast that a red shimmer blurred her eyes. "That was *my* money. *My* account. Entirely my personal funds. Alfonso had no right to do anything with it. How could you let him?"

"Please, don't excite yourself, señora. There has been a slight mistake. I'm sure that's all. Go home and talk to Señor de la Portilla. He has your money."

"*You* should have my money!" she exclaimed, rising so fast that her chair shot backward on the slick marble floor. "You were criminally negligent to give my funds to another person."

"He is your closest male relative now."

"What does that have to do with anything?" she demanded, her green eyes blasting him with scorn.

The man appeared shocked. "Well, naturally he would be expected to assume the burden of your financial affairs now that your husband is—is—gone."

"My husband is dead," Valerie said flatly. "Why does everyone in this country have such an aversion to speaking plainly? Alfonso has nothing to do with my financial affairs. For that matter, my husband didn't, either, except to offer advice now and then. I manage my own funds, and grief hasn't made me lose my mind. I'm still capable of taking care of my money."

The officer wet his lips nervously. "Please, if you will sit down, I'll telephone Señor de la Portilla and we can straighten this matter out."

"Don't you dare!" Valerie snapped. When the young man stared at her in astonishment she went on more calmly, "I can straighten it out without your help, thank you. I don't want you involved in my finances any longer. You will be contacted by my attorneys concerning your negligence. Good day."

Valerie stalked out of the bank, buoyed by her righteous anger. As she strode along, however, the full force of her predicament sank in on her. Her steps slowed. What was she to do now? She had no money except the relatively small amount in her purse. No credit cards. She hadn't used them here and had allowed them to lapse. How could she leave the country without money?

She stopped suddenly. The American embassy! Of course. Why hadn't she thought of it earlier? She would explain who she was, and the embassy would help her. Money could be wired to her from her trust account in New York. Valerie whirled around and headed in the opposite direction, raising a hand to hail a taxi. She jumped in and told the driver to go to the American embassy, then leaned back, closing her eyes in relief. As they turned onto Calle Libertad, the street where the foreign embassies were located, she sat up eagerly, waiting for the pale gray brick of the American embassy. But when she saw it the smile died on her lips. Across the street from the embassy was a long black limousine which Valerie immediately recognized. Her throat closed. "Drive on past," she directed the driver hoarsely.

He shrugged and went on, not even slowing down. Peeking cautiously out the window, Valerie spotted Alfonso in the back of the waiting car. His face was pulled into a dark frown. He was too busy staring at the gate to the embassy to notice the cab that passed him. Another option was closed. If she stepped out of the cab at the embassy, she had no doubt that Alfonso would seize her before she could reach the gates. The marines on guard wouldn't stop him. They weren't supposed to get involved in internal matters.

Valerie chewed at her lower lip, frantic with fear. Where was she to go? What was she to do? She had failed utterly in her attempt to free herself. Her happy confidence of the afternoon before now seemed absurd. She had accomplished nothing except to get two long, raw scrapes across her palms. How typically inept she had been. She should have known that Alfonso would draw out her money to keep her helpless. Why hadn't she taken her jewelry along to pawn?

Valerie glanced down at her hands. She could pawn one of her rings. It would bring enough money for a flight to Mexico City. Once she was out of the country she could have money wired to her. But she hesitated at letting go of her wedding ring or the special ruby ring Felipe had given her. They were rich in sentimental value. She rubbed the bright ruby thoughtfully and, like a genie out of a bottle, a picture of Ashe Harlan flashed into her mind. Ashe. She had no choice but to turn to him. She would explain the whole situation, and he would have to help her, however much he resented her. Relief flooded her and Valerie wondered whether she had longed for this result all along.

She had the driver go to the modernistic El Jefe Hotel, which was preferred by most Americans. When she asked the desk clerk for Ashe Harlan's room number, she was informed that no one by that name was registered there. She turned away, momentarily dismayed. Where would he stay? Oh, dear God, she

hoped he hadn't left La Luz already. It occurred to her
that Felipe might have recommended one of the older,
aristocratic hotels more commonly used by South
Americans. If he had, surely it would have been El
Palacio, for it had all the modern conveniences Americans demanded, as well as a stately grace and beauty.

It was a short walk from El Jefe to El Palacio, so
Valerie didn't take a cab. She strode down the street
and into the elegant marble-floored lobby of the
Palacio. She approached the counter, where a thin,
haughty clerk took in her designer pants suit with an
experienced eye and obligingly looked at the register.
"Yes, señora. Señor Harlan is in room 1164."

"Thank you." Good. She was in luck. She dialed his
room from a house phone. There was no answer.
Valerie sighed and looked around her at the grand
lobby. She spotted an empty corner from which she
could see both the revolving front doors and the
elevators. She'd be sure to spot Ashe when he entered
the hotel. She crossed to the corner and sat down to
wait.

The hours passed slowly. Valerie fidgeted. The longer she sat, the more uneasy she became. Ashe was
probably in day-long negotiations with a government
official or the de la Portilla lawyer. He wasn't likely to
return in an hour or two. What if Alfonso thought of
sending a man to look for her at Ashe's hotel? She
shouldn't remain there for the whole afternoon like a
sitting duck.

Valerie left the hotel and ambled along the street,
casually glancing in storefronts. When she caught sight
of a movie theater she ducked inside gratefully. It was a
way to occupy her time in a place where Alfonso
wouldn't dream of looking for her. The movie was a
long Mexican epic, and since she had entered halfway
through, Valerie had little idea of what was going on.
But it suited her needs perfectly, providing dark ano-
nymity for several hours. She relaxed, even dozing off

for a few minutes. At about four-thirty she emerged
from her haven to return to Ashe's hotel. She studied
the street in front of the hotel for a sign of Alfonso or
one of his men but saw nothing suspicious. Inside the
lobby she again rang Ashe's room and received no
answer.

Her corner seat was taken, and she had to be content
with a more conspicuous one. Hands clenched in her
lap, she watched the slow, steady movement of the
revolving doors, afraid to glance away and perhaps miss
Ashe's entrance. She was aware of the appreciative
male stares cast her way, and they increased her
nervousness. A woman conspicuously alone would be
fair game to most of the men there. What if one of them
made a pass at her? She was sure she would handle it
badly in the state she was in. If only Ashe would hurry
up! What if he went to someone's house for dinner, or
decided to eat before he returned to the hotel? What if
he had made a quick trip to another part of the country
and wouldn't be in at all that night?

She was trying to quell her panicky thoughts when
Ashe Harlan's lanky, undeniably American form
strode through the revolving doors. His forehead was
creased, his eyes hard and dark. Valerie released a
despairing sigh. Obviously this wasn't a good time to
approach him. However, she couldn't put it off, so on
trembling legs she crossed the lobby to intercept him
before he reached the bank of elevators. She didn't
know what to say to make him believe her. He might
turn her away. He might not give her a chance to say
anything. Her anxiety made her rigid and set her face
into a lovely cold mask resembling a store manne-
quin's. It was a front she often presented to the world,
the only way she knew to hide her fear.

Ashe stopped, his eyes fixed on Valerie, his carefully
blank face revealing none of the turmoil inside. Since
she had left the U.S. he had almost been able to forget
how lovely she was and how eagerly his body respond-

ed to her. But the evening before her beauty had struck
him anew, and it had required all his willpower to
retain an indifferent attitude. Now she seemed even
more enticing, although her outfit was not provocative.
The V neck didn't reveal even the beginning slopes of
her breasts, and the slacks completely covered her legs.
But the soft velvet top was pulled taut across her
breasts by the heavy belt around her waist, emphasizing her very feminine form. Ashe experienced an
almost overwhelming urge to spread his fingers across
the jacket and feel the even softer curve of her breasts
beneath.

He cursed silently. She looked as cold as ice. Why
hadn't he noticed that before? A marble goddess. She
was a deceitful seductress who had sold her body to an
old man for his money while she sought sexual amusement with other men such as himself. Then, not two
weeks after she had kissed Ashe so passionately, and
before her husband was even cold in his grave, she had
coolly agreed to marry Felipe's nephew.

When Ashe had gone to Alfonso de la Portilla's
home he had yearned to see her, though he had done
his best to hide it. A small, unquenchable spark of hope
had flamed deep inside him. Perhaps Valerie would be
pale and grieving and turn to him to ease her sorrow.
Instead she had been beautiful, perfectly made up, with
every hair in place, obviously needing no comfort from
anyone. And then Alfonso's wife had announced that
Valerie intended to marry their son. Ashe's insides had
turned into a block of ice. She was a heartless gold
digger and always would be.

Nor was she any more inclined to be faithful. Barely
widowed and newly engaged, she was nevertheless
seeking him out at his hotel. Last night he hadn't fallen
at her feet, which made him a challenge. She wanted to
add him to her trophy collection. The awful thing was,
he knew it would take little effort on her part to do so.
He stiffened unconsciously, bracing himself against the
force of her allure.

Valerie stopped a few feet away from him. "Hello, Ashe."

"Valerie." He offered no encouragement.

The slate gray suit he wore made him seem a stranger. There seemed to be no connection between this cool, efficient businessman and the lover who had held her in his arms and kissed her until she couldn't speak or think, only tremble. How could she hope for his aid?

"I—I need to talk to you," she continued hesitantly.

"We have nothing to talk about." He walked past her toward the elevators.

"Ashe!" The tremor in her voice stopped him. He turned and came back slowly.

"Valerie, this is pointless."

"Please, listen to me for a few minutes. I need your help—desperately."

He raised one cynical eyebrow. "That sounds a little melodramatic, don't you think?"

"Yes, but it's the truth. Please, Ashe."

"All right. Start talking."

"Not here." She cast an agonized glance around the busy lobby.

His smile was knowing. "Where would you suggest then? My room?"

It was the place she would have suggested, for she wouldn't be seen there, but after the innuendo in his tone she didn't dare. "No, of course not. Just some-place private."

He sighed and nodded toward a hall leading off the lobby. "All right. Let's go to the bar. There shouldn't be many people there this early."

"Okay." She walked after him passively as he strode across the lobby and down the hall to the hotel lounge, not once looking back to see if she was following. The lounge was a dim, narrow room dominated by a huge wooden bar lined with high rattan stools. Beyond the bar lay a sunken conversation pit containing several chairs and a few tiny tables. Against the far wall high-backed semicircular booths stretched the length of the room. Designed for privacy, the minuscule tables held no lights, making each booth a pool of darkness. Ashe led her to the most distant one, screened from view by a large palm tree, and they slid in, facing each other warily.

"Well?" he began. "What is it you want to talk about?"

"I need your help."

"You said that." He reached inside his jacket and extracted a crumpled package of cigarettes, expertly tapping the end and drawing one out. He leaned back to dig into a trouser pocket for his lighter, pulled it out and lit the cigarette. Valerie watched him, noticing the rough grace of his movements and the strength of his hands. Ashe cupped his hands around the lighter as if he were in a high wind, and she could easily imagine him lighting cigarettes in the windy oil fields. An ache blossomed in the center of her chest.

The waitress arrived to take their drink orders, which gave Valerie a breathing space to pull her thoughts together. When the waitress left Valerie launched into her story. "I need to get out of the country."

"What?" Whatever Ashe had expected, it wasn't this. He stared. "You sound like someone in a spy movie."

"It's the truth," Valerie flared. "They're trying to force me to marry Carlos."

A harsh burst of laughter shot out of him. "Come on, Valerie, you can't expect me to buy that."

"But it's true," she protested. "Alfonso locked me in my room until I agreed to do it, but I wouldn't. I escaped this morning and was going to fly out of San Cristóbal, but he's closed my bank account. Please, hide me. Help me get out of here."

"What's the matter? Wouldn't your fiancé come through with enough money? Did he find out about your little peccadilloes while you were married to his uncle? I understand most Latins take such things seriously. Or perhaps you realized that Carlos wouldn't die as quickly as Felipe, since he's a young man."

Valerie gasped at the insult and turned her head away to hide her hurt. The waitress brought their drinks, and Ashe told her to leave them alone, that they would let her know if they wanted another round. Valerie sipped her drink slowly, buying time to absorb the pain and build up new courage. Ashe studied her, fighting the wave of sympathy her vulnerably bowed head produced in him. He couldn't let her fool him again.

Valerie lifted her head proudly. "Well, will you help me? I'll repay you as soon as we get to the States."

"How? With your body? That's the way you usually do it, isn't it?"

Valerie's eyes widened and her stomach twisted in humiliation. Ashe slid around to the center section of the banquette and reached out to run a careless finger down her cheek, a gesture that was more an insult than a caress. With one sinewy hand he grasped her arm and pulled her closer. His back was turned to the room, and she was totally hidden from view by the palm, the shadows and the broad width of his back and shoulders. His face loomed nearer and nearer until she closed her eyes against him. Then his lips were on hers, as firm and warm as she remembered, transporting her to a warm, breathless night in Dallas. She stiffened, resisting both the memory and the man, but something gave inside her and she melted into him.

His arms encircled her, pressing her to him, as he sucked her lower lip into his mouth, massaging it with his lips and tickling with his tongue. He dug in more deeply, his tongue thrusting. Valerie tasted the acrid flavor of Scotch and cigarettes mingled in his mouth and found it strangely sweet. She shifted restlessly as Ashe continued to kiss her, his hands roaming her back as his lips moved from her mouth to her cheeks and ears, nibbling, testing, learning the contours of her face.

He released her and gazed at her for a long moment, his face flushed and his eyes glittering through the dimness. Then he laid his hand on her shoulder and let it drift down over the velvet jacket, luxuriating in the plushness that covered her rounded breasts. He molded the material to her curves, moving from one breast to the other. Her nipples hardened under his touch. Lazily his fingertips teased the hard buttons until they stiffened into diamond points of desire.

Ashe's breath rasped in his throat, loud in the stillness, as he moved his hand to the bare skin above the top button. Moving down into the dark cleft, his skillful hand unsnapped the front fastening of her bra, giving him free access to the silken skin of her naked breasts. Valerie thought she heard him whisper her name, but she couldn't be sure, for the pulse in her ears drowned out all other noises.

Valerie closed her eyes at the onslaught of the delicious sensations his stroking aroused in her. His hand slid up out of the jacket and down to her hips, curving over her abdomen. He dipped to the junction of her legs and coaxed them apart, sliding down one thigh and back up, then down the other. Valerie clasped her legs together to stop his caresses, but her movement only clamped his hand against her most vulnerable spot. Ashe chuckled softly, his hand pressing hard against her. Valerie gasped at the sparkles of light that shot through her at his intimate touch.

He moved to unzip the side opening of her slacks. "No, Ashe, please. We're in public," Valerie pleaded breathlessly.

"No one can see us," he assured her thickly, his fingers slipping beneath the flimsy lace of her panties to work their magic. His callused fingertips created a silken friction, rousing her past any point of desire she had ever dreamed of reaching. Valerie caught her underlip between her teeth as tiny whimpers escaped her.

"Look at me," he commanded, and she opened her eyes, unable to deny him. His shadowed gaze was a midnight hue, dark and compelling, fathomless. Slowly he stoked the flames within her until an inferno raged in her abdomen.

Valerie could feel something building inside her to a peak of ultimate pleasure, and as it did his touch lightened to the merest brushing. Valerie twisted in frustration, murmuring, "No, please . . ."

His magnetic eyes seemed to swallow her as he suddenly pressed down hard, catapulting Valerie into a blinding flash of pleasure. Tremors shook her and she strained back against the high leather seat.

Valerie didn't know how long they sat in silence after that, so stunned was she by the explosion that had wracked her body. She felt Ashe's hand slide away and heard the rasp of the zipper as he refastened her slacks. Eyes closed, her face a study in sated content, she floated on gentle waves of pleasure, unaware of the open yearning on Ashe's face.

By the time she lifted her heavy lids he had composed his features into their former harsh blankness. His mouth curled cynically. "You've got what you came for. You won't need to peddle your little stories anymore."

Valerie gasped, the coldness of his contempt shattering her pleasure. She realized that Ashe had toyed with her, forcing her to expose her deepest, innermost yearning, while he remained perfectly aloof. He had demonstrated his control over her, then had dismissed her with contempt. Her face flooded with shame. "You coldhearted bastard! God, how I hate you! I came to you in desperation, pleading for help, and you—" She broke off on a sob and jumped out of the booth. Head down, she ran from the bar.

Behind her Ashe half rose, his reserve cracking. "Valerie, wait!" But she was already out of the room. He slid out of the leather seat and hastily tossed several bills onto the table, not knowing whether the unfamiliar San Cristóbal currency over- or underpaid the bill. He hurried into the lobby. Valerie wasn't there, and he ran out the front door. Standing on the sidewalk, he scanned the street. It was useless. She was out of sight. He sagged against the wall.

Chapter 8

WHEN VALERIE LEFT THE BAR SHE RAN BLINDLY ACROSS the lobby of the hotel and burst out the front door. She had no idea where she was going or what she would do without Ashe's help. She knew only that she couldn't stay with him a second longer. Tears blurred her vision as she stepped onto the sidewalk, so that Alfonso was beside her before she saw him. When he grabbed her arm she whirled and recognized him with horror. Vainly she struggled to pull away, but he was stronger and completely determined. It took only a moment for him to whisk her into the black limousine idling at the curb. He hopped in after her and slammed the door. The car pulled out into traffic.

Valerie slid across to the opposite door and glared at Alfonso. He returned her gaze with equal animosity. "I should have known you would run to that Yankee. It's unfortunate that I didn't realize it earlier. It would have saved me some trouble."

Valerie pointedly turned her head to stare out the window. Alfonso continued, "That was a foolish thing to do, Valerie. I thought you had better sense. Even though you had foolishly independent American ways, you never seemed so recalcitrant before."

"I didn't need to be. Felipe never tried to bully me," she flared.

"Well, a few weeks on the plantation should help change your mind. Perhaps being with your future husband will persuade you."

Valerie folded her arms and mutinously thrust out her chin, struggling not to show her fear. God, how she hated going to the plantation! With Felipe it hadn't been too bad, although she disliked the isolation of the place. But Carlos was in charge of the plantation now, and with him around all the time it would be awful! He was a brutal man. She wouldn't put it past him to rape her in the hope that the dishonor and possible pregnancy would force her to marry him.

And there was no possibility of escape. The family traveled to the plantation by boat, for the only land route was through an almost impenetrable jungle. It took two days to traverse the narrow, rutted trail through the jungle by donkey, as the archaeologists had done. It took even longer on foot—even if you didn't get lost. From the small village of San Mateo on the edge of the jungle, one could drive the rest of the way to La Luz, although the roads were poor. But to do that required a car, which wasn't easily come by in San Mateo. No, there wasn't a prayer of escape.

Unconsciously Valerie sighed and tears welled in her eyes.

"Ah, so you see how idiotic your little escapade was," Alfonso remarked unsympathetically. "Believe me, it will get worse the longer you continue to resist me."

"I refuse to marry Carlos," she ground out. "You can't make me do it."

Alfonso made no comment, maintaining his silence throughout the rest of the ride. They turned into the dock area and drove slowly along the marina. When they reached the long wooden pier where the de la Portilla family boat was moored, Alfonso helped Valerie out of the car, his fingers wrapped around her wrist. Valerie stumbled after him docilely, knowing that any struggle now would be futile. Her only chance was to lull his suspicions by appearing acquiescent while she made new plans to get away. Alfonso marched her onto the large motorboat and pulled her down the narrow steps into the single cabin.

"Now," he told her with satisfaction, "I have ordered the crew to leave immediately. I'm afraid I won't be able to accompany you. I must stay behind to keep an eye on things. The political situation is grim at best, and I'm not at all sure that Esteban isn't straying from the de la Portilla stronghold. I have heard rumors that he is secretly adhering to the Caballistas." He named the current regime's followers. "Remember that it would be pointless to try to escape. The boat won't stop until tomorrow afternoon, when you reach the plantation. The crew won't help you. They're completely loyal to me." He grinned humorlessly. "Good-bye, little sister. Sleep well." Alfonso nodded to her and left the cabin.

Valerie expelled her breath in a despairing sigh and flopped onto the narrow bed. Alfonso had spoken the truth. If there was enough gas on board, they wouldn't have to stop. And Alfonso's men would be completely bound to him by money and threats. She was trapped on this boat. Valerie curled up on the bunk. She let her tears come now, clutching the bedspread and pouring out her pain and sorrow in wracking sobs. Finally, drained, she drifted to sleep.

When she awoke the next morning she groaned and stretched, remembering where she was and where she was going. She arose and washed her face, then idly tried the cabin door. To her surprise it was unlocked. But, after all, what was the use? She wasn't likely to jump into the Rio Miedo, which was rumored to be infested with crocodiles and water snakes. She stepped across the hall into the galley and poured herself a cup of hot coffee. Cup in hand, she climbed to the deck. Strolling to the rail, she sipped her coffee and stared at the scene before her. The Rio Miedo, on which the boat traveled, was a dank, dark river. Valerie could

well understand its name, Fear River. It started high in
the distant Sierra Azul mountains as a sparklingly clear
stream, but by the time it had twisted its slow, serpen-
tine way through the lowland jungles to the Gulf of
Mexico it had become sluggish and impenetrable, carrying the rich silt of the farming region to the ocean.
Felipe had once joked that the Rio Miedo gave away
the few riches that the outsiders had not already taken.

Valerie shivered. She hated this river as much as she
hated the jungle. The air was hot and moist, oppres-
sive, and the thick growth on either side of the water
created a closed-in, claustrophobic atmosphere. Spider
monkeys chattered in the treetops at the intruding
boat, and colorful parrots and macaws flapped away,
screeching, at their approach. Beautiful, colorful, lush
—yet to Valerie it was decaying and hostile. Every time
she came to the de la Portilla plantation she hated the
jungle more. This time most of all. She would be a
prisoner, with no kind husband to suggest a trip to one
of the coastal resorts or to La Luz for a shopping spree.

Late in the afternoon, as the sun sank behind the tall
trees, beginning the long, dim, jungle twilight, the boat
docked at the de la Portilla banana plantation wharf.
Valerie was dismayed to see Carlos waiting to help her
disembark. His short, stocky figure filled her with
dread, although his face wasn't ugly, despite its rather
square formation. His legs were heavy and muscular, as
were his arms, which were covered with thick, curling
black hair. Valerie thought with an inward shudder that
his arms reminded her of an ape's. His small brown
eyes darted everywhere, never still, giving him a nervous, suspicious manner. He made Valerie uneasy, and
he bored her. He was a man of no great wit and still less
charm. Too often she had seen him explode into a rage
and beat an animal or worker half to death. It was
dreadful spending even a few days in his company. She
hoped that he would largely ignore her as he had in the
past.

However, Carlos evidently had been instructed to

charm her into marrying him. He was dressed in immaculate planter's whites, with a new wide-brimmed straw hat on his head and high, glossy leather boots on his feet. He talked ceaselessly as they strolled to the house, and Valerie was thankful when they reached their destination and she could escape to her bedroom. Once inside the familiar pastel room she sank onto the bed with a sigh. The firm bunk bed of the boat hadn't given her a restful sleep the night before, and she had been troubled by vague, frightening dreams. It was pleasant to relax on this soft mattress. Her eyelids closed and she drifted in a half-sleeping, half-waking mist. She thought of Felipe, recalling the times they had spent there in that house, and suddenly her eyes popped wide open.

Carlos had taken over the master bedroom, Felipe's bedroom. She had noticed his possessions there as she passed it coming to her room. That meant that she would be sharing a connecting bathroom with Carlos! She scuttled off the bed and bent to look at the lock on the bathroom door. Thank heavens it *had* a lock, though it was less sturdy than she would have liked. She fastened the lock and then, no longer sleepy, inspected the door from her room into the hall. Like the doors in the town house, it locked with an old-fashioned key. If she had the key, she could fasten it from the inside to keep Carlos out, which was more her concern now than being closed into her room by him. The less she had to do with him, the better. However, she had never locked her door and had no idea where the key might be.

She turned to the long shuttered doors leading onto the second-story verandah. They locked with a bolt from the inside, thank goodness. The nights were warm, however, even in the spring, and she was used to sleeping with the outer doors open and a mosquito netting draped over her bed. Well, she would simply have to suffer a little heat. She must make sure that Carlos couldn't get into her room. She didn't trust

him one bit. He would soon tire of wooing her.
Before long, she was afraid, he might decide to give up
the effort and take the quicker, more aggressive
course of raping her. His medieval mind would doubtless consider it an excellent way to bring her to heel.
What else could she expect from a man raised by
Alfonso, who, despite his sophisticated veneer, was
capable of imprisoning her?

How in the world had she gotten into this? Although
Alfonso was the perpetrator of the scheme, she knew
that somehow she was responsible for it. She had an
ability for getting into awful situations. Look at her
failures: an engagement to a fortune hunter; her impet-
uous marriage to Felipe, which had wound up immur-
ing her in San Cristóbal; her infatuation with Ashe
Harlan; now this. She didn't know how she could have
avoided it, but she must have made the wrong decisions
or given off signals that she was an easy mark.

Valerie stepped out the French doors onto the verandah and crossed to the railing. A grassy side lawn
dotted with flowering fruit trees stretched beside the
house, hacked out of the thick jungle. Beyond it
loomed an impenetrable wall of vines, brush and trees,
broken only by the narrow trail to the river dock. A
brightly feathered parrot landed in a distant tree,
flashing red against the deep green. Oh, what she
wouldn't give to see the concrete of New York City
again, or her mother's trim green estate in Connecticut.

She went inside, more depressed than ever, and
began to dress for dinner. She pulled a simple yellow
sundress from the closet, where she kept a complete
wardrobe of casual clothes for plantation wear to avoid
the tiresome chore of packing and unpacking every
time she went back and forth to La Luz. The sundress
was full skirted and had a short jacket that she could
wear to cover the bare expanse of her back. After
washing her face, she slipped into the dress and flat
white sandals, not bothering with makeup or jewelry.

The last thing she wanted to do was impress Carlos with her looks.

She spent a tiresome half hour on the side porch of the downstairs verandah, where the de la Portillas were accustomed to having their predinner drinks, sipping a glass of white wine and listening to Carlos drone on about the work he had been doing on the plantation. When at last the butler announced that dinner was served she jumped up as if on springs and hurried into the dining room adjacent to the porch. She picked at her food and downed another glass of wine. Fortunately Carlos didn't attempt to engage her in conversation, preferring to devote his attention to his food. As soon as the dessert and after-dinner coffee had been served, she announced that she was tired and would retire early. There was a flicker of relief in Carlos's eyes before he politely begged her to stay. She refused equally politely and left the table.

Valerie ran upstairs, took a quick bath and retreated to her bedroom, locking the door to the connecting bath and propping a heavy straight chair under the knob of the hall door. She checked to make sure the outside doors were locked before she dressed for bed and curled up in the high-backed wicker chair to read. The wine had made her sleepy, however, and the book didn't hold her interest. Soon she gave up the effort and crawled into bed, thinking that at least one day had passed. How long did they plan to keep her there?

Two days inched by, filled with tedium. Although she was free to roam the house, she was likely to run into Carlos. He seemed to pop up wherever she went, so Valerie spent most of the time in her room, reading and staring out the verandah doors. She wondered how long she would have to keep up a pretense of passive acceptance before Carlos would be lulled into believing she wouldn't try to escape. And once he was lulled, how could she leave? There was no satisfactory answer

to that question. Steal a donkey? Stand on the dock and
hitch a ride on a passing boat? It was absurd, impossible.

With the time dragging heavily she found her mind
returning again and again to her meeting with Ashe.
Valerie refused to think about the indescribable sensations his hands and mouth had aroused in her, just as
she wouldn't admit that she dreamed each night about
those kisses and caresses and awakened taut, sweating
and dissatisfied. No, all she allowed herself to remember was the humiliation. He had made a fool of her,
treated her with cruel contempt. She hated him! She
was sure she hated him. She didn't need or want his
help. She would get out of San Cristóbal without him.
Yet deep down she knew that if he walked up the
driveway that instant, she would run to him and beg to
be taken away. She was that cowardly.

When she actually saw Ashe walking toward the
house late in the afternoon she thought for an instant
that she was hallucinating, creating him from her
constant thoughts. She blinked and ran to the porch
rail. It *was* Ashe, his golden hair glinting in the tropical
sun, strolling up the path from the docks, Alfonso's
compact form beside him. Valerie gripped the railing.
What was Ashe doing there? Why on earth would
Alfonso bring him to the plantation, knowing that she
had gone to Ashe for help?

The answer was obvious: Alfonso would do it only if
Ashe insisted on it. Ashe must have wanted to come.
Did he know she was there? Had he begun to believe
her? Demanded to see her? Valerie whirled and darted
into her room, cheeks flushed and mind buzzing. She
flung open the closet doors and searched her wardrobe
for the perfect dress for dinner. It must be lovely, but
not sexy or inviting. Something virginal. White. She
settled on a white cotton dress, full-skirted, with a
wide, stiff belt. The bodice was covered with white
eyelet embroidery and the sassily starched cap sleeves

were unlined eyelet. It was pretty, proper and utterly feminine.

She checked the lock on the connecting door into Carlos's room and took a long bubble bath, emerging rosy and sweet smelling. She dressed, her fingers trembling, her mind in turmoil. One moment her cheeks flamed and she was certain she couldn't face Ashe, remembering how wantonly she had responded to him. She was too embarrassed to see him again. But the next instant she dreamed of sailing down the stairs, of Ashe taking her in his arms to whisper an apology and assure her that he would whisk her away to safety. That was idiotic, of course, she reminded herself, but she ought to be practical and seek his help again, forgetting her pride. Underlying each attitude—dreaming, pragmatic, shamed—was a pulsating excitement at the thought of seeing Ashe, of hearing his voice and feeling his skin brush against hers.

As she was arranging her hair there was a thunderous knock on her door and Alfonso barged in, scowling blackly. He closed the door behind him and whipped around to face her. "What the hell is going on?"

Valerie raised her eyebrows. "I don't know what you mean." She turned her attention back to her mirror and began brushing her hair.

Alfonso growled. "Don't lie to me. That American, Harlan, insisted on visiting the plantation today. He practically forced me to bring him."

Valerie shrugged. "I'm afraid that's your problem, Alfonso, not mine."

"Damn it, he keeps asking about you! He wants to know if you'll be at dinner. He's made it clear that he wants you to be there."

"Well, as you can see, I'm dressing for dinner."

"Did you tell him?"

"Tell him what?" Valerie asked innocently.

"About our wanting you to marry Carlos."

"You told him I was marrying Carlos. I didn't deny it, if you'll remember."

"Yes, but you went to him when you ran away from the house." He paused and asked suspiciously, "Are you having an affair with Harlan?"

"That's none of your business!" Valerie snapped, buoyed by the implication of what Alfonso had told her. "But suppose I am? It would make me quite unfit to be a de la Portilla wife, wouldn't it? So I think I shall answer yes."

"Don't joke with me!" Alfonso roared.

"Alfonso!" Valerie exclaimed with mock horror. "Careful, Mr. Harlan will hear you. He'd be doubly suspicious then."

Alfonso glared and pointed a stern forefinger at her. "Listen to me. You will come to dinner tonight and behave as a de la Portilla woman should. I will have none of your boldness or lies, no tricks, do you understand me? If you try to get Ashe Harlan alone or pour out a sad story to him, I'll make certain it's the last thing you do. Do you understand me?"

Valerie lowered her lashes demurely. "Certainly. I won't say a truthful word. I'll lie so readily that you'll think I'm actually one of your family."

His fists clenched. She was afraid she had gone too far and that he would strike her. However, Alfonso was satisfied with a final glare before he slammed out of the room. Valerie released a long, shaky breath, her heart knocking against her ribs. Alfonso had scared her, however little she would admit it to him. But warring with her fear was the knowledge that Ashe must be suspicious or he wouldn't insist on seeing her. Valerie applied a light film of makeup and added lipstick and mascara. Heavy makeup didn't work in the moist jungle heat. Besides, she preferred a fresh, clean look, particularly tonight. She would use anything, including makeup and costume, to convince Ashe that she was an innocent victim.

Valerie linked a fragile chain with a pearl drop

around her neck and placed matching earrings in her ears. She took a few minutes to calm her shaking nerves before she hurried down the stairs to the side porch. At the sight of Ashe lounging against the white wooden railing she stopped, almost losing her courage. There was something hard and tough about him, an unrelenting strength. He couldn't have reconsidered and decided to believe her. Would Ashe Harlan ever change his mind about anything?

Swallowing nervously, Valerie stepped onto the cool tiles of the porch. Ashe spotted her and immediately straightened, his eyes boring into her as if he could read her soul. "Valerie." She quivered at his husky voice curling around her name. It never sounded that way when anyone else said it.

"Hello, Ashe." She was surprised that her voice didn't shake, because she was brimming with conflicting emotions. What did Ashe think? Did he regret not believing her? Was he remembering the way she had moaned beneath his expert hand?

Alfonso fixed a smile on his face and turned to her. "Ah, Valerie, my dear, join us. Shall I pour you a glass of wine?"

"No," Valerie replied firmly. "I'd like a Manhattan, please."

"But . . ." Alfonso started to protest, frowning. He didn't consider it ladylike to drink anything stronger than wine. Clearly this was a gesture of defiance from Valerie, but he couldn't remonstrate with Harlan watching. Alfonso put the best face on it he could and mixed Valerie a weak drink.

Valerie accepted the glass and smiled a polite thanks at Alfonso. She didn't care if the drink was weak. She truthfully wasn't fond of liquor. Her request had been exactly what Alfonso had thought it to be. And she had won, which was all she wanted.

"You are very lovely tonight, my dear," Carlos offered stiffly. They were speaking English for Ashe's benefit, and Carlos was not at ease with the language.

Nor was he comfortable in his crisp white suit, for he kept tugging surreptitiously at the collar. If Valerie hadn't disliked him so, she would have laughed. He looked like a buffoon beside Ashe's lean strength and casual handsomeness.

"Thank you, Carlos. It's kind of you to say so." She hadn't needed his compliment to know that she was at her best. The quick flare of light in Ashe's eyes had told her that far better. She turned to Ashe, forcing her gaze to meet his levelly. "Ashe, it's nice of you to come all this way."

"I'm interested in the farm. I've never seen a banana plantation. In fact, I haven't seen anything like this whole area." He indicated the jungle beyond the carefully kept lawn.

"Yes, it's certainly different from Texas," Valerie teased, giddy with happiness. Ashe was there and not glowering at her. He didn't act as if he despised her, nor had anything in his eyes or words hinted that he remembered his conquest of her body. Suddenly she was sure that things would come out right.

"You're right about that. Do you plan to live here?"

"No, I'll be returning to the United States soon. I plan to study archaeology." There. She had made it clear. She wasn't tacitly going along with Alfonso as she had at the other dinner party. Alfonso took up a position by a porch column and directed a black look at her. Valerie carefully avoided it. She refused to let him intimidate her.

"Archaeology?" Ashe seemed genuinely amazed. "You're joking. Isn't that digging up old bones or something?"

Valerie instinctively rose in defense of her interest. "I imagine you're thinking of anthropology, which is the study of the origins of man. While it's closely related to archaeology, they're not the same thing. Archaeology is the study of ancient people and their cultures. Archaeologists excavate sites where historic or prehistoric people lived. Their interest is to establish the way of life of those people through the artifacts they left." She stopped abruptly, realizing that she sounded like a textbook. Ashe's eyes twinkled. "You wretch. You knew all along what it was. You're putting on your good-old-boy act."

He chuckled. "No, I didn't know exactly, though I was teasing you a little. Sorry, I know you prefer to be serious."

Valerie couldn't resist his grin, which crinkled the corners of his eyes. She smiled back. "I thought you were the serious one."

Carlos interrupted sulkily. "It's time to eat."

"Yes, yes," Alfonso chimed in more smoothly, not liking the friendly tone of the conversation between Ashe and Valerie. The last time, he could have sworn they disliked each other. But now . . . "I believe the servants are ready to serve dinner."

Alfonso led them to the dining room and indicated everyone's place at the table. He placed Carlos beside Valerie and Ashe across from Carlos, with the intention of stopping any talk between Ashe and Valerie. But his hopes were dashed as soon as they were seated, for Ashe carelessly shoved aside the tall centerpiece blocking his view of Valerie and asked, "How did you get interested in archaeology?"

"Actually, Felipe was the one who was interested in it." Ashe's face stiffened slightly at the mention of her dead husband, and she hurried on. "A group of archaeologists from an American university began a dig not far from here. Felipe went to meet them, and I accompanied him."

"Close to this plantation?"

"The group here is studying the Mayan civilization, which developed around the third century A.D. and continued until the tenth century. It was an interesting and advanced culture. They built cities, temples and farms in this lowland jungle." Valerie caught herself before she could romp off too far on her hobbyhorse. She had been seized by inspiration. It was obvious that Alfonso wouldn't leave Ashe alone with her for an instant, and she needed to talk to him in private. "Perhaps you'd like to visit the dig. I'm sure the American team would love to meet you. They could explain far better than I."

Alfonso forced a laugh. "Now, my dear, I'm sure Mr. Harlan isn't interested in broken pieces of pottery. You must excuse her, Ashe. She and Felipe thought everyone was as mad on the subject of ruins as they were." He gave Ashe a smile so stiff it resembled a grimace.

Ashe smiled slowly. "On the contrary, Alfonso, I'm very interested. Doubtless Valerie thinks I'm a philistine, but actually her field and mine have some similarities. I'm concerned with ruins in the earth that are a few million years older than hers."

"What?" Alfonso looked puzzled; then his face cleared and he coughed up another chuckle. "Oh, yes, I see—geology and oil. Of course. However, I assure you, this spot isn't worth the time. Very small. Very insignificant."

"Oh, no, Felipe believed it would prove to be one of the best finds in San Cristóbal," Valerie protested. She wasn't about to let Alfonso win this contest. "They're excavating the ruins of a Mayan temple. Many of the original walls are still standing, but they were so overgrown with vines that the site was lost."

"It sounds very interesting. I'd love to go," Ashe agreed.

"But, Ashe, the well," Alfonso protested, his hand clenching around his fork. "You wanted to inspect the land where the well will be dug."

"I can see it the following day," Ashe replied easily, breaking a roll and buttering one side.

"But the jungle heat—it's so far to ride. You would have to take donkeys. You can't reach the site in a car. It's an all-day trip. If you wish to see artifacts, it's far better that you go to the National Museum in La Luz. It's a beautiful new building, with all the most important finds, and it's air-conditioned."

Ashe chuckled with something close to real amusement. "Not all Americans are addicted to air conditioning. I grew up without it and survived. I've lived in Texas, Oklahoma and Saudi Arabia. I think I can take a spring day in the jungle. It'll be a little vacation for me. Provided, of course, that you'll lend us some donkeys to ride."

Alfonso smiled sickly. "Of course. Carlos will accompany you."

Carlos looked appalled at that piece of news but nodded. "My pleasure."

"Nonsense. No need for you to go. I'm sure you'd be bored by all of us jabbering English at each other. Besides, I wouldn't dream of taking you away from your work. I'm sure you're quite busy this time of year. Valerie can show me all the sights, I'm sure. No pun intended."

"Excuse me? Oh, yes, I see. Sights. Sites." Carlos tried a small laugh, though it was marred by his frown.

"Then it's settled." Ashe smiled at Alfonso. "Valerie and I will visit the site early tomorrow morning."

"Yes, certainly." Sweat dotted Alfonso's upper lip. "I'll see that the donkeys are ready."

Relief flooded Valerie. For a while she had been afraid that Ashe would be deterred by Alfonso's obstacles, but he had persisted. Each new rebuttal had made her more positive that Ashe wanted to speak to her alone. Didn't that prove he believed her? And tomorrow he would help her get away!

Chapter 9

VALERIE SLEPT PEACEFULLY FOR THE FIRST TIME IN WEEKS and awoke feeling almost cheerful. She bathed quickly and dressed in blue jeans and a scoop-necked pink cotton blouse. She twisted her hair into a knot atop her head, slipped on socks and laced her feet into sturdy walking boots. A wide-brimmed natural straw hat with a bright pink ribbon hatband completed her ensemble.

She clattered lightheartedly down the stairs and into the dining room. Ashe sat alone at the table, absorbed in a pile of papers, a cup of coffee beside his hand. He resembled a planter himself this morning, for he was dressed in white denim slacks tucked into boots and a white shirt open at the throat. The contrast between the dazzling white shirt and the darkly tanned skin of his throat warmed Valerie's stomach, and suddenly happiness seemed to be bubbling in her. She strode to the sideboard to pour herself a cup of coffee, asking brightly, "Hello, how are you this morning?"

Ashe looked up from his work and a slow smile spread across his face. "Not as well as you, apparently."

His blue eyes were startling in his tan face, and his lazy grin squeezed her heart. Valerie wondered if it had the same effect on all women, or if only she was this crazy. She returned his smile, berating herself for her weakness and stupidity. She ought to be furious with him for the wounding things he'd said and done to her, but at the moment she couldn't work up a single negative emotion. All she wanted was to watch him and listen to the rough timbre of his voice. Her coffee cup rattled on the saucer, and she realized that her hands were trembling. Quickly she set the cup and saucer on the table and slid into a chair. "I'm looking forward to today. I imagine that's why I feel good."

"I'm looking forward to it, too. Would you like breakfast? I think the maid said to ring if we did. My Spanish isn't the best," he added ruefully.

"This is fine." Valerie picked up a small crystal plate and filled it with freshly cut fruit and a sweet roll from the two platters in the center of the table. "This is what I normally eat for breakfast. Where are Alfonso and Carlos?"

"The fields, I guess. They weren't here when I came down. And I thought I was rising early."

Valerie smiled. "Around here you start before dawn so you can do most of your work before the day gets broiling hot. In the afternoon, when it's hot and sticky, everybody rests. The *siesta* makes sense."

Valerie ate her light breakfast while Ashe stacked his papers in his briefcase and locked it. Then she shoved back her plate and stood. "I'm ready."

"That was fast." He rose and followed Valerie through the hall to the front porch. Three donkeys waited patiently on the graveled drive, a servant holding their reins. The man swept off his straw hat and bobbed his head to Ashe and Valerie.

"Señora, señor."

Valerie had a sick premonition of disaster. Three donkeys? Why three, when only she and Ashe were going to the dig? "Hello, Joaquín."

"Señor Alfonso, he said I am going with you. I bring a lunch, see?" Joaquín pointed to a straw basket strapped onto the back of one mount.

Valerie bit her lip. Alfonso had managed to thwart

them after all. He was sending a servant to spy on them. Joaquín was one of the few servants who understood English. Struggling to remain calm, she told him, "That's kind of Señor Alfonso, but we don't need a guide. I know the way to the archaeologists' camp. You can put the basket on my donkey."

"Oh, no, I cannot!" Joaquín protested, shocked. "Señor Alfonso ordered me to guide you and make sure nothing happened. Sometimes the jungle is not such a nice place, you know?"

"We won't stray from the path, I assure you. I've ridden to the dig by myself many times."

"But Señor Alfonso said I was to go," the man insisted stubbornly, his pleased expression changing to a worried frown.

Valerie could have screamed with frustration. The servants were too frightened of Alfonso and Carlos to disobey them. She was a mere woman, whereas Alfonso had power. Joaquín wouldn't want to argue with her, but he would refuse to stay behind even if she ordered him to.

Ashe made an impatient gesture. "It doesn't matter. Lead on, Joaquín, we'll follow." He shot Valerie a firm glance and trotted down the steps to the animals. Valerie's spirits lightened. Ashe would find a way to get rid of Joaquín so they could talk. That was what his look had meant. Any further efforts to leave Joaquín behind would appear suspicious.

Valerie followed Ashe and let him help her onto the sturdy back of one of the donkeys. When Ashe hopped onto his animal a giggle escaped Valerie. He looked ridiculous atop the little donkey, his long legs trailing almost to the ground. Ashe gave her a forbidding frown at her laughter. "Are you sure this thing is strong enough to hold me?"

"Oh, yes. It seems cruel, but apparently they're quite strong. They carry burdens far heavier than you all the time."

Ashe shrugged. "Okay. Let's go."

With Joaquín in the lead, they set off down the driveway and along the narrow road. Soon they turned off onto another path through the thick undergrowth. Since it was much narrower, they proceeded single file. Valerie and Ashe talked little, now and then commenting on a bird with stunning plumage or an unusual plant. Ashe asked some general questions about the history of the area, and Valerie did her best to answer them as casually as he had asked them. He seemed so normal and unconcerned that doubt kept pricking at her. Did he really mean to help her?

It took several long hours to reach the archaeological dig. Just before the ruins came into view they happened on a middle-aged man in a pith helmet squatting beside the trail and studying a large rock in the middle of a patch of vines. He glanced up at their approach and adjusted his wire-rimmed glasses, smiling vaguely. "Ah, Valerie, nice to see you again."

"Hello, Dr. Samuels. Doctor, this is Ashe Harlan, an American friend of mine." Valerie swiveled toward Ashe. "Dr. Samuels is an expert in hieroglyphs."

Ashe made a polite comment, but the man had already resumed his study of the rock, lost to the rest of the world. Ashe cocked an eyebrow at Valerie and grinned. Valerie barely restrained a giggle. After they were past him, she told Ashe, "He's always like that. I'm surprised he remembered my name. He's one of those scholars whose head is in the clouds. Or, rather, in the mists of the past."

The trail broke into a clearing. Along one edge of the open area were several large tents. A small tin shed stood at right angles to a long one. Opposite the tents stood a man-high wall with a jagged top. A shirtless, tanned young man dressed in hiking boots and khaki shorts was seated in front of the wall, his back to them, drawing on a pad. The portion of the wall he was drawing was cleared, but a few feet on either side it was obscured by clinging green vines. Two native workers were carefully peeling away the encroaching vines.

"Hello, Mike," Valerie called, and the shirtless man turned. A pleased grin creased his face.

"Valerie! Hey, it's been forever since you were here." He loped over to help her dismount. A pleasant-featured young man in his mid-twenties, he had dark brown hair with sun-bleached streaks of auburn on top. A reddish beard adorned his cheeks and jaw. He wore sunglasses, which he now pushed on top of his head to reveal warm brown eyes. "I heard what happened. I'm sorry. I mean, about Felipe."

"Thank you. Mike, I'd like you to meet a friend of mine from the United States, Ashe Harlan. Ashe, this is Mike Paretti. He's in graduate school."

"Hi." Mike extended a large hand in greeting, as puppyishly friendly to Ashe as he had been with Valerie. "Dr. Robertson's inside." He motioned with his head toward a large opening in the wall. "Come on in."

Ashe and Valerie, with Joaquín in their wake, followed him through the gap. Ashe turned toward Valerie. "What is this place?"

"It used to be a Mayan temple," Valerie explained. "That's what brought the team here originally, but after they arrived they discovered something more important nearby: a Mayan cave. Up till now they've spent more time in the cave than here."

"What was Dr. Samuels doing out on the trail, then?"

"There are remains of other buildings scattered around, probably outbuildings in the courtyard of the temple. He was working on a cornerstone's hieroglyphs. Last time I was here they were speculating whether the stone was part of the outer wall."

"You mean he's been at it since then?"

Valerie laughed. "I'm sure not the whole time, no, but it does take a lot of time to decipher some drawings. They can get pretty complex."

The room they had entered had walls but no roof.

Vines and underbrush had been cleared away, but the floor was rough and uneven. Mike explained that the roof had collapsed sometime in the past, leaving rubble all over the floor which had to be removed and examined carefully. A man and a woman squatted in the center of the room, bent over a large map. When Mike announced Valerie de la Portilla they looked up, smiled and rose. The man wore a straw cowboy hat pushed back on the crown of his head. He took one of Valerie's hands in his and expressed his sorrow at Felipe's death. They spoke for a few minutes about Felipe and his interest in archaeology; then Valerie turned to introduce Ashe. The man shook his hand firmly. "Mr. Harlan, I'm Dr. Robertson. Nice to meet a friend of Valerie's. Have you come to look over the site?"

"Yes, if you don't mind," Ashe replied.

"Not at all, not at all," Dr. Robertson assured him heartily. He stuck the pencil he carried behind one ear and rolled up the map. "I'll be happy to show you around myself. Gloria and I were stuck, anyway." He introduced his companion, then motioned to Ashe and Valerie to follow him.

For the remainder of the morning Ashe was treated to a detailed lecture on the Mayan culture in general and that site in particular. Dr. Robertson showed them the temple and outer grounds, winding up in the cleaning shed, where he explained the process by which the bits and pieces of artifacts were cleaned and identified. Proudly he displayed several of the more important pieces to Ashe. All through the tour the servant Joaquín stayed at their heels.

At about one o'clock the crew quit work and strolled to a rough wooden table in the shade of a large tree. They sat down to eat a lunch made up primarily of canned foods. Valerie and Ashe joined them, sharing the lunch they had brought from the plantation house. Ashe ate quickly, and Valerie followed his example.

They had finished their meal by the time Joaquín had dished up his food and settled under a nearby tree among the dig's native workers. Ashe glanced at him out of the corner of his eye, then addressed Dr. Robertson. "Valerie's been telling me about a cave you discovered."

"I think it's the most important find here, perhaps the biggest one I've ever made. Of course, we've had a problem with vandalism. Not long ago thieves destroyed some of the best carvings by trying to hack them out with an axe. Left big scratches."

"Oh, no!" Valerie gasped.

"Yes, I'm afraid so."

"Why?" Ashe asked, puzzled. "It seems like a lot of trouble to come all the way out here just to wreck something."

"Their purpose is to steal, not wreck, although they usually manage to do the second while accomplishing the first. You see, the San Cristobalian government tries to control the outflow of artifacts to other countries. They've built a lovely new museum in La Luz, and they want all the nation's treasures to be placed there."

Ashe flicked a glance at Valerie as they both recalled with amusement Alfonso's advice that Ashe visit the museum in comfort instead of trekking to the dig in the heat.

Dr. Robertson went on, "They even assign a government official to every dig to make sure we aren't pirating artifacts to our universities' museums. One can hardly blame them. But their real problem isn't archaeologists, but thieves, who know they can sell stolen artifacts to museums and collectors at nice prices, no questions asked. In swiping them, though, they damage much of what's left. So the government loses doubly—and so does archaeology, as in this case. They severely damaged one whole wall trying to cut out a piece of stone."

Ashe sympathized with him over the damage, then went on, "Nevertheless, it sounds as if the cave is worth seeing."

"Sure, if you're game to do a little climbing. It's in one of those low cliffs to the east."

"Sure. I don't mind a climb. Valerie?"

"I'd love to."

Ashe rose from the rude bench on which they sat and extended a hand to Valerie to help her up. Her hand tingled as his rough skin met hers, and she unconsciously folded her fingers over the palm he had touched. Ashe swung toward their shadow, Joaquín. "Señora de la Portilla and I are going to look at the cave."

Joaquín, disappointed, started to set aside his plate and rise. Ashe waved him down. "No need for you to come. Stay and eat. Mike will show us the way."

Valerie started to protest that she knew the way, but Ashe clasped her hand and squeezed. She closed her mouth on the words. Joaquín hesitated, then bowed his head and continued eating. Despite Alfonso's orders, he was too accustomed to obedience to defy Ashe's calm authority. He could ignore *her,* Valerie thought huffily, but not a man. Ashe glanced inquiringly at Mike, who jumped to his feet, grinning. "Sure. I'll be glad to."

Mike struck out through the underbrush, taking a narrow, recent trail. The thick undergrowth gradually thinned as they reached rockier soil. Before long they came upon a creek bed, which contained only a trickle of water. On the other side of the creek rose a small bluff, and about halfway up it lay a dark, round hole. "That's the cave." Mike pointed to the hole. "We have to cross the creek and climb those rocks."

Ashe turned to him. "Mike, Valerie and I needed an excuse to get away from Alfonso's watchdog back there." He grinned, man-to-man. "We'd like a little time alone. Think you could wait out here for a while?"

Mike stared for a moment, startled, then grinned slyly. "Sure. No problem. I've been wanting a rest, anyway. Here, better take my flashlight."

"Thanks. Valerie?" Ashe took her hand and led her across the stream. They climbed the heavy boulders at the bottom of the cliff, then half crawled the rest of the way up, holding on to a rope the archaeologists had left dangling out of the cave. After they pulled themselves onto the ledge at the entrance to the cave they dusted off their clothes, and Ashe held the flashlight out to Valerie. "Okay, let's go inside. Might as well see it since we're here."

Irritably Valerie snatched the light from his hands. "Why did you say that to Mike? Now he thinks you and I are having an affair."

Ashe shrugged. "So what? It's the easiest explanation for wanting privacy. Would you rather he came with us and listened to our discussion?"

"No, but you didn't need to have a suggestive look on your face when you asked him. You did it to be spiteful."

He muttered a short expletive and motioned her forward. Valerie shone the light into the cave, and they started down a steep slope to a large, flat-floored chamber.

"The archaeologists named this the Passage Chamber because it has so many scenes representing passage into the world of the dead. You see, the Mayans believed that caves were entrances to the underworld and feared them greatly. However, an underground spring opens into this cave, and in times of drought it was their only *cenote,* or well, which also made the cave a place of life." She led him through the chamber and along a narrow passage, pointing out the glyphs of ballplayers on the walls as they passed.

They emerged into a rounded chamber whose dripping stalactites were colorful in the glow of their flashlight. "This is named the Jaguar Room because of the glyphs representing the jaguar."

"Wait." Ashe grasped her arm, turning her forcibly toward him. "I didn't come here for a lecture on archaeology. Damn it, Valerie, I'm risking a big deal for you. You better play straight with me."

"I'm surprised you'd be so chivalrous," she countered coldly. He didn't believe her. Her chest ached at the thought.

Ashe blew out an exasperated breath. "Look, I want to help you—if you need help. When I heard that you'd decided to 'retire' to the plantation for a while I began to suspect that you were telling the truth the other night. Then Alfonso was so reluctant for me to visit or for us to be alone together that it confirmed my suspicions. But the way you're acting now makes me wonder. Was your story the truth?"

"Yes, of course. I've never lied to you!"

"No, certainly not." His mouth turned down in a grimace. "You simply neglected to inform me that you were married, even after I began making love to you. What do you call it when you imply a falsehood, if it isn't lying?"

"I don't know! I didn't . . . mean to hurt you. I didn't expect it to happen. It just got out of control."

"Forget it." His mouth clamped into a thin line. "Let's stick to the here and now, okay? Do you think we could talk without you arguing or snapping my head off?"

"I'm sorry. I didn't mean to snap." She moved away, her voice dropping. "I'm on edge because I feel unsure around you. I don't know what to say or do. I'm aware that you hate me. After the other night, I swore I'd never turn to you again." Tears sprang into her eyes. "But I need help badly. I've messed up everything, as usual."

Ashe crossed his arms over his chest and stared down at the floor. His voice was as quiet as hers when he spoke. "Valerie, I want to apologize for the way I acted in the bar. It was inexcusable. I wanted to hurt you back. I assumed that you were lying again to win my sympathy. That's why I was harsh. I'm not an especially kind man, but I'm not usually cruel, either. I'm sorry."

Valerie turned. Her eyes were wide and soft in the dim light, tears sparkling like diamonds on the ends of her lashes. "I'm sorry, too. What I did in Dallas was wrong. Please, do you think we could call it even and start over?"

Unconsciously his face slackened as he gazed at her, and his eyes darkened. Then he pulled back, shaking his head as though to clear it. "All right. Agreed. We'll start fresh. Now, tell me again what you said the other night at the hotel."

Obediently Valerie launched into her story, ending with a description of her escape and visit to the bank before she came to Ashe for help. "When I—when I left the hotel, Alfonso was waiting. He sent me here, where I can't escape. Even worse, I have to be around Carlos all the time." Valerie shuddered. "I dislike him. I always have. Even Felipe called him a brute. I'm afraid. . . ."

"Of what?"

"Of what he might do to force me to marry him. Right now he's trying to charm me, but you must have seen how incapable he is of that. Once he realizes it he's likely to resort to other methods. I'm afraid he'll rape me."

"No!" Ashe growled. "I'll get you out."

"But how?"

Ashe shrugged confidently. "Tomorrow I'll tell Alfonso that you're returning with me. Carlos may be a dangerous type, but so far Alfonso hasn't attempted violence. I don't think he'll try to stop us. His worst threat would be dropping the deal with Stone Oil. Even if he's inclined to violence, he must know he can't make me disappear and hope no one will notice. Alec wouldn't rest until he either found me or found out what happened. And then he'd hound Alfonso to his grave."

"But why?" Valerie blurted out. "I mean, I know Alec wouldn't want one of his employees to disappear, but would he really launch a big investigation and punish Alfonso?"

"Of course. Alec's not a soft man. He'd want full measure for losing a son."

"What!"

Ashe's brows rose in surprise. "You mean you didn't know? I'm Alec's son." Valerie stared, dumbfounded. How could he be Alec's son? All those years when she had visited Laraine and Alec in the summer, there had never been any mention of a son. Nor had she seen Ashe around. There had been only Alexis, Morgan and Cara. At her stunned look Ashe added sarcastically, "Don't get excited, baby. I'm his *illegitimate* son. I won't inherit Stone Oil."

"Oh!" Valerie exclaimed. "As if I cared whether you inherited anything. I haven't the slightest interest in you."

Ashe grinned. "Oh? Tell me another one."

Valerie recalled her behavior at the bar the other night and how much interest she had shown in him. Even now, in the midst of danger, she had been very aware of the firm muscles beneath Ashe's tanned skin, the touch of his hands as he helped her up the cliff, the line of sweat down the front of his shirt from the exertion of the climb. She ached to touch the dampness, to lean her head against his chest and feel the warmth, hear the hard thud of his heart, smell the acrid scent of his sweat. She blushed to the roots of her hair and whirled away, shining her flashlight around the walls. "We better run through the rest of the cave. Come on."

Valerie led him through the cave, pointing out a few places of interest, and headed for the entrance. The sunlight pouring into the entrance dazzled their eyes after the darkness, and they had to pause to let their eyes adjust before climbing down. Mike waited for them on a large boulder, hat tilted over his eyes, dozing like a cat in the sun. When they approached he stretched and rose, protesting that his rest hadn't been long enough.

Mike and Ashe chatted as they hiked to camp, but Valerie was silent, mulling over the bombshell Ashe had handed her. So Ashe was Alec's son. It made a lot of things clearer, including Laraine's asking an oil executive to fix her car. She glanced surreptitiously at Ashe. Yes, the resemblances were there, if only she'd had the sense to see them. The pale blue eyes were Alec's although lighter in shade, and he had the same loose-jointed walk, the same deceptively slender body encasing hard-as-steel muscles. A smile twinkled in her eyes as she noted that the determined set of his chin was Alec's—and Cara's—to a T.

No wonder Valerie had been so immediately attracted to Ashe and had felt so at home with him. Subconsciously he had reminded her of Alec, whom she had adored for years. It explained her feelings. It wasn't Ashe himself but his resemblance to her teenage idol that evoked such emotions in her. It wouldn't last, as she had been afraid it would, nor would it deepen just by being around Ashe. The more he became his own person and less Alec's image, the less attracted she would be. The thought was reassuring. The last thing she wanted was to be hopelessly in love with a man who despised her.

Deep in thought, she stumbled over a thick tree root and Ashe's arm reached out to steady her, his hand encircling her wrist. Embarrassed, she raised her eyes to his. "Thank you," she murmured, intensely aware of Mike watching and waiting for them. But Ashe didn't drop her wrist and walk on. Instead he stared into her face, and his thumb began to draw a lazy, hypnotic circle on the inside of her wrist. As plainly as if he had spoken, she knew that he wanted to kiss her. And just as plainly she knew that she wanted him to.

After a long, silent moment he released her wrist and

started down the path. Valerie followed, folding the opposite hand around the wrist he had touched as if he had burned or marked the flesh. If what she felt for Ashe was caused by his resemblance to Alec, why had she never known that same sizzling, choking yearning around Alec?

Chapter 10

BY THE TIME ASHE AND VALERIE RETURNED TO THE plantation house it was almost dark. Carlos and Alfonso sat on the front porch, predinner drinks clutched in their hands, and glowered at the group riding toward them. When they reached the porch Ashe slid from his donkey and turned to help Valerie off her mount, ignoring Carlos's thunderous face, while Joaquín rode on toward the barn. Alfonso smiled stiffly, more adept than his son at hiding his emotions but unable to erase the suspicion from his eyes. "Well, hello," he greeted them heartily. "We were afraid something had happened to you."

"No," Ashe replied easily. "After all, we had Joaquín with us. But the site was so interesting that we stayed longer than I had expected." He launched into an account of the dig and the archaeologists' story of the art thieves in the Mayan cave, giving Valerie a chance to slip away to her room. She took a leisurely bath and changed into a sky blue sundress, quite unconcerned at making Alfonso and Carlos wait.

By the time she returned to the verandah Ashe had also cleaned up and changed, and the men were ready to go in to dinner. The atmosphere was reasonably friendly, except for Carlos's sulking, and Valerie relaxed. Apparently Ashe's unconcerned tone had convinced Alfonso that she hadn't revealed the story of her imprisonment. Soon after supper Valerie excused herself and left Ashe to talk to Alfonso. His nerves were better than hers. She had difficulty even meeting Alfonso's eyes, much less conversing naturally with him. Anxiety gripped her stomach as she packed a small suitcase for the trip the next day. Despite Ashe's confidence, she couldn't believe that leaving would be as easy as he predicted. She found it difficult to concentrate on anything, but neither could she go to sleep. After several fruitless hours of waiting and worrying she forced herself to go to bed and eventually slipped into an uneasy sleep.

The sun streaming through the wooden shutters awakened her the next morning, and she sat up in alarm. It was far later than she normally awoke. She leaned across the bed to grab the small alarm clock and gasped when she saw its face. Nine o'clock! She had intended to arise early and be downstairs, ready to go whenever Ashe indicated it was time. Valerie jumped out of bed and rushed through her morning routines, not bothering with any more makeup than a dab of lipstick. She slid on off-white slacks and a simple blue knit top, stepped into flat white sandals and picked up the matching suit jacket. She hurried to the door and turned the knob. It wouldn't open.

For a moment it seemed as if everything had stopped —her heart, her breath, her hearing—and there was a peculiar droning in her ears. Her hand trembled on the doorknob. Then common sense reasserted itself. Alfonso couldn't do this to her again, not with Ashe in the house. She had merely turned the knob in the wrong direction. Valerie twisted it the opposite way, but the door remained as solidly closed. She was locked in. What if Ashe was gone? She was late. Would he assume that she didn't want to go with him? No, surely not. Their conversation the day before had convinced him that she was telling the truth. But what if Alfonso had

made up a story that convinced Ashe she was lying?
Ashe didn't have much faith in her. Valerie felt
physically sick. She sank into the nearest chair and
lowered her head. She mustn't faint now. And she
mustn't give way to panic, either. She had to think.
Had to act. Only what was she to do?

Ashe jumped out of the Jeep, landing lightly on his
feet, and bounded up the front steps. Behind him
Alfonso climbed out more slowly.

They had arisen early to drive to the site of the
proposed well. Ashe had glanced over the area and
announced that he was ready to leave. Now Alfonso
cursed under his breath. Harlan had insisted on coming
to the plantation to view the site, had forced Alfonso to
wake up at dawn to drive him there, and after all that
he had hardly looked at it. It was crazy. Worse than
that, it was suspicious. Alfonso had almost been lulled
into believing that Ashe knew nothing about Valerie,
but now he was glad he had taken the precaution of
locking Valerie's door that morning. Underneath his
appearance of ease and friendship, Harlan must be
planning something sneaky.

Wiping his forehead with a limp white handkerchief,
Alfonso trailed Ashe up the steps. Ashe glanced at his
watch and went to his room to gather his belongings.
He carried the bag downstairs and strolled through the
house, looking for Valerie. He wound up in the dining
room, where Alfonso and Carlos were waiting for him
to join them for breakfast. Glancing around, he asked
mildly, "Where's Valerie?"

"She is not well today," Alfonso explained. "The
maid told me she's still in bed. She had a rather rough
night, I understand. Migraine headache." He shot
Ashe a sly glance. "She is often subject to them. She
hasn't been herself since Felipe died. Such a tragic loss,
and to one who is"—he paused meaningfully—"shall
we say as high-strung as Valerie? . . . it was crippling."

Ashe's expression did not change. "Indeed? I'm

sorry to hear that. You see, I need to discuss family business with her. Alec specifically cautioned me not to come home without her answer."

"I am most sorry." Alfonso sighed and shook his head. "I fear she isn't capable of giving her opinion on anything today. Perhaps when you return."

The movement of Ashe's lips was a grim imitation of a smile. "Apparently I'm not making myself clear. I must speak to Valerie before I leave."

"But, Ashe, you have to understand. Her mental health is, well, to put it bluntly, precarious at the moment. Business problems would disturb her."

"That's odd." His tone was crisp. "She seemed all right yesterday. And she asked me to take her with me today. Valerie told me you were holding her prisoner."

Alfonso heaved a sorrowful sigh. "So she is doing that again? I am sorry. I wanted to shield her, but I see I must tell you. Valerie suffers from recurring delusions of persecution. She thinks we are trying to harm her. As if I would harm my dear brother's widow! This isn't the first time she's asked a stranger to help her escape. You must believe me. It's for Valerie's own good. I think she will recover, given time and our loving care. I can't bear to send her away for mental treatment. Please, don't make this a legal issue."

"Are you threatening to have Valerie declared insane?" Ashe's brows rose incredulously. "I would be most interested in the judge's opinion after he speaks to Valerie. And I imagine the judge would be interested in how much Stone Oil wants her out of the country." His jaw hardened, and the gaze he leveled at Alfonso was chilling. "Look, de la Portilla, let's stop the ridiculous fencing. Valerie's informed me of your scheme to force her to marry Carlos. She also told me that you kept her a prisoner in her room back in La Luz. So I'm not likely to believe your story about migraine headaches."

"Are you calling me a liar?" Alfonso puffed indignantly.

"Yes, I'm also calling you a lot of things far worse, such as kidnapper, thug and coward, to name a few." The other man began to splutter, his face growing alarmingly red, but Ashe paid him no attention. "Let's conclude the whole sorry affair in as adult and reasonable a manner as possible. Valerie is leaving with me."

"You are destroying our deal!" Alfonso growled. "I refuse to do business with a man so easily swayed by a silly girl's stories."

"I'll regret losing the well for . . . oh, maybe thirty seconds. Stone Oil doesn't need you nearly as much as you need us. You might remember that." Ashe stood up and leaned on the table, looming over the older man. "You interfere with me and there won't be much of you left to cry over. If by some chance you managed to stop *me*, you'd have put yourself crosswise with Alec Stone, who eats little guys like you for breakfast. He's very fond of Valerie. Now, I'm going up to get Valerie. Excuse me."

Ashe pushed himself away from the table. Carlos impulsively rushed to block the door with his heavy frame. Ashe glared at him, his stone-cold fury as awesome as any ever displayed by his father, and after a long moment Carlos stepped aside. Ashe strode across the hall and up the stairs, ignoring the other two, who followed on his heels, exchanging hot words in Spanish. "Valerie!" he called as he reached the top of the stairs and faced numerous doors that lined the hall.

Valerie lay curled on her bed, her face sodden with tears, her hair fanned out across the comforter. When she had first realized that she had been locked in again she had beaten on the door and screamed in panic, but her efforts had brought no one. Not knowing that Ashe was out of the house with Alfonso, she had burst into despairing tears and thrown herself onto her bed. Almost three hours had passed since she had woken up, and by now she was convinced that Ashe had left her behind. Numb and hopeless, she lay waiting for her brother-in-law to show up to gloat. Then she heard the pounding of feet on the stairs and Ashe's voice shouting her name.

For a second she was so stunned that she could do nothing, but when he called her name again Valerie sprang off the bed and rushed to the door. "Here, Ashe! I'm in here!" she yelled back, beating a tattoo on the door with her fists.

The doorknob rattled violently. She heard Ashe's voice, so low and icy that it sent a shiver down her spine. "All right, unlock it."

"Please, Señor Harlan, you must understand. . . ."

Ashe cut Alfonso off with a short, vivid expletive. "Stand back, Val."

Valerie obeyed and watched in amazement as the door shuddered under a crashing impact. It was rammed again and then flew open. Ashe stumbled in. Over his shoulder Valerie could see Carlos's and Alfonso's grim faces, but they were nothing compared to Ashe's steely expression.

"Come on, we're getting out of here," Ashe snapped, picking up Valerie's jacket and tossing it to her. "Is this your suitcase?"

Valerie nodded, struck dumb at witnessing Ashe's full fury. He seized her bag and marched out of her room. Valerie grabbed her purse and darted after him, hardly glancing at her former in-laws. Downstairs, Ashe swung his waiting bag onto his shoulder and continued out the door, Valerie trotting at his heels. He strode full steam across the porch and along the path to the dock, his long legs forcing Valerie almost to run to keep up with him. She heard Alfonso and Carlos emerge from the house and knew that the two men were staring at their backs. She swallowed hard and concentrated on not thinking about her exposed back.

They reached the motorboat, an older, slightly smaller vessel than the de la Portillas' gleaming craft. Valerie was relieved that Ashe hadn't come to the plantation in Alfonso's boat, but she wondered if the crewmen had been hired by Alfonso. Ashe tossed their bags into the boat and pivoted to help Valerie step onto the deck. A member of the crew stood there, and Ashe barked out a rapid succession of orders to him in Spanish. The man scurried to cast off, and Ashe helped untie the heavy rope, which bound the boat to one of the pier beams. They pushed away from the dock and the engine coughed to life. The crewman guided the boat out into the wide brown river. Valerie looked back at the shore, shading her eyes. She couldn't see anyone following them and sagged against the rail in relief.

She was safe. Ashe hadn't deserted her. Her legs began to tremble uncontrollably as her adrenaline drained away. Ashe crossed the deck to her as the boat gained speed. "They aren't pursuing us. We're all right." He saw her white face and the shudders that racked her, and his face softened. "Poor baby. Did you think I'd forgotten you? Sorry. I didn't realize he'd locked you in or I'd have gotten you out sooner. I put in a token appearance at the well site this morning. That's why I was late."

"Are you—is the crew loyal? Did Alfonso hire them?"

Ashe chuckled and pulled her close, wrapping both arms around her securely. "Yes, he's loyal. It's only one man, and I hired him myself. No need to worry. We're home free. Got your passport?"

She nodded, lulled by the steady rhythm of his heart and the warmth of his chest. "In my purse." She cuddled closer, needing him too much to be embarrassed at her boldness.

"Good. We're in great shape. When we reach La Luz I'll finish my negotiations with the government and we'll head home. Okay?"

"Okay." His arms remained tightly around her even after her shivering stopped. Valerie made no protest. As far as she was concerned, the moment could go on forever.

* * *

She didn't know how long they remained clasped in one another's arms, but finally the one-man crew called out a question to Ashe and he released her with a sigh. "Back in a minute."

While he conferred with the man Valerie glanced about her, taking stock of her surroundings. The boat wasn't swift, but it appeared sturdy enough to get them to La Luz. That was all they needed. Alfonso and Carlos could catch them in their swifter craft, but surely they wouldn't try. Alfonso might intimidate a woman without any qualms, but he wouldn't be so crazy as to go up against Ashe Harlan and Stone Oil. Now that Valerie was away from him and able to think more rationally, she realized that.

They puttered down the river, and with each passing mile Valerie grew more relaxed. She and Ashe leaned against the railing and talked lightly, discussing the wild plants growing in profusion beside the river. The sun glinted off his golden brown hair, highlighting the paler streaks, and Valerie yearned to reach up and brush back the lock that strayed across his forehead, but she was too afraid that he would recoil in distaste. He already thought she was a sex-starved adulteress. No point in confirming his bad impression.

"What's that?" Ashe pointed to a tree leaning over the riverbank.

Valerie laughed. "I don't know. Some kind of palm. Honestly, Ashe, I'd have to be a member of the Botanical Society to keep up with you."

He glanced sideways at her and caught his breath. Her hair was whipping around her delicate face, glittering almost white in the glare of the sunlight. Her silvery green eyes were almost translucent, her pale lashes sparkling like golden halos around them. Her lips parted slightly as she smiled, and a dimple flashed at one corner of her mouth. She dazzled his senses, and unconsciously he leaned closer to her. As he moved he glimpsed a flash of metal amid the heavy foliage of the riverbank. Before his brain could register it as a thought he instinctively stiffened and grabbed Valerie, pulling her back with him.

"What—" Valerie began in bewilderment just as something popped loudly. A chunk of the wooden rail they had leaned against flew into the air, and Ashe realized what he had glimpsed: the barrel of a rifle.

He shoved Valerie to the deck and stretched out on top of her. More shots blasted out, gouging holes in the railing and deck. Valerie and Ashe scrambled over the planks on their stomachs and reached the shelter of the cabin wall. Shielded by the cabin, Ashe crouched over and ran toward the opposite end of the boat. There was a high-pitched scream from the direction of the boatman. Valerie covered her ears and closed her eyes, not daring to look. What was going on?

Suddenly Ashe was back at her side. "The owner went overboard." His voice was taut and grim. "Shot. We're out of control, and I'm afraid any minute they'll hit the gas tank."

"What's happening?" Valerie wailed.

"Somebody's firing at us! What do you think's happening?

"I know that!" Irritation reduced her panic fractionally. "I mean, why? What are we going to do?"

"Swim," he snapped. "You can swim, can't you?" Valerie nodded mutely. "Okay. We'll jump into the water and head for the opposite shore. For a time the boat should protect us, but then we'll be sitting ducks until we reach the bank."

"Great."

"If we stay here, we may go up in flames any minute."

"You've convinced me." Valerie kicked off her shoes and turned to Ashe, her eyes wide in her paper-white face. "I'm ready."

"Okay. Let's go." Ashe dumped his shoes beside hers and crossed the deck in a flash. He leaped lightly onto the railing and arced off it in a clean dive. Beside him Valerie ran bent over across the deck, ducked under the railing and made an ungainly dive into the muddy water.

The water was as murky as it appeared from above, making it almost impossible for her to see where she was going. She surfaced and tossed her wet hair out of her eyes, treading water in the shadow of the boat as she oriented herself. She wondered how far she could swim and still be blocked from the view of the gunmen by the boat. Ashe looked over at her, nodded and struck out toward shore. Valerie sucked in a deep breath and followed him. Fortunately, swimming was one of her few accomplishments. All those years at summer camp were finally paying off, she thought grimly as she raced through the water.

She felt the warmth of the sun strike her head and knew she had emerged from the boat's shadow. Almost immediately a tiny geyser spewed up beside Ashe. The riflemen had spotted them. Valerie dived deeply, as did Ashe. She swam underwater for as long as her lungs allowed before she broke the surface. As she sliced through the water she glanced around her. The current had carried her downstream, but she was also much closer to the opposite shore. Apparently the attacker had lost her, for there were no shots yet. Ashe popped out of the water several feet away from her.

Valerie concentrated on the shoreline, willing herself not to think about how many years it had been since she had swum this kind of distance or about the rumors of water snakes and crocodiles in the Rio Miedo. Now the shots started again, and the water splashed around Ashe as if a handful of pebbles had been thrown at him. It took Valerie's fright-numbed brain several seconds to realize that their attacker was firing only at Ashe. She angled toward him until she reached his side, and the bullets stopped instantly. Ashe glanced at her in surprise.

The bank loomed up before them. Ashe encircled

one of her wrists with his iron hand so he wouldn't lose her as he grabbed at the end of a log wedged into the soft bank. He worked his way along the log, and Valerie latched onto it behind him. Their feet and legs made contact with roots and soft silt, and once— Valerie choked back a scream—something slithery brushed her and moved away. Ashe heaved himself out of the water, bracing his arms on the log. It shifted and pulled loose from the shore. But Ashe grasped a large branch bending over the water and reached back with the other hand to clasp Valerie's arm. She clung to him tenaciously as she fought for traction in the sticky mud of the bank. Sliding and falling, they crawled up the root-clogged riverbank and sank onto the ground, lungs gasping for air and limbs trembling with exertion. Finally Ashe sat up, shoving wet hair from his face. He rose to his knees and peered across the river.

It was a long way to the opposite shore, and the other side was thick with heavy undergrowth. He couldn't see anything useful. "How quickly could they cross the river?"

Valerie struggled for the breath to answer. "If they have a boat, immediately. If not, they'll have to go—oh, miles and miles back to reach even a foot-bridge. The nearest ferry is past the plantation, and a bridge capable of supporting a car is way downstream at Piedra Roja."

"Could they have gotten to that bank by car?"

"Probably not. There's a village fairly close on the other side. It's a notorious hideout of thieves and guerrillas. They must have come from there, and the fastest route would be on foot or by donkey. There's a road a Jeep could navigate running from the village to Piedra Roja. But it would take hours that way. Their best bet is to get across the river by boat. I'm sure they wouldn't hesitate to commandeer one if they'd go around shooting at people."

"Then we'd better get out of here." He rose to his feet and extended a hand to pull Valerie up.

She rose with his help and ran her fingers through her wet hair. "Where are we going?"

"You tell me. You're more familiar with the area than I am."

"I've never gone tramping through it on foot!" she retorted. It had taken all her strength of character to stand and agree to follow him through the jungle. "I don't know where to go!"

"Then think. We need a place to hide in case they look for us. We can make our plans for reaching civilization after that."

Valerie glared at him, then closed her eyes, examining a mental map. She began tentatively. "I think we had just passed the big curve in the river when they started firing. That means the archaeologists' camp should be almost directly behind us." She pointed into the thick jungle. "Well, no, a little bit that way." She swung her arm a fraction further. "The camp's almost due north of the bend, if I remember the map correctly."

"Let's hope you do. You think the archaeologists will hide us?"

"I'm sure they would—although I wouldn't want to place them in any danger." Valerie frowned.

"How about the cave?"

"The cave?" Valerie repeated blankly.

"The one you and I went to. We could climb into it and pull up the rope after us. They're less likely to look for us there than at the camp, which is where we'd naturally go for help."

"You're right." Like Ashe, Valerie avoided naming the faceless "they." She couldn't face it yet. Later, when they were safe . . . "And the cave is actually closer to where we are. It lies between the camp and the river."

"Can you find it?"

Valerie's stomach trembled. How could she manage it? But it was up to her. Ashe had no idea where they were. "I'll have to, I guess," she murmured.

Ashe's arm encircled her shoulders, and he squeezed her hard, as if he could imbue her with his own confidence. "I'm good at telling directions. What general direction do we need to walk?"

"Northwest, mostly north."

Ashe tilted his head to look at the sun, then glanced down at his watch. He grinned and pointed. "Okay, Tonto, let's go thataway."

Valerie returned his smile weakly, and they set off through the brush. It wasn't easy going; the only paths were small ones that had been made by animals. Often they had to push their way through bushes or vines. Beneath the luxuriant trees it was difficult to tell the location of the sun, and Valerie could only hope that Ashe was better able than she to determine their direction. Once or twice they stopped and Ashe climbed a tree to get a better view. When he came down he altered their course slightly and they started off again.

To make it worse, Valerie wasn't sure how far it was to the cave or precisely how to get there. What if she had miscalculated? What if they had passed the bend a long time before the shots, or hadn't reached it yet? She had been concentrating on Ashe, not the surroundings. She could be miles off course.

It seemed as if hours had passed. The jungle darkened around them, increasing Valerie's fears. She stumbled as she walked, her legs aching from the swim followed by the long hike. The ground wasn't hard on her bare feet, but now and then they were scratched and bruised by branches or rocks lying on the path. Her mind felt equally numb and weary. They passed several familiar trees and rocks before Valerie was aware of a lightening in the area of her heart, followed by the conscious realization that she recognized their location.

"Ashe!" she cried. "Wait! I think we're almost there."

"What?" He whirled. "You mean the cave?"

"No. The dig. I must have miscalculated. Let me

think." She looked around her, placing herself in the familiar framework. "If we're where I think we are, we're practically in the camp. See how we've wandered onto a trail? It's much better marked than anything we've used so far."

"You're right." He glanced down at their feet. "I hadn't noticed. Is the camp down this trail?"

"Yes. I've been thinking. We'll need some food and blankets tonight, and I'm sure we can trust the archaeologists. They're all friends of mine. They liked Felipe, but they don't know Alfonso, and they actively dislike Carlos."

"Mmm. He has such a winning personality."

Valerie giggled and clapped her hand over her mouth to silence the hysterical laughter bubbling in her throat.

Ashe continued, "I think you're right. But if Alfonso sends out search parties, we'll be safer at the cave. Why don't I go into the camp, find Dr. Robertson, and get blankets, food and clothes? Then we can head for the cave. Okay?"

Valerie nodded dumbly and slid down to sit on the dirt path. No doubt any self-respecting female would insist on accompanying Ashe, she thought, but frankly she was too tired to care whether she was being weak and dependent. She sat with her legs up and her chin propped on her knees. Soon she dozed. It seemed only seconds later that Ashe was shaking her shoulder. She pulled away with something very close to a growl.

"Come on. Up and at 'em. It's less than a mile, Dr. Robertson tells me."

Valerie came to full consciousness. "Oh, I'm sorry. Heavens, I fell asleep, didn't I?"

Ashe pulled her to her feet and handed her a canned soft drink. "Here. All the comforts of home. It'll perk you up."

Valerie realized how extremely thirsty she was and seized the drink, turning it up to gulp the cool sweetness. Ashe was right. It did revive her. She followed him with more energy as he struck out once more. He carried a blue nylon pack on his back, and Valerie occupied her brain guessing what food was hidden inside. Since her stomach was growling viciously, the thought was enough to keep her on her feet and moving at a reasonable pace.

Finally the small bluff containing the cave loomed up and their tired feet quickened. They crossed the almost-dry stream and began the climb to the cave's mouth. It wasn't an easy slope, and today Valerie thought it was more than she could do. But when she lagged behind Ashe helped her, pushing, pulling and tugging as well as murmuring both encouragement and threats in her ear. With a last supreme effort they scrambled over the lip into the cave, and Ashe yanked the knotted rope up after them. Valerie dropped to the floor inside the dark entrance and leaned against the cool, uneven wall. Even the jagged rock felt heavenly. They were safe.

Chapter 11

Ashe flopped down beside Valerie and slid the pack off his shoulders. He dug into it and hauled out a box of crackers, a jar of processed cheese, a knife and a hard roll of summer sausage. It didn't take long to demolish half the sausage and crackers, and most of the cheese. They washed the food down with bottled water, and Valerie sighed with contentment. She leaned against the cave wall, her eyelids drifting shut. Ashe shook her unsympathetically. "Just a minute. Let's move farther in, so the flashlight won't be seen from outside."

"A flashlight? You got that, too?"

"I thought of everything," he assured her with an almost boyish grin.

"I think you're actually enjoying this," Valerie grumbled.

He chuckled. "Well, at least it's a change in routine. Anyway, what's to be gloomy about? We have warm blankets, full stomachs and a light. After this afternoon I'm beginning to appreciate the little comforts of life."

He motioned to stand up, and Valerie complied with a groan. Ashe switched on the flashlight, breaking the gathering gloom, and they made their way down the sloping floor of the cave entrance to the flat, wide room inside. Ashe pulled several tightly rolled blankets from

153

his pack with a magician's flourish and shook them out. He spread one on the hard floor, handed Valerie another and began to wrap the third around himself.

"Are we both going to sleep on that?" Valerie eyed the single blanket with some misgiving.

"Don't worry. I'm not in the mood for ravishing tender maidens at the moment. Your virtue will be safe."

Valerie grimaced and followed his example of winding the blanket around her. She settled onto the edge of the spread blanket as far from Ashe as possible, rolled onto her side and immediately fell into an exhausted slumber.

It was several hours later that she awakened, cold and cramped. It was utterly dark. She couldn't see even her hand, and she panicked. "Ashe! Ashe! Where are you?"

His voice was instantly alert. "What's the matter?"

She scrambled clumsily in the direction of his voice, hampered by the blanket wrapped around her. She bumped up against Ashe and his arms enfolded her. His voice was gentler as he asked again, "What's the matter?"

"I woke up, and for a second I didn't know where I was, and it was so dark, and the ground was cold." She shuddered.

He squeezed her tightly. "It's okay. Don't worry. I'm here." She snuggled against his side and pillowed her head on his chest, her fear banished. Again she fell asleep.

The next morning Valerie awoke with her face burrowed into Ashe's side. Every muscle in her body ached from the physical exercise of the day before, and her bones and flesh were equally sore from a night spent on a hard floor. It took a moment to remember where she was and why. She groaned and rolled away, fighting free of the encumbering blanket. It had been juvenile to snuggle against Ashe in the night. No doubt, in his usual egotistical way, he had thought she was after his body.

However, her physical discomfort was enough to take her mind off her embarrassment. The ball she had curled into in the night was hard to unwind. Arms, back and legs straightened, but not without creaking protests. When she managed to stand up she shuffled up the incline to the beckoning light of the cave entrance. She stepped onto the narrow outcropping of stone, which formed a porch for the cave. The sun struck her full force, and for several minutes she simply stood, absorbing its warmth like a cat dozing in the sun. It helped her joints and muscles, but at that moment she would have traded almost anything for half an hour in a hot tub.

There was a noise behind her and Ashe joined her on the ledge, lifting his arms in a bone-cracking stretch. He rotated one arm as he kneaded the shoulder. Valerie watched him. His clothes were muddy, wrinkled and torn, and his gold-brown hair was dark with dirt. Yet the large expanses of flesh that the rips revealed, combined with the intimacy of his sleep-stamped face, sent a tongue of desire licking through her.

Ashe smiled, eyeing Valerie. "Good morning." He shot another glance at her and grinned. Valerie grimaced, very conscious of her disreputable appearance. Mud, river slime and dust covered her once-white slacks. Her bare feet were so coated with dust that she couldn't even see her skin, and her hair hung in dank, dirty strings. It didn't raise her spirits to have Ashe laughing at her. "You don't look any better, I hope you know," she snapped.

"Sorry. I didn't mean to be rude. But it's nice to find anything humorous in our situation."

"Well, I hate to spoil your fun, but I intend to bathe and change if Dr. Robertson included any clothes for me."

"Yes, he did. One of the women archaeologists donated a set of clothes. But where are you planning to accomplish this feat?"

Valerie smiled, giving her face such a glow that Ashe forgot the streaks of dirt on it. "Wouldn't you like to know?" she teased.

"Yes. And since I possess the flashlight, food and clothes, I suggest you tell me," he retorted with a grin as sly as hers.

"Oh, all right, if you're going to be that way. Follow me." She went back to the large chamber inside, where Ashe produced a set of clothes for each of them from his magical sack.

"You mean you didn't bring soap?" Valerie joked, taking her clothes and the flashlight from him.

He shook his head. "No, they didn't have any of those little flower-shaped, scented ones, so I said, 'no soap.'"

Valerie groaned comically and set off through the tunnel pathways, winding farther and farther back into the cave until Ashe was beginning to wonder whether she was playing a joke on him. At last she stopped beside a low hole in one wall and ducked down to crawl into it. Ashe raised an eyebrow skeptically but followed her. Inside was a small, dark chamber with plenty of headroom to stand. Water sprang from the far wall about seven or eight feet up, splashing into a small black pool below. Valerie played the light over the miniature waterfall. "See? The perfect shower. The only problem is, it's cold as ice."

Ashe frowned. "Valerie, are you sure it's safe? How deep is the thing?"

Valerie chuckled. "It's dark because the rock is practically black. But the water is clear and pure. It's only two feet deep. See?" She shone the beam straight down on the oval of water, and Ashe peered over the edge. She was right. He could see the bottom of the rock pool through the clear water and it was quite shallow.

"Where does it go? I mean, why doesn't it flood the whole cave?"

"It's like a bathtub. At the opposite end is a drain—a hole about two feet wide. Apparently the water goes down it into another chamber, and somewhere it comes out on the surface or goes underground. But don't investigate the hole. It's the only dangerous place. It has a lot of suction. The photographer lost some equipment down it." She paused, and they glanced at each other, then away, suddenly awkward. How were they to bathe with only one flashlight? Valerie couldn't ask Ashe to loiter in the pitch-black hall while she scrubbed herself clean, and she certainly had no desire to do so while he bathed. But if they both remained, how could they undress and bathe in privacy?

Finally Ashe cleared his throat and asked, "Shall I turn my back like a gentleman?"

"I—I'd rather you did. Please."

Obediently he swung around and squatted on the floor, staring fixedly at the wall. Valerie stepped to the edge of the pool and stripped, shivering in the cool air. Taking a deep breath, she hurried into the thin rushing waterfall. It was like being struck full in the face with a load of snow, but she gritted her teeth and combed through her wet hair to let the torrent sweep away the grime. When her hair was clean she washed the rest of her goose-pimpled body. Hopping out, she pulled on the clean denim trousers and blouse. They didn't fit her especially well; the jeans were too large and the shirt too small. Nor did they provide enough warmth. Valerie's teeth chattered as she informed Ashe that she was through.

He swiveled back, and his eyes swept over her. Valerie realized with horror that he might as well have seen her stark naked. Because they had no towels and she hadn't been inclined to drip dry in the chilly room, Valerie had donned her clothes while she was wet, with the result that the thin cotton shirt clung to her breasts, outlining the thrusting nipples, hardened by her shivers. There was no hope that Ashe had missed it. His gaze lingered on her chest before moving up to her damp face and dripping hair. She could feel the drops from the ends of her hair splashing onto the curves of her breasts and rolling down over the hardened peaks.

Ashe's throat bobbed as he swallowed. He moved forward slowly, as if drawn against his will. In the dim light his eyes were black and huge, his lean face a stark sketch of shadow and light. He stopped only inches away, and the heat from his body warmed her. Without touching her, he leaned down and brought his mouth hard against hers. His lips tasted of dust and the salt of sweat. They stung her own dry, chapped lips, but the tiny pain only intensified the incredible delight of his warm, seeking tongue. Valerie's whole body shook, and she went up on tiptoe, wrapping her arms around his neck. "I'll get you dirty," he mumbled in feeble protest.

When Valerie didn't draw back his arms encircled her fiercely. Ashe twisted, caressing her engorged nipples with his chest as he kissed her again and again. His mouth was wild and hungry, moving insistently against her lips until they opened to accept his tongue into the wet heat of her mouth. His tongue tangled with hers, stroked, withdrew to enter anew. Their joined mouths were a furnace, their dancing tongues the flames within. His hands dug into her blouse, bunching the material as his fingertips massaged her back. His hands came up to clasp her face on either side and he followed the whorls of her ears with his index fingers, lightly pinching the lobes. He eased away and unbuttoned her blouse, his fingers brushing her skin with fire. Valerie stretched her arms back to let the blouse slide down them, and the movement thrust out her breasts.

Ashe groaned softly. "You know what I thought about when the bullets started hitting the deck? I thought: I'm going to die, and I never tasted Valerie's breasts." His eyes flashed in the dimness. "It's true. I touched you, but not with my lips. I've regretted it a million times. I've dreamed what your skin tastes like and awakened so hot I—" He broke off and bent to take one nipple in his mouth, laving it with molten heat. Valerie drew in her breath sharply. His lips were a velvet circle centered by a lashing flame. The contrast melted her, and she would have sunk to the floor if not for Ashe's steely arms supporting her.

He left one nipple to explore the other, and the cold air on her wet peak thrust another stab of longing through her. His hand played with the free breast, cupping it and rolling the center button between his thumb and forefinger. In frustration Valerie rubbed her hands over his back, tugging at his shirt. She wanted him—oh, how she wanted him. There was a helpless, moist ache between her legs urging her to grind wantonly against him and beg to feel his fullness. But afterward he would like her no better. Her body aroused him, but Ashe felt no emotion for her except contempt. He would use her to ease the desire in his body, but his mind and heart would reject her. Tears choked her throat.

"Ashe! Please, no!" She squirmed in his arms, pushing vainly at his shoulders. "Let me go. Stop."

His only answer was to burrow his face into her chest, pulling her nipple even more deeply into his mouth, the suction so fierce it stopped barely short of pain. His hands slid to her hips and lifted her, digging into the soft flesh. Pleasure rocked her, and Valerie knew she was only a step away from mindless ecstasy. She had to end it now or she wouldn't be able to stop at all.

"Ashe! Let me go!" She shoved harder and twisted.

Suddenly he released her, almost flinging her away, and whirled quickly, turning his back. His curse exploded in the small chamber. "Damn you, Valerie! First you throw your arms around my neck and moan as if you want me as much as I want you. Then, when I'm almost crazy, you shove me away and order me to stop. What is it you want? To show how much power you have over me?"

Valerie admitted that there was some justice to his words. She had urged him on after his token protest that his hands were dirty. But he was wrong and unfair about the reason why she had stopped him. "That's more your style," she lashed out sarcastically.

"So you're playing a little game of revenge, huh? I should have known. My apology wasn't enough. You have to have your drop of blood."

"I'm not after your blood."

"No. You'd just like to add my heart to your collection. Well, lady, I can tell you, you'll never get that."

"I know." Valerie kept her back rigid and pulled the sides of her blouse together, struggling for dignity. "You've made that perfectly clear. But the one thing you want from me you can get from a lot of other women. I suggest you try one of them. I refuse to be a meaningless one-night stand!"

He pivoted to face her, his face set and blank. Without a word he unbuttoned his shirt and flung it on the floor. Valerie's breath rasped in her throat, and her heart began to pound. Was he going to force her? His hand moved to the belt of his slacks. He undid the snap, then jerked down the zipper. Valerie watched, mesmerized and trembling, as he skinned out of the mud-stained slacks and shucked off his underwear. His body was golden in the faint glow, the hairs catching the pale light and glinting it back. Hard muscles encased his chest and stomach and bulged in his arms. His legs were long and lean, with no spare flesh.

Valerie found it difficult to breathe. Her mouth was dry and the skin on her face strangely tight. She wanted to touch him, to run her hands down his chest, feel the crisp spring of the hair beneath them, the solidity of bone and muscle. She ached to caress the sharp jut of his hipbone and slide her hands around to his tight buttocks. . . . Valerie clasped her hands together behind her back.

Ashe turned and walked in the other direction to step under the waterfall. Valerie sank to the floor. He had deliberately tried to frighten her, she thought. She tried to work up a satisfactory indignation, but she was too honest not to admit that the emotion pounding in her throat had been more excitement than fear.

Valerie dropped her head to her hands. Why did she make things so difficult? Why wasn't she the kind of woman who could take what Ashe offered and be content? Why couldn't she accept the shattering pleasure he could give her as just that and nothing more? Other women no doubt went to bed with him, enjoyed the experience and didn't cry when he left. Why couldn't she? Why did she have to yearn for love as well?

Valerie heard the slap of wet feet on stone and knew that Ashe had stepped out of the pool and was dressing. She picked up the flashlight and cast a sideways glance at him. Seeing that he was dressed, she stooped to go through the exit and began wending her way back through the tunnels. Ashe followed silently. When they reached the main chamber they ate the remaining sausage, crackers and cheese. Afterward Ashe stuffed their supplies into the knapsack and spoke for the first time since their argument beside the bathing pool. "All right. What's the best way to La Luz?"

Valerie's first instinct was to throw up her hands in despair and cry that she didn't know. Then she stifled the impulse and forced herself to think calmly. Ashe didn't know the country. She was the one they had to guide them back to civilization. Valerie chewed at her underlip and suggested, "I think we ought to take the jungle route. It'll take a couple of days to get to San Mateo, and we're more likely to get lost than if we followed the river, but if there are search parties, I imagine they'd concentrate on the river area."

"I agree." Ashe rose and slung the knapsack onto his back. "Will the archaeologists give us more help?"

"Yes, I think so. I could send them the money to pay for the supplies we take.

"Okay. Let's pay them a visit." He strode toward the entrance.

"Ashe?" Valerie's hesitant voice stopped him, and he swung around, his face carefully indifferent. Her expression was almost pleading, and the sight pierced his chest. He started toward her, then stopped himself.

"Yes?"

"Do you—is it Alfonso?"

"Who else could it be?"

"Bandits? The area is full of them. That part of the river is well known as a hideout for bandits and guerrillas."

He shrugged. "It's possible, but I doubt it. I know it's hard to accept the idea that someone you know would want to kill you, but the coincidence of bandits attacking us an hour after we escaped from Alfonso's house is too much for me to swallow."

"I guess you're right." Valerie stared at the floor. Why did they hate her so much? Wouldn't it be easier to find another American wife? Sighing, she followed Ashe out of the cave.

When they approached the archaeologists' camp they slowed down. Ashe took the lead, watching for evidence of a search party's presence. They peered through the bushes into the camp but could see only normal activity. They glanced at each other and Ashe shrugged. He stood up and sauntered toward the dig, Valerie on his heels. Dr. Robertson emerged from the temple as Ashe and Valerie entered the clearing. When he saw them, he hurried forward, almost quivering with suppressed excitement, and led them into the small shack that served as his office.

Ashe's eyes were immediately drawn to the wireless radio set on the counter. "Can you get La Luz on that thing?" he asked, pointing to the set.

"What? Oh, yes, of course. Listen, I have something important to tell you. This morning your brother-in-law was here, Valerie, looking for the two of you. We revealed nothing, of course, just as Ashe warned us. Alfonso told us that guerrillas had fired on your boat and you had escaped. He said he wanted to find you before the guerrillas got to you so he could protect you. He asked us to send word to him if we saw you."

Valerie sighed and rubbed her hands wearily across her face. Ashe growled, "That proves it. How could he have gotten word so quickly unless he was in communication with the men who fired on us? Someone finding the wreckage of the boat wouldn't have known it had anything to do with the de la Portillas. I hired it myself."

"Dr. Robertson, we need your help." Valerie leaned forward earnestly.

"Of course. Anything I can do . . ."

"We need supplies for a trip to San Mateo and transportation, if you can spare a couple of donkeys. And boots." Valerie thrust out one foot with a laugh. "Ashe neglected to mention that we lost our shoes along the way."

"Good heavens. It must have been quite an ordeal. Are you sure you're up to making the trip?"

"I have to be."

"Uh, yes, I see. Now let me think. Two donkeys to ride and one for supplies. Bedrolls would be better than the blankets I grabbed last night. A small tent." He hesitated, his glance flicking toward Ashe and back to Valerie. "Or should that be two? I have a couple of pup tents."

"One'll be enough," Ashe replied shortly. "I'll exercise restraint. I don't want to carry anything but essentials."

"Of course." Dr. Robertson took a memo pad and began to make a methodical list. "Coleman stove?"

"Not necessary. I can light a fire," Valerie replied. Ashe glanced at her in surprise and she raised her eyebrows, clearly pointing out his ignorance of her.

"Dr. Robertson," Ashe cut in on his oral list, "I have to contact La Luz. We'll need transportation when we reach the village—San Martin or whatever."

"San Mateo," the archaeologist corrected absently. "Yes, that's true. The Jeeps we came in were driven back to the city, or you could have used one of them. They would have been stripped to their framework if we'd left them there."

"Can we get a plane? Is there a landing strip near San Mateo?"

"Not what you or I would consider one, but San Cristobalian pilots claim to be able to land there. We had considered flying to San Mateo but found it was too expensive. I could contact the flying service if you'd like."

"Great. See if you can rouse them now."

Dr. Robertson called La Luz on his wireless and before long had the flying service patched in. The pilot at the opposite end was reluctant to fly to San Mateo before receiving payment until Ashe informed him that he couldn't be late for an appointment with his good friend Señor Carraboza in the Ministry of the Interior. Then the man grudgingly agreed. After the call Dr. Robertson set Mike to rounding up the supplies Ashe and Valerie needed, warning him to avoid the dig's government inspector. Although he didn't know for sure that the San Cristobalian official would inform Alfonso of their presence, it was safer if he remained ignorant.

By noon the supplies and donkeys were ready. Valerie and Ashe grabbed a hasty lunch of sandwiches and left. The trail was well marked, since it was used daily by the native workers at the dig. Armed with a map and compass, Valerie felt reasonably sure that they could find their way even after they passed the workers' tiny village. They jounced along on their donkeys side by side, leading the third donkey, which carried their supplies. They were still frozen into awkward silence by the incident at the cave pool.

After a long two hours Ashe commented, "Valerie, this doesn't make sense."

"What?" Valerie was relieved at the opportunity to discuss anything.

"Shooting at us. Don't you find it rather extreme to kill us because the de la Portillas need to funnel money into the U.S.? Besides, if Alfonso had gotten rid of you, he'd have lost his connection to the U.S."

"Didn't you notice? When we were swimming I realized that they were firing only at you."

He twisted in the saddle to stare at her, his brows drawing together. "No, I was too busy dodging bullets. You mean they didn't shoot at you?" Valerie shook her head. Ashe paused for a moment. "Was that why you swam over to me?"

"Yes. I figured they must have had orders not to kill me, so if I was close to you, it'd be too risky for them to fire."

"That was a dangerous thing to do."

Valerie shrugged. "Not really. I was pretty sure they'd stop."

"But a chance bullet could have struck you before they saw you were there. Or they could have been confident that they could hit me without touching you."

"I couldn't watch them kill you if I could stop it," she pointed out mildly.

There was another pause. "Well, thank you. You're full of surprises."

Valerie couldn't keep from giggling. "That was a backhanded compliment if I ever heard one."

Ashe's features relaxed into a grin. "I'm sorry. I do appreciate it. But I feel guilty. You risked your life to save mine, then I was nasty to you at the pool. I apologize."

Valerie stirred uncomfortably. She hated to think about the effect his lovemaking had had on her or the pain of his accusations. "I wish we could keep on like we are now. I enjoy your company. It seems crazy, considering the way we're always at each other's throats. But we'd have fun if it weren't for the—"

"The sexual issue?" he finished for her. "You're probably right. The only problem is, I apparently have trouble avoiding that."

A blush tinged Valerie's cheeks, and she held her breath, waiting, hoping. But whatever she wanted didn't come. Ashe studied the gray neck of his mount, then glanced toward the trees. He began again. "What I said is still true, Valerie. Even though they didn't try to kill you, this cloak-and-dagger routine seems excessive. Surely they could find another American woman willing to marry Carlos. Somebody'd be bound to do it for the money."

"I thought that myself. Alfonso assumed I was more biddable than I am, despite my American ways. I guess it was because I never argued with Felipe. Maybe he believed I'd go along with the plan out of grief and a sense of obligation to Felipe's family. Once he'd started, he couldn't stop, so he had to take more drastic action."

"Maybe." Ashe didn't sound convinced. "But I suspect there's another motive behind it."

"Like what?"

"Like an inheritance. If Felipe left his money to you, the de la Portillas could get it back if you married Carlos. Is that how Felipe's will reads?"

"I don't know. I haven't seen the will. But, it wouldn't make sense for Felipe to leave me money. I mean, logically he'd give it to his son, wouldn't he?"

Ashe's face was etched with disbelief. "Come on, Valerie. Do you expect me to believe that? You marry a guy for his money, and then you don't bother to read his will? It's not very consistent behavior."

Valerie's jaw dropped. "Is *that* what you think of me? That I'm a gold digger? That I married Felipe for his money?" Her voice rose with each question until it reached a high-pitched shriek.

"Why else marry a man twice your age?" Ashe countered bluntly.

"For lots of reasons! Because I loved him, for one thing."

Ashe snorted. "I'm the one you kissed in Laraine's garden, remember? That wasn't wifely devotion you were demonstrating."

Blood rushed into Valerie's face. "You are the crudest man I know! What I did was wrong. I admit it. I almost violated Felipe's trust in me, and I can't forgive myself for that. You—you have a very powerful effect on me. But I wasn't in the habit of—of betraying my husband. You were the only man I so much as looked at the whole time we were married. Maybe I didn't feel the passion for him that I did for you. But there's more to love than sex, you know! Felipe befriended me when all Mother's other friends avoided me like the plague. He was warmhearted and compassionate. And I loved him! I certainly didn't marry for money. Why would I? I already have plenty."

"Are you trying to tell me you were wealthy before you married de la Portilla?"

"Yes! I'm Darryl Stanton's daughter."

"Darryl Stanton? The head of Statco?"

"Yes."

Ashe whistled. "My God, I should think you didn't need the de la Portilla money."

Valerie glanced at him. Ashe seemed stunned. "I can't believe Laraine didn't tell you."

"Why should she?"

"Well, since you're Alec's son and I'm Laraine's cousin, I thought she might have let you in on the family secrets."

"You're Laraine's cousin?" That news startled him even more.

"Yes, of course. Ashe, why are you staring at me that way?"

"Oh, my God!" He tilted back his head and laughed mirthlessly. "What a mess I've made of it."

Chapter 12

"WHAT'S SO FUNNY?" VALERIE DEMANDED.

"Nothing." Ashe's face sobered. "Absolutely nothing. I thought you'd been Alec's mistress."

"What!" Valerie whirled on him furiously. "His mistress! You have a pretty peculiar opinion of your father!"

"No," Ashe replied grimly. "I have a very realistic opinion of him."

"I'm half his age, and he's married. How could you possibly think—"

"Your husband was twice your age, too, if you'll remember. I thought you'd married Felipe for his money. When Alec told me he was very fond of you, well . . . knowing Alec, I assumed you'd had an affair with him."

"And settled for Felipe because he offered me marriage? You're big on judging people, aren't you? No need to know the facts to make up your mind. Tell me, what magical power do you possess that enables you to know a person's character by merely looking at them?"

"What else was I supposed to think? It's suspicious for a beautiful young woman to be married to an older man who's in failing health. And after you lied to me, I found it difficult to impute the highest motives to you. As for being Alec's mistress—if you'd take Felipe, why

169

not Alec? He's handsomer, more dynamic. Women always fall for him. He wouldn't hesitate because he was married. Fidelity has never been part of Alec Stone's creed."

"Are you implying that he's unfaithful to Laraine?"

Ashe made a cynical grimace. "Why not? He certainly was to his first wife. He didn't acquire a bastard son by sleeping at home."

"One love affair doesn't mean he's a philanderer."

"Believe me, there was no love involved, at least on his part. It was one in an endless string of affairs. Ask his daughters. They'll tell you. Their mother divorced him because she couldn't take it. Alec Stone doesn't know the meaning of the word faithful." Valerie stared at her hands, amazed and chastened. After a moment Ashe made an impatient gesture. "Oh, hell, how did we get off on this subject? It's so old and worn that even I'm tired of hearing it."

"Ashe, I'm sorry. I had no idea. I've always thought of Alec as perfect."

"Perfect? Alec?"

"Yes. You see, I used to visit him and Laraine in the summers when I was a teenager. It got me out of Pamela's hair. And Alec was so nice to me. He'd take me out to lunch at a businessmen's club, and I felt like a princess. He noticed what I wore and complimented me on how I looked. He laughed when I said something funny. He used to tell Laraine she'd better watch it or I'd steal him from her. He was so—so suave and handsome. And he paid attention to me! He treated me like a person, a *special* person. I ate my heart out envying Cara and the others. They had him all the time."

Ashe gazed at her for a long moment. "Funny," he said finally, "how different another's viewpoint is. I used to hate Alec with every fiber of my being. To me he was a wicked man who'd 'trifled' with my mother and heartlessly left her to bear his son in shame and poverty. The only thing I wanted from him was to get even. But when I met Cara, I saw the other side of the coin. To her, he was the father who had no time for her, who was always at work. None of his daughters believed he loved them because he desperately wanted a son. He'd hurt their mother by having affairs with women like my mother. And now here you are, thinking he was debonair and charming and a father to envy." He shook his head. "The weird thing is, I guess he was all three."

"He was everything my father wasn't. He cared. He was *there*. His charm was just a wonderful bonus."

"You weren't around your father much?"

Valerie shrugged. "My parents were divorced when I was six. Before that he was rarely home, and afterward he didn't ask me to visit him."

Ashe sighed. "Fathers. They haunt your whole life, don't they? I'll tell you something, Valerie. Darryl Stanton's the one who lost out, not you."

She turned to Ashe, surprised. The lines were deep in his weathered face, and he seemed older, tired. Sympathy mingled with the warmth his words created inside her. There was so much hidden in Ashe, revealed only in flashes. It would take a woman years to know him fully. Suddenly, with a deep ache inside her, Valerie wished she could be the woman he allowed to stay with him for that long.

They stopped when the late afternoon gloom of the jungle settled upon them. Ashe untied the supplies from the back of the extra donkey and began to set up the low, narrow tent. Valerie helped, calling on the knowledge she had gleaned at summer camp long ago. She gathered branches and brush for a fire while Ashe tended to their mounts. Soon she had a respectable fire going and a pot of soup hanging over it, and Ashe squatted down beside her. He smiled. "You surprise me. I wouldn't have figured you for an outdoor girl."

Valerie laughed. "I'm not."

He held up one hand and ticked off his points. "You

swam across a wide river. You set up a tent, and you built a fire. You're even cooking over it."

She smiled, happy to be in his company and to have him joking with her. "The result of years of summer camp."

"You must have been the star Girl Scout."

"Hardly. Number one, I wasn't a Girl Scout. Pamela wouldn't have let her daughter join anything so ordinary. I went to a posh summer camp in Maine, where everything was of the finest quality and completely lacking in comfort. Secondly, I was a miserable camper. Swimming was the only thing I could do well. We were also expected to play tennis, badminton and volleyball. We were supposed to learn how to paddle a canoe, hike, set up our tents, sing camp songs and, joy of joys, shoot archery. Or whatever it is you do with archery. I was terrible, the worst archer in the place for seven years running. Then Thelia Wilcox came to camp and took the honor away from me. I never hit the bull's-eye, but *she* managed to graze an instructor with a wild arrow."

Ashe laughed. "Come on, you couldn't have been that bad."

"Oh, but I was. The counselors hated to see me arrive. All I wanted to do in the summer was lie around a pool and read, or go to the movies. Something nice and placid. I hated hiking through the foothills and singing like the Family Von Trapp." She giggled at a memory. "The first time I picked up a bow and arrow and nocked the arrow against the string, instead of pointing forward, the arrow swiveled back and bumped me in the nose." When Ashe smiled, she related episode after bumbling episode, recounting her own and others' disasters. Ashe laughed so hard he had to hold his sides, and Valerie joined him gleefully. Her heart swelled with happiness. It didn't matter that they were in the middle of the jungle and on the run from killers. The only important thing was being with Ashe and hearing his unbridled laughter. It astonished her that she could make him laugh. She couldn't remember any of the sophisticated young men she had dated finding her clever. She was stiff as a board around them. But Ashe put her at ease. With him she could be herself and chatter without worrying whether she sounded stupid. She could joke without fearing that he would find her sense of humor too caustic or too juvenile or too absurd. It was a lovely, happy feeling— and he seemed to enjoy it as much as she did.

"Wait, wait," Ashe protested, gasping for breath after a spasm of laughter. "It couldn't have been that horrible. Why would you go back summer after summer?"

"Not because I wanted to, believe me. Mother sent me." The lightness vanished and her face closed. "It was a good way to get rid of me for two months a year."

Ashe saw the glow disappear from her face and could have bitten his tongue for asking the question. Quickly he changed the subject with a growling inquiry as to when the food would be ready. "You'll notice I didn't say edible," he pointed out. "After the examples you just gave me of your failures over the campfire, I'm almost afraid to taste it."

Valerie stuck out her tongue and removed the pot from the fire to dish up the soup. They opened a can of dried beef and ate it doubtfully. After that, the soup tasted glorious. The bizarre meal was topped off with pull-top cans of chocolate pudding. The fire died down and the evening cooled. Valerie carefully banked the glowing coals so she could start a fire in the morning, then they stood up and moved toward the tent, suddenly awkward.

Silently Ashe unspread their bedrolls side by side, while Valerie, clutching the flashlight, ventured timidly into the jungle, cursing the thing she had always disliked most about camping. Motor homes or campers with toilets, cute little sinks and tiny showers were the only way to rough it, as far as she was concerned. When she returned Ashe departed without speaking to or glancing at her. Valerie crawled into the tent and took off her boots, then slid inside her bedroll fully clothed. It was an awkward enough situation without her being only partially dressed. She recalled that morning and wondered what would happen in the close proximity of the tent.

She had rejected Ashe that morning because she had thought that he held her in contempt. Now that she had cleared up his misconceptions, wouldn't he feel differently about her? Surely he no longer despised her. After all, look at the fun they had shared that evening. If he didn't dislike her, that would change everything about his lovemaking. She could share that tumultuous pleasure with him without feeling that she had demeaned herself. Of course, revising his opinion didn't mean he'd fallen in love or wanted a long-term relationship. Ashe Harlan could have any number of women. Even if he wanted her now, he would tire of her. He would miss the sophisticated beauties he had known and find her naive inexperience a bore. It wouldn't last. It couldn't. She would be setting herself up for heartache if she let him make love to her. But Valerie couldn't help wishing that when he returned he would crawl into her bedroll instead of his.

She saw the flashlight beam bobbing outside and heard the scrape of Ashe's boots. She flipped over onto her side and closed her eyes. The light snapped off, and Ashe crept into the tent on hands and knees. It was pitch black inside, the dense foliage outside shutting out the stars and moon. Ashe fumbled blindly with the ties of the roll-down cloth door, and Valerie heard a wordless sound of disgust grated out through clenched teeth. He crawled onto his bedroll and yanked off his boots, so close that she could hear his breathing. Valerie lay rigid with tension. She heard him pull aside the top layer of his bedroll and slide into it. There were a few more rustles, then the tent was silent. Valerie sagged. Ashe wasn't going to visit her bed that night.

When Valerie arose the next morning she ached even

more than she had the morning before. New muscles had been affected by the long ride, and a second night of sleeping on the ground hadn't helped. Combing back her hair, she braided it in one long plait. It was cooler up, the way she had worn it the day before, but she'd lost half her hairpins in the course of the ride and the work she had done. She straightened her clothes and ventured forth, feeling very unready to face the day. However, after she had the fire going and breakfast cooked, things looked brighter. The coffee helped wake her up, and Ashe had smiled at her, praising her scrambled eggs.

She helped him dismantle the tent and reload the supplies. Soon they were on their way. The air was steamy and thick, but at least the foliage of the trees prevented the sun from baking their brains. The trail grew so narrow that they had to ride single file, and there were times when Valerie knew a throat-filling terror that the path would disappear altogether, leaving them stranded. She put a tight rein on her fear and plodded along, her eyes fixed on the back of Ashe's shirt, where a line of sweat formed along his spine.

Ashe rode easily, one hand on the reins and the other braced on his thigh. His muscles strained against the too-short blue denim jeans he had borrowed from Mike, and below the cuffs his lean brown legs emerged, covered with curling golden brown hairs. Valerie idly wondered what color his moustache would be if he had one, then shook her head impatiently. What in the world was wrong with her? One minute she was scared to death that they would be stranded or Alfonso's men would find them. Moments later she was enthralled by Ashe's physical appearance. It was crazy to even think about desire while they were being chased by killers.

But she felt so safe with Ashe that it was hard to believe in the real possibility of the killers finding them. It wasn't a reasonable belief. Ashe wasn't used to the jungle, and she doubted that he was accustomed to dealing with kidnapping or attempted murder, either.

But he possessed such a firm quality of command—even ruthlessness—that it made her trust him to handle almost anything.

They stopped briefly at noon to stretch their aching muscles and eat a cold lunch of canned meat, crackers and bottled water. Valerie dreaded remounting the donkey, but she forced her tired legs to climb on. As they continued the journey she noticed a gradual widening of the trail. By late afternoon they could again ride side by side. "Do you suppose the road's getting better because we're nearing San Mateo?" Ashe asked as his donkey dropped back even with hers.

"I don't know. It seems logical, but I'm not familiar enough with the area to say. I've been this way only once, when Felipe and I traveled to a new resort on the Pacific coast. Then we had a guide and several local servants." She refused to raise her hopes or she would expect the village to appear every time they rounded a bend in the road. The ride was becoming more tiring and painful to her abused muscles every second, and disappointed hope would only make it worse.

"If we're close enough, we wouldn't have to stop at dusk to camp. We could keep riding until we reach San Mateo."

Valerie contemplated the issue. They should leave the jungle as soon as possible. Alfonso would probably concentrate the search on the river area, but when he failed to find them, he would turn next to the jungle route. Yet she hated to lose another night alone with Ashe.

That was the dumbest thing she'd dreamed up yet, she told herself derisively. There had been nothing special about the other two nights with him. He hadn't even touched her last night. Apparently he no longer wanted her. Her rejection beside the cave pool must have destroyed his desire. His present disinterest made her yearnings ridiculous. She couldn't let herself want him, because once he returned her safely to the United States, she wouldn't see him again.

"Let's try for San Mateo," Valerie voted.

Ashe smiled. "Good. I hoped you'd say that. But I didn't want to tire you."

"I'm okay." She saw him stiffen. "What's the ma—" He raised an imperative hand for silence, and she broke off. For a long moment they stood stock-still, the limitless quiet broken only by the shrill chatter of the monkeys overhead. Then Valerie detected the far-off rise and fall of laughter. She gripped the reins and turned frightened, questioning eyes to Ashe. He responded without hesitation, motioning for her to follow him as he slipped off his donkey and led it through a narrow gap in the undergrowth. Lifting a heavy curtain of vines, he guided the reluctant animal behind its cover. Valerie stuck to his heels, the metallic taste of fear in her mouth. Quickly Ashe went back to fetch the pack animal and drag it into hiding, too.

Breathlessly they waited, huddled behind the fall of leafy vines, their hands on their mounts' muzzles to keep them silent. Valerie glanced over at Ashe. His face was mottled with light and shadow, a stranger's face. How could she have fallen in love with a stranger, Valerie thought, then blinked, amazed. In love with Ashe Harlan? She couldn't be. Yet in this moment of stress she hadn't the strength to deny it. However crazy it might be to love a man she barely knew, it was what she felt. The emotion inside her was no juvenile infatuation, as her love for her former fiancé had been, no blind grabbing at someone, anyone, to love her. Nor was it the gentle, almost filial love she had known for Felipe. This was a strong, forceful love, a woman's blending of physical desire and heart's yearning. Ashe was no stranger to her inner self, no matter how short the span of their acquaintance. Her soul had recognized him from the instant they met. She was unsure of his feelings for her, but she was absolutely sure of hers for him.

The wave of strong emotion made her forget momentarily that danger might be moving along the path toward them, but the sound of voices nearby roused her from her thoughts. She peered through the vines as Ashe did, but saw nothing. The noises grew louder, and she could distinguish a word now and then in guttural Spanish. The accent was so thick she couldn't decipher the words, but it was obvious that there was more than one man. Were there donkeys, too? Horses? She couldn't hear the clink of bridles or the thump of hooves. But the dirt trail muffled noise.

A man's head came into view: a square, blunt face underneath a wide-brimmed straw hat, thick black hair poking out from under it. Then the rest moved into her range of vision. There were three—no, four of them, and they were walking. They wore the San Cristobalian peasant garb of loose white trousers, and open-throated shirts belted by bright strips of cloth. Woven straw sandals adorned their feet. A single-file train of four small burros trailed behind them, heavily laden with sacks.

Valerie crumpled to the ground in relief. It was the monthly load of supplies for the dig. Ashe squatted beside her, reassured that the men were not a search party out hunting for them. Yet he and Valerie didn't emerge from hiding until the men were well out of hearing range. Valerie turned toward Ashe, trembling and limp in the aftermath of fear. Ashe winked, grinning, and squeezed her shoulders with one arm. "That's my girl. Come on, we have to make San Mateo tonight."

Warmed by his words, Valerie followed Ashe out to the path and swung up onto her mount. She called herself all kinds of fool for treasuring half a hug and an impersonal statement of encouragement. He would have said the same to anyone.

They urged their donkeys to greater speed, spurred by the moment of danger. The illusion of safety that the thick, quiet jungle created had been shattered by the approach of the supply train. Dusk came with its usual swiftness, and soon they traveled the path in velvet darkness, moving as much by sound and feel as by sight, trusting their animals not to stray from safety.

San Mateo appeared without warning. In the dark they hadn't noticed when the trail widened further and the jungle thinned around them. Suddenly the trees ended, and before them lay a creek bordered by flat, cultivated fields. Beyond the fields stood a small hill, low mud buildings crawling up its side. "San Mateo," Valerie announced flatly.

Ashe cocked an eyebrow. "You were right. It's not much. Let's hope our pilot's there. It doesn't look like too many motel rooms will be available."

Valerie giggled, and again the laughter of hysteria crowded her throat. She bit her lower lip and shifted on the blanket covering the donkey's back. Her legs and feet had no feeling left, she noticed, too tired to be concerned by it. Even though their goal was in sight, her numbed mind expected her to ride forever. They crossed the creek and ambled along the trail, which had become something almost deserving of the name "road."

"Look!" Ashe's voice was low, but he couldn't conceal the undertone of excitement. He pointed at a field of stubble, and Valerie's gaze followed his finger. A small airplane stood in the field. She swallowed, her stomach knotting.

"Can that thing get off the ground?"

"I certainly hope so. It looks tiny because we're at a distance," Ashe reassured her, but she suspected that he was as uncertain about the craft as she was. There was no sign of a person around the plane, and they agreed that the pilot would be in San Mateo, seeking out whatever refreshments and amusements the village had to offer. They urged their donkeys forward.

When they reached the village all the buildings were dark. The villagers obviously retired early. In the center of town they finally found a house with one dimly glowing window. Ashe knocked at the door. He learned that it was the home of the village *alcalde*, or mayor, and also the spot where the pilot from La Luz had chosen to wait for his customers. At the sight of Ashe's blond head the pilot leaped to his feet, grinning from ear to ear.

"Señor! You must be the man who desires a plane," he exclaimed in English.

"Yes. Are you our pilot?"

He sketched a bow. "Geraldo Munez, at your service. Thank God you came tonight. I think any more of the local hospitality would make me—how you say?"

"Bored?" Ashe ventured.

Munez chuckled. "No. Crazy, I think."

"Can we leave in the dark? I mean, can you take off?" Valerie asked, exasperated by the two men's joking.

The pilot assumed an aggrieved expression. "Of course, señora, of course. I am an expert pilot, the best at Cavaldos's Flying Service—even if he is my brother-in-law."

Valerie suppressed a groan. Geraldo Munez was small, brimming with vitality and full of a bumptious confidence that reminded her of the de la Portilla chauffeur's behavior in traffic. It was an attitude she had seen often in San Cristolbalian men, and to the best of her knowledge it was usually unfounded. But she kept her mouth shut, knowing that there was no point in antagonizing the man who was their sole hope of escape.

They left their donkeys and remaining supplies with the *alcalde,* who assured them that they would be returned to the American archaeologists. Then the three set forth on foot, cutting across the field to the plane. The closer they drew, the smaller and more disreputable the aircraft appeared. Valerie's fears must have shown on her face, because Ashe slipped his hand around hers and squeezed lightly. She tried to smile for him, but the muscles of her face refused to respond.

Ashe helped her into the small cockpit, which would

seat four, and he took the copilot's seat beside Señor Munez. Munez released the weights holding the plane to the ground and hopped in. He started the engine, and the propeller rattled to life, whirring into a silver blur. As he chatted merrily to Ashe above the noise of the engine, he taxied across the field. The plane jumped and bounced on the broken land, and Valerie closed her eyes, certain that they were more likely to capsize than take off. But the plane gained speed and left the ground, hovering for a heart-stopping second before it rose steeply. When they leveled off Valerie glanced down at her hands, which were clenched so tightly on the back of Ashe's seat that they were bloodless. She forced them to unfold. She was glad that it was night, so she couldn't see the ground rushing past below.

Valerie was so numb and tired that she should have fallen asleep, but her nerves wouldn't let her. Ashe and Munez talked, and she was glad she wasn't expected to join in. She dreamed of a bath and a clean bed. Even more, she dreamed of firm ground beneath her feet again. A daredevil plane trip at night was not her idea of fun. Could the tiny light on the plane possibly help him to see? Was it enough to warn larger planes of their presence? It seemed unlikely.

Much to her relief and amazement, they landed without mishap at a small private airport north of La Luz. Valerie had to admit that it was as smooth as any landing she'd experienced. Geraldo Munez shot them a victorious look, which made her wonder if he had been as unsure of the outcome as she. Ashe's wallet was still a little sodden from its dunking in the Rio Miedo, and the paper money inside was crumpled and dirty, but Munez happily accepted it. He even telephoned for a taxi to drive them to the hotel.

Valerie fell into the back of the cab and didn't even notice the hair-raising ride to Ashe's hotel. When they arrived at the Palacio they stumbled up the steps and into the lobby. The desk clerk shot them a shocked glance and immediately surveyed the lobby to make sure no one saw the disreputable couple enter his establishment. Valerie had to cover her mouth to keep from exploding into giggles. They must have looked awful in their dusty clothes, with their hair tangled and dirty. She wouldn't have been surprised if the clerk had ordered them out of the place. Ashe strode to the desk to pick up his key, his chilly glance quieting any questions or protests the clerk was about to make.

Valerie waited for Ashe by the elevators and let him lead her upstairs to his room, too numb to think or move without guidance. Her mind and her body felt equally bludgeoned. When they reached his door Ashe slid the key into the lock and stood aside for her to enter. Valerie saw nothing of the room but the large, inviting bed. Dirty as she was, her need to sleep claimed first priority. Valerie collapsed onto the clean bedspread and was asleep by the time Ashe flopped down beside her.

Chapter 13

THE SUN SIFTING THROUGH THE SHEER CURTAINS WOKE
Valerie. She opened her eyes and stared, struggling to
orient herself. It took a moment to remember that she
and Ashe had reached the safety of his hotel room the
night before. It quickened her breath to think of him
lying beside her all night, though they had been so dead
to the world that their behavior couldn't have been
more proper if they had slept in different hotels. She sat
up, yawning, and shoved her hands into her matted,
tangled hair. A bath was what she needed now—a long,
soaking scrub—followed by a hearty breakfast.

She stood up gingerly, renewing acquaintance with
her assorted bruises and strained muscles. If not for
their presence, she might have wondered whether the
past few days had been merely a nightmare. Looking
back on it, what had happened seemed absurd. The
creamy walls and thick carpet of the Palacio didn't
house people who'd been chased through the jungle,
shot at and forced to swim the Rio Miedo.

She creaked over to the European-style telephone
and ordered a breakfast sent to Mr. Harlan's room.
Where was Ashe, anyway? The room was obviously
empty except for herself. The bathroom door stood
open, and she peeked in, not really expecting to find

him there. But he hadn't left the bathroom long ago, for the air smelled faintly of shaving cream and men's cologne. Valerie sniffed the scent, a faint smile on her lips, then caught sight of her image in the mirror and shrank back. Heavens, she looked horrid! How had Ashe stomached looking at her?

No wonder his desire had vanished. There was a yellowish bruise on one cheekbone where a branch had snapped back and hit her, a smudge of dirt on her chin, a red streak across her neck and a coating of dust all over her face. Her hair, also liberally sprinkled with dust, had come loose from the neat braid and hung snarled and twisted around her face. The blouse was too tight, as well as being ripped, stained and muddied. Her jeans, while equally dirty, were as baggy as the blouse was tight. On her feet she wore heavy, muddy hiking boots with a strip of tan socks showing above. Just what the well-dressed woman would be wearing this year, she thought derisively.

She shucked off the offending clothes and stepped into the shower to wash away the grime of her travels. A thorough soaping made her clean again, although it set up a fierce stinging in the more livid scratches on her hands and arms. There was a small bottle of shampoo, which she used gratefully, despite its decidedly masculine smell. However, there was no creme rinse to dissolve the tangles. It took a good fifteen minutes with Ashe's comb in front of the steamy bathroom mirror to return her long tresses to their usual sleekness.

Before she was through combing room service knocked on the door and Valerie frantically cast around for something to wear. She found a soft navy silk robe hanging in the closet and shrugged into it, wrapping it around her as she scurried to the door. The bellhop rolled in the cart, his impassive face revealing no hint that it was unusual to bring food to a young woman whose hair was half-combed and half-wild and who wore a man's robe. Valerie thanked him with a tentative smile, and he held out the ticket for her to sign.

Nerves began to blossom in her stomach. How should she sign it? The room was registered in Ashe's name. Mrs. Ashe Harlan? Her own name? Finally she scribbled her maiden name at the bottom. Then she remembered that she should give the bellman a tip, but she had no money! She had left her purse behind when she jumped into the Rio Miedo. Valerie glanced around the room, hoping that Ashe had left some loose change lying around. She opened the drawer of the nightstand and the top drawer of the dresser, mentally cursing Ashe for not leaving her some cash. Hadn't he realized that she would have food sent up to the room? She turned toward the waiting bellhop with an embarrassed smile. "Is it all right if I add the tip to the bill?"

"Of course, señorita," he answered gravely. Obviously he had no illusions that she was Mrs. Ashe Harlan. She calculated the tip in her head and jotted it onto the bottom of the bill, unsure whether she had figured it right, as always. The man smiled and bowed as he left the room, so she supposed it must have been enough. Probably too much. She constantly overtipped out of nervousness.

Why was it that bills and tipping and such things made her feel inadequate? It was part of her general ineptitude in handling daily life. There were times when she wondered how she would have survived if she hadn't been born a Stanton and blessed with her grandparents' trust funds from the day she was born. First lawyers, bankers and accountants had handled everything for her, then Felipe had taken over. Was that one reason why she had married him? Not for love or money, or even to soothe her broken heart, but simply for the security of having someone run things for her? What a lowering thought. It sounded even worse than what Ashe had thought about her.

Valerie finished combing out her hair before she ate. She didn't want it to dry all tangled, making it even more unmanageable. By the time she was through the

coffee and eggs were cold, but she was too hungry to
care. She stuffed every bite down her throat and leaned
back with a satisfied sigh when she had cleaned the
plate. Again she wondered where Ashe was, and a hint
of fear disturbed her stomach. He wouldn't have left
her to fend for herself—not after helping her out of the
jungle. That was silly. Too idiotic to think about. But
she couldn't hold the dread of abandonment completely at bay.

He was probably making arrangements to fly to the
U.S., that was all. Or had soldiers taken him away to be
questioned at the Presidio? No, that was ridiculous.
The government had no quarrel with Ashe. He was
negotiating an oil deal with them. The ruling junta
certainly wouldn't arrest him as a favor to the de la
Portillas. No, she was making up worries. Ashe could
take care of himself. And he *would* come back to her.

She pulled the robe more tightly about her and
cinched it shut with the sash, which was its only
fastening. What she ought to worry about, she thought,
was her wardrobe. She couldn't continue to wear
Ashe's robe, which gaped at the top as well as being
ludicrously long on her. It wasn't exactly indecent,
because it covered her body, even hiding more of her
legs than a dress would, but when she walked her legs
were revealed halfway up her thighs, and the too-large
top showed a tantalizing glimpse of her shadowed
breasts. Valerie looked with disgust at the pile of
muddy clothes she had dropped on the floor. There was
no way she could put those things back on.

Sighing, she rose and examined Ashe's closet again,
but she could find nothing to satisfy her needs. The
only other thing she could wear would be one of his
shirts, which would cover all the essentials but leave
her legs bare almost to the hip. No, wearing a man's
shirt was too suggestive. She admitted defeat. She
would have to ask Ashe to buy her something—if and
when he returned. She washed out the lacy panties and

bra, the only garments that were her own. It took three
soapy scrubbings to remove the river silt and dust, but
finally they were clean enough to satisfy her and she
slung them over the towel rod to dry.

Valerie sat down cross-legged on the bed to wait, full
of a curious mixture of boredom and anxiety. Almost
thirty minutes passed before there was the scrape of a
key in the lock. She straightened, modestly stretching
out her legs and covering them with the robe. An
inexplicable fear that it would not be Ashe seized her,
and she sagged with relief when he ambled in. He
stopped dead still, and a slow grin spread across his
face.

"You look better."

Valerie tried to smile. "So do you," she countered in
a small voice. It was true. Shaved, washed and wearing
a perfectly tailored suit, he hardly resembled the
hard-bitten man of the trail. He was devastatingly
handsome this way, the sharkskin suit veiling his toughness; but, strangely, she thought she preferred the
other Ashe, stubble and all.

"Thank you." His eyes strayed to the robe's neckline. Self-consciously Valerie pulled the sides together
and held them with one hand. Ashe tossed a sack onto
the bed beside her. "I bought you something to wear.
Your clothes are about done in."

"Oh, Ashe! Thank you." Valerie's eyes sparkled as
she ripped open the sack. Inside were simple rope
sandals and a skirt and blouse of coarse cotton in an
off-white shade. The blouse tied at the neck, leaving a
scoop of chest visible, and the neckline was embroi-
dered with bright flowers, as was the hem of the full
skirt. Such outfits, deceptively peasant-styled, were
a favorite of the tourists at the resort towns of San
Cristóbal because of their beautifully hand-done embroidery. Valerie had always wanted one, but natives
like the de la Portilla family considered them common
and "touristy." Now she jumped up, careless of the

expanse of leg she showed, and ran into the bathroom to try it on.

Ashe shrugged out of his coat, unknotted his tie and kicked off his shoes. He really wasn't meant for civilized clothes, he thought, especially in the hot, muggy climate of La Luz. He unfastened the top button of his shirt as well as his cuffs, which he then rolled up above his elbows. Slouched in a chair, he waited for Valerie to emerge from the bathroom, eager to see her in the clothes he had chosen. When he had spotted the skirt and blouse in the window he had pictured Valerie with her pale hair loose and flowing, her feet bare, an image of innocence, yet conversely sensual as well.

It was crazy. She wasn't his type. He was uncomfortable around rich girls, didn't understand them or know what they wanted. Sooner or later he'd do something to embarrass or offend her. Besides, he'd already soured her on him by making stupid assumptions about her character. It had been even dumber to admit what he had thought. She must despise him for believing she was both a gold digger and Alec's mistress. Plus, he had been unkind and cutting to her in his hurt. It made him sick when he thought of the night she had come to him, begging for help, and he had teased and taunted her, pretending she would have to pay him with her body. Even at the time he'd hated himself, had done it as much to hurt himself as her. How could he expect her to welcome him into her bed after that? She would think he was demanding his price for rescuing her. No wonder she had rejected him that morning in the cave. He had accused her of punishing him. Well, maybe she was, but he deserved it. She probably couldn't stand his touch after what he'd done in the bar.

Ashe closed his eyes, massaging his creased forehead with long, supple fingers. Valerie was so lovely, so vulnerable and fragile. Married to an old man. Had she known any other man's touch? Someone before Felipe? A suave preppie like Nick Fletcher? He wondered how his own hands had felt to her. Had she despised their roughness? Had he been too crude, too swift? The night in the garden flooded his mind. He recalled the touch of the breeze on his scorching neck, her hands digging into his back, her small body arching passionately against him.

He opened his eyes and shook his head to clear it of the vision. It was dangerous, thinking like that. The sight of her in his robe had already aroused him enough. He'd be as randy as a teenager if he kept thinking about the passion she had shown him. Better to remember what had occurred since, like her pushing him away at the cave pool. It didn't matter that she'd been full of desire several weeks ago. He'd spoiled it since then. The best course was to steer clear of her. Valerie Stanton wasn't for the likes of him.

The bathroom door opened and Valerie danced out, twirling like a child, arms outspread. The full skirt whirled above her knees, showing an expanse of slender white thigh. Ashe swallowed. She was everything he'd imagined. Better. She was real and standing three feet away from him. He tried to assume a casual pose by propping his feet on the table and lacing his hands across his stomach. "Nice, very nice."

Valerie finished her pirouette and smiled, her face tinged with color. "Really? Do you like it?"

"Yeah, I like it," he rasped, and clenched one hand to combat the desire pooling in his gut. He wanted her like nobody he'd ever known. She posed before him, slim and straight, bare-legged, her cornsilk hair tumbling over her shoulders. The light from the window behind her outlined her legs and the curves of her body. Ashe swallowed. Not only her feet and legs were bare. She was naked beneath the dress. He'd forgotten to buy a slip or underwear. The dress wasn't sheer, but with the light behind her he could glimpse enough to set him to imagining what he couldn't see. The blouse gathered and tied above her bosom and was caught by the waist of the skirt, so that it was pulled taut across her full breasts. He could detect the darker circles of her nipples beneath the cloth.

Ashe cleared his throat and tore his gaze away, focusing on the other window. "We better buy you some more clothes, I guess."

Valerie slumped. She didn't know what she had hoped for, but this noncommittal response was not it. Really, she scolded herself, what had she thought Ashe would do? Grab her and throw her onto the bed, enraged by lust? Maybe wearing nothing beneath her blouse and skirt had seemed daring to her when she realized that her panties and bra were too damp to put on, but Ashe wasn't as backward as she was. He'd been around far bolder, sexier women. Morgan and that crowd. The kind of women who sunbathed nude on the Riviera. Despite her wealth and her mother's glamorous life, Valerie had been sheltered and retiring. She probably bored him. She wet her lips and matched his casual tone. "Okay."

"Let's go." He rose, tossing his tie, which hung untied around his neck, onto the bed. He opened the door and Valerie passed through, each carefully managing to avoid brushing against the other. Ashe held the elevator door for her when it arrived and again when they stepped off, his hand hovering at the back of her waist without touching her. A gesture of pure politeness, not interest, Valerie thought glumly as they strolled through the gracious lobby and out into the glaring San Cristóbal sun.

They walked stiffly down the block and turned the corner into the area Felipe had laughingly called "Designer Alley." There were small intimate shops and huge department stores, even a couple of smaller representatives of famous American stores. Their first stop was to buy sunglasses for Valerie, who could barely see in the fierce sunlight. Next they went into a department store, where Valerie stopped at the lingerie department to buy satin underthings. Ashe stood, arms

crossed across his chest, seemingly oblivious but co-
vertly watching her from the corner of his eye as she
picked out a rainbow collection of intimate apparel. He
could imagine the slick garments under his gliding
hand, and it took all his control not to drag Valerie
back to their hotel room. The last straw was a nightgown she held up to study, a maroon satin so dark it
was almost black. The gown fell straight down from her
bosom, so narrow that he knew it would cling, and its
bodice was unlined maroon lace. Ashe swung away and
strode to the cashier's counter to wait for her.

Valerie joined him soon, and Ashe paid for the stack
of lingerie. As they strolled away Valerie told him,
"You don't have to buy me anything else. I have
everything I need. Since we'll be leaving soon, this one
dress should do."

He frowned. "We probably won't go as soon as you'd
like. There's a slight complication: your passport."

Valerie's eyes widened, and her mouth formed a
startled "Oh." "It's in my purse."

"Which is on the boat or at the bottom of the Rio
Miedo."

Deep fear filled her eyes. "What am I going to do?"
she whispered, one hand unconsciously grasping his
shirt sleeve.

"It's okay, I'll take care of it." Ashe covered her
hand with his.

"But in San Cristóbal a person without a passport or
a national ID card is nothing. I'll be stuck here forever!
No ID and you're in prison," she whispered. "It's one
way they catch the guerrillas."

"Slow down. I didn't mean to upset you. Let's have a
cup of coffee somewhere, and I'll explain everything."

Valerie led him to an elegant pink and white tea shop
on the mezzanine overlooking the main floor. Ashe
ordered coffee and pastry and reached over to enfold
Valerie's hands in his. He shook them lightly. "Will you
relax? Everything is under control. It'll simply take
longer than we'd like, that's all. I visited the

American embassy this morning and explained that you lost your passport. I tossed around the name Stone Oil and mentioned a certain senator, who I understand is Laraine's uncle.''

Valerie nodded. "He's Pamela's uncle, too."

"Even better. Anyway, they promised to get you a replacement pronto, which apparently means a couple of days. Just to insure it, I put in a call to Alec and explained the situation." He grinned. "I could hear the steam hissing out his ears. I suspect the embassy will receive a few calls today."

Valerie giggled. "Really? I'll have a new passport in two days?"

"Guaranteed. If not sooner. Next I spoke with my friend in the government."

"The man whose name brought the pilot to San Mateo?"

"The same. The name Carraboza seems to have a certain persuasive quality to it. . . ."

"Try fear."

"Don't knock it. It was on our side this time. Alec may not be too pleased with the terms I'm giving San Cristóbal, but Carraboza promised to have a special stamp put on your passport to get you through customs, since the new passport won't have an entry stamp. There, you see? It's all worked out."

Valerie managed a quavery smile. "I hope so. Ashe, you don't know this country. It breeds fear. I won't feel safe until we land in Dallas."

He squeezed her hands. "Val, I promise to get you out, even if I have to smuggle you over the border. *Comprende?*"

"*Sí, comprendo,*" she replied docilely, her smile more certain now. She believed that Ashe *would* smuggle her out if it came to that. "What would I have done without you?"

"Don't think about it," he commanded. "Now, as to the rest of my activities this morning . . ."

"You did more?" she teased. "My, you certainly were a busy boy."

"Some of us got up earlier than others I could mention. I paid a call on your husband's attorney, who is also the executor of his estate. He seemed surprised that you weren't aware of the terms of the will. He wouldn't reveal them to me, but I made an appointment for you to meet him tomorrow morning at ten. I think he'll be straight with you. He seemed honest when I talked to him a few days ago. Alfonso introduced me to him, since he's the man we'll be working with now that . . . uh . . ." He paused awkwardly.

"Go ahead, you can say it. I've accepted Felipe's death. So much has happened since then that it seems a lifetime ago. I won't weep all over you and make a scene."

"I didn't think you would. I just didn't want to hurt you. I'm really not an ogre."

Her eyebrows shot up. "I never thought you were."

"That's hard to believe. I know I seemed unfeeling." He stopped abruptly, turning his gaze down to the tabletop. When he spoke, his voice was low, and Valerie knew how much the words must have cost him. "I'm not the greatest guy alive, but I'm not usually a brute. Abusing women isn't one of my hobbies."

"It's okay, Ashe. You've already apologized. I understand why you distrusted and disliked me. I wronged you first, although I didn't intend to. Anyway, you didn't 'abuse' me. The only thing you hurt was my pride."

"Sometimes that can be the worst kind of injury."

"Look, let's forget it. It's over with. I don't—I couldn't hate you. After all, you saved my sanity by getting me away from Carlos and Alfonso."

"Okay, I'll accept it as a fair trade. Now, how about buying you some more clothes?"

They strolled through the fashionable stores in a more congenial mood. Ashe rested his hand on her back as they walked, and once reached down to clasp her hand. Valerie vibrated with life. They went through shop after shop, Ashe lounging in the comfortable waiting areas set aside for the cash-carrying males who accompanied their spending women, while Valerie modeled clothes for his approval.

Sometimes Felipe had shopped with Valerie, particularly when they were first married and Valerie's tastes had not settled into his mold yet. He, too, had watched as she pivoted for inspection, but his eye had been critical and artistic, concerned only with style. With Ashe the process was far different. Valerie tried on jeans, shorts, skirts, dresses, even an evening gown, and emerged from the dressing cubicle to show him. Ashe's eyes took her in, his face a study of lazy enjoyment. He let out a short bark of laughter at one absurd creation and gave her a wink to indicate that she looked particularly good in a certain dress, but he didn't critique, only watched. A primitive thrill surged through her as she paraded before him, as if his appraisal indicated his ownership of her, made her his possession.

She purchased several blouses, shorts, jeans and slacks, as well as a jacketed lavender dress suitable for her conference the next day with Felipe's attorney. The dressier outfit meant a stop for shoes to match, and she ended the spree by buying a purse. "Though I don't know what I'll put in it," she joked to Ashe, "since I haven't any money or a passport."

"Your hairbrush?" Ashe suggested.

"Oh," Valerie gasped. "That reminds me. I need to buy a hairbrush and some makeup."

"Ah, I see you're dragging out the heavy ammunition. Who do you intend to entrance? Mr. Gutierrez?"

"The attorney? Maybe." She glanced at him sideways, not daring to admit that he was the only one she cared to charm.

"You look fine to me the way you are. But feel free."

He motioned toward a counter lined with perfumes and vials of cosmetics.

"Just the essentials," she assured him as she selected lipstick, mascara and foundation, then checked another counter and found a hairbrush.

They caught a taxi back to the hotel. When they reached their room Ashe dumped the sacks in the center of the bed. Valerie happily sorted through them as Ashe stepped into the bathroom. Through the closed door he could hear the rustle of clothing as Valerie changed. The thought turned his mouth dry. He ran cold water in the sink and washed his face, as much to clear his head of his imaginings as to clean the film of sweat and city grime from his face. As he reached for a towel his hand grazed the underthings drying on the towel rack. He stared at the sheer, lacy panties and bra while he mechanically dried his face and hands. The familiar hot throbbing started in his abdomen. He reached out to touch the satin material, then jerked his hand back. God, he'd turn into a pervert soon if he kept that up.

Valerie, unaware of his yearnings, slipped on a set of her new undergarments and refastened the skirt and blouse Ashe had bought that morning. She didn't want to take the outfit off yet; it was special, chosen by Ashe himself. A faint smile curved her lips. How different he had been that afternoon. In the morning he had looked right through her, his eyes offering no opinion of her looks. But later, in the stores, he had surveyed her as if she belonged to him, his eyelids heavy and drooping over glittering eyes, his lips relaxed and sensual. Nothing overt had happened or been said, but the air had been charged with sexual tension, and she had felt as if she flirted dangerously with his control when she modeled for him.

But when he sauntered into the bedroom a moment later, she wondered if she had imagined his interest in her. His face was taut, mouth thin, and the blue eyes were frosty. "Ready?" he asked, impatience tinging his voice. "I thought we'd go out to dinner."

"All right." Valerie swallowed her disappointment and trailed after him to the door.

They ate dinner in an elegant French-style restaurant on the top floor of the El Jefe. Ashe was polite, almost formal, and Valerie despaired of recapturing the afternoon's mood. What had changed him? Was he simply moody? Or had she imagined his earlier interest?

After the meal they rode down to the lobby in the glass-encased elevator and strolled across the cool glazed tiles to the front door, passing the hotel's nightclub on the way. The door opened as a couple went in, and they glimpsed the dim interior, the dance floor glowing with jewel-like colored lights. The music throbbed heavily. Valerie cast a wistful eye inside. "La Luz is famous for its nightclubs," she told him. "Different ones specialize in different kinds of Latin dances. Not this one, of course. It's American."

"Did you visit them often?" he asked, reaching to open the front door for her."

"Heavens, no. They were too *nouveau riche* for the de la Portillas. Or at least the nice ones were. The rest were too lower class. So Felipe wouldn't take me. Besides, he couldn't dance because of his heart."

"Did you want to go?"

Valerie shrugged. "It doesn't matter. It's all past now, anyway."

"Not if you want to go dancing. I'll take you."

She glanced up, startled. "Oh, no, I didn't mean to hint."

"I didn't say it because you hinted. Just answer me. Do you want to go to a nightclub?"

Valerie's eyes shone. "Yes, I'd love it."

They jumped in the first cab available, and Valerie gave the driver the name of the most popular club, La Gaviota. Named after the white gulls wheeling and diving above it, La Gaviota was situated on the edge of the sea, and one side of the building had a long bank of windows looking out on the ocean. The music was loud and vibrant. Ashe and Valerie joined in the fast dancing, doing their best to imitate the others and bursting into laughter at their mistakes.

They had a drink and were persuaded by another couple to learn the dance from them. When the man returned Valerie to Ashe, flushed and laughing, and retrieved his own date, Ashe whipped Valerie onto the floor, fitting her against his body. Her teacher had held her the same way, but it hadn't had the effect it did with Ashe. Her throat constricted. Ashe's breath fanned her cheek as they executed the fast steps with their bodies molded together, his arms like iron around her, supporting her. When the dance ended he pulled away reluctantly, sliding one hand down her bare arm to clasp her hand.

"Let's go." Ashe's voice was rough and his eyes gleamed with a dangerous light. Valerie decided not to protest his decision. They stopped by their table to pick up her purse, then stepped into the moist night air and hailed one of the waiting cabs. Ashe almost shoved Valerie into the back and climbed in after her, barking out the name of their hotel to the driver. Valerie glanced at him surreptitiously. His skin was stretched tightly over the wide bones of his face, and color flamed high on his cheekbones. A fine film of perspiration lay on his upper lip. Was he angry? Or was his body rigid with sexual frustration?

But there was no reason for him to be frustrated. He must have realized how easily she would fall into his arms after the other times she'd done it. If the dance had aroused him as it had her, he would have kissed her, or held her tightly and whispered that he wanted to take her to the hotel to make love. He wouldn't have tersely commanded her to leave the nightclub or practically jerked her out the door. He must be angry. Because she had danced with the other man? But Ashe had danced with the man's partner! Surely he couldn't be harboring his old suspicion that she was promiscuous.

Resolutely Valerie folded her arms and stared out the opposite window. She wasn't going to attempt to drag Ashe out of his sullens. Whatever his reason, she refused to cater to his moods. They rode to the hotel in silence and maintained it from the car to their room. In the elevator Ashe kept his eyes on the numbers flashing by as if they were the most important thing in the world. Inside the room, he tossed the key onto the table and ripped off his suit jacket. He pulled out a package of cigarettes and lit one as he strode to the far window. He stood looking out, grimly drawing in smoke, as he unfastened his tie and collar.

"I would have gotten you a separate room, but it's safer to have you here with me," he said suddenly. Valerie stared at him, not knowing how to reply. What did this speech mean? The whole day had made no sense. He went on, "You can have the bed. I'll sleep on the floor."

Sadness crept through her. "There's no need. I can—"

"You'll do as I say," he snapped. "I've slept worse places than the floor of this room."

"All right." Valerie tilted her chin up, willing the tears not to come. She grabbed the nightgown and matching robe she had purchased that afternoon and marched into the bathroom to change. When she came out she discovered that Ashe had pulled a couple of blankets and a pillow from the closet and made a crude bed on the floor in front of the hall door. He sat on a chair, untying his shoes, and glanced up briefly when she entered, then returned to his task. With trembling fingers Valerie untied the ribbons of her robe and slipped it off. After laying it across the foot of her bed, she turned back the covers and slid inside. Rolling onto her side with her back to Ashe, she pulled the covers over her shoulders, blocking him out. She waited tensely, listening to the sounds as he undressed, until he turned out the light and lay down. Hot tears burned behind her eyes, but Valerie clamped her lids shut and refused to let them come. She wouldn't let him hear her cry.

Chapter 14

VALERIE OPENED HER EYES TO DARKNESS AND BLINKED, wondering why she had awakened. Groggily she rolled onto her back, then gasped. A man stood beside her bed, a dark, faceless outline against the faint light filtering in through the window. She was frozen with terror for an instant before she saw the moonlight glinting off his hair. She sagged with relief. "Ashe. You scared me."

"Sorry. I was just checking on you."

"Why?" she retorted, irritable with the aftermath of fear. "Did you think someone had swung in the seventeenth-floor window and kidnapped me? Or opened the door and walked over you without waking you up?"

"No, of course not. I couldn't sleep and decided to have a smoke." He raised a hand to show the glow of the cigarette in the dark. "While I was up, I thought I'd make sure you were okay." He shrugged.

Valerie shoved herself to a sitting position, fluffed up a pillow at her back and switched on the bedside lamp. It cast a muted circle of light over the bed and floor, but Ashe retreated as if it had been a spotlight.

He slumped into a chair several feet from her bed, shading his eyes. "Do you have to turn on the light?"

"Yes," she retorted firmly. "You're not an owl. You

can stand it." Valerie studied him. His face was drawn, as if he hadn't slept, and there were blue smudges beneath his eyes. He looked tired. Worse than tired. She couldn't think of a word for it. Haunted? "Ashe, what's the matter with you? You've acted like a nut case today. First you're friendly, then angry, then polite, then . . . well, seductive."

"No one's ever described me as seductive before," he countered in an amused tone, but Valerie caught the underlying strain. "That's more *your* style."

"I'm not seductive and you know it. At best I'm ladylike."

His laugh was a short, harsh sound. "Believe me, baby, at the moment you don't look very ladylike."

Valerie glanced down at herself, realizing that she was clad in a sheer nightgown. Her white breasts gleamed through the openwork of the maroon lace bodice. She flushed, embarrassed, but her nipples tightened and shoved against the lace at the thought of Ashe seeing her like that. He would see that, too. Valerie grabbed for her robe at the foot of the bed, but Ashe was there before her, his widespread fingers pinning the satin garment to the bed. "No!" His voice was low and rough. "At least let me look."

Valerie drew back uncertainly as he sank once again into his chair. His words confused her even as they melted her. The implication was clearly sexual, but he'd made it clear that he didn't want her. "You don't make any sense!" she snapped.

"I don't know what you're talking about."

"You must be aware of how moody you've been today."

"I'm not moody."

"I hadn't thought so 'til now. I would have said you were steady to the point of stubbornness, but today you've been up and down like a manic depressive."

He groaned. "I'm only human, Val. And I'm not an old man!"

"What's that supposed to mean?"

"Nothing. Forget it."

"Ohhh!" Valerie slammed her fists onto the bed in frustration and shot up from her sitting position to kneel at the edge of the mattress. Leaning forward earnestly, she pleaded, "Why won't you tell me? Why are you being secretive?"

"You're killing me," he rasped, his hands clenching on the arms of the chair. His forehead was beaded with sweat.

"Ashe, what's wrong?" Valerie started off the bed, reaching out to him, and Ashe flung himself out of the chair with an oath, stalking away. Tears gathered in Valerie's eyes as she sat back on the mattress. He couldn't stand for her to touch him.

"What's wrong?" he repeated with thick sarcasm. "You've been married. Don't you know anything about men?"

"I—I guess not," Valerie replied shakily, struggling to speak around the tears clogging her throat. "Ashe, I'm sorry I'm so stupid, but I truly don't understand. Tell me what I've done to make you angry."

"I'm not angry!" he roared, flinging his arms wide; then he whirled away and slammed his fist against the wall, punctuating each word with a resounding thud. "You're driving me out of my mind."

Valerie swallowed, frightened by his barely controlled violence. "A—Ashe, please, tell me what I'm doing and I'll stop. I promise."

He sighed, his shoulders sagging, and turned to her. "I don't want you to stop. You couldn't if you tried. It's everything about you." He stubbed out the cigarette, grinding it into the ashtray, and walked toward the bed, his barefoot tread as noiseless as a cat's. Fear prickled the back of Valerie's neck. Ashe had put on blue jeans when he got up, but nothing else, and the bare flesh of his chest and arms, taut with muscles, seemed strangely menacing. His pale eyes glittered, colorless as ice, and she sensed that his control had slipped away with his sigh.

Valerie swallowed. "What are you talking about? Do you—hate me?"

He laughed, the sound loud and humorless in the still night. "No, Valerie, I don't hate you." Ashe stopped beside the bed, looming over her. She slid back, turning her head aside, unable to meet his bright gaze. His voice was low and rasping, oddly lulling. "I don't hate you at all. I wish I could, for the way you've tormented me today, but you don't even know you're doing it." He placed one finger on her bare shoulder and ran it lightly down her chest, over the swelling top of her breast into the deep décolletage of her gown. "Are all your nightgowns like this?"

"Like what?"

"Sexy. Enticing."

"I—well, yes, I suppose so."

The tip of his finger crept beneath the cloth to circle her breast's sensitive tip. "You never cheated on Felipe?"

"No! Never! I've told you before. Why are you starting again?" Valerie jerked away from his teasing hand and crossed her arms over her breasts. "Leave me alone."

He went on as if she hadn't spoken. "What about before? Surely you had men before you married."

Valerie stuck out her chin rebelliously, not answering. Suddenly Ashe was on the bed on his knees, towering above her as she sat with her legs curled beneath her. He began to knead her arms gently. Her breath caught in her throat and she stared fixedly at his stomach, very aware of the heat from his body and his tight, revealing jeans. "Tell me, Valerie," he ordered, his voice no less steely for its low tone.

"All right!" she snapped. "Yes, I slept with one man before I married Felipe. David. My fiancé."

"Your fiancé? You didn't marry him?"

"No." She dropped her head, humiliated to admit the story to Ashe, who was so streetwise, so pragmatic, so experienced—all the things she wasn't. He had to bend his head to hear her words. "I discovered that he didn't really love me. I—we made love, but he didn't want me. I was too stupid to realize he was only after my money. I walked in on him one day when he was in bed with a girl. A very pretty girl he'd dated before me. A bunch of us were spending the Christmas holidays at my mother's ski lodge in Vermont." She laughed harshly and sniffed back the tears welling in her eyes. "In my own house! He didn't have enough consideration to hide."

"Oh, baby." Ashe pulled her to him roughly, his hands knotting in her loose hair. Her tears splashed onto his bare stomach. "I'm sorry. The lousy son of—" He broke off and grasped her arms, lifting her to her knees. An insistent hand in her hair tugged her head back so she was forced to look at him. She didn't know what she had expected to see on his face, but it wasn't the peculiar mingling of desire and sorrow she glimpsed.

Valerie swallowed and wet her lips. "It's okay. Not your fault."

A funny half-sigh, half-moan escaped his lips. "Do that again."

"What?"

His tongue touched his lips in imitation of her. Valerie frowned, puzzled, and tentatively repeated the motion. But this time his tongue met hers and followed its path across her lips, starting an explosion of shivers through her. "No wonder you have such innocence. You've never known a man, only a heartless boy and an old guy who treated you like a daughter. Haven't you wondered how it would be—having a man who wanted you, who was so hot for you he couldn't sleep at night?" He traced her lips again, gently pressing them farther apart, his tongue sliding in between to fill her mouth.

Ashe bent over her, molding her body to his, kissing her more and more hungrily. (His mouth tasted faintly of cigarette smoke.) Valerie's arms stole around him, her fingers digging into his back. She reveled in the feel of his warm naked flesh, slightly damp with the sweat of desire. He made an inarticulate noise deep in his throat and broke the sweet seal of their mouths to drop soft, openmouthed kisses across her face to her ear. Valerie shivered and twisted in his arms, enjoying what he did so much that it frightened her. Her movements rubbed her breasts against his chest, and the friction of the lace gown against her nipples caused them to swell further. She remembered his mouth on her breasts by the cave pool, and she yearned to experience it again. She hoped he would touch and kiss her breasts, but she was too shy to ask him.

His hands glided over the smooth satin gown down to her hips and up again. He cupped her breasts in their lace covering and teased the nipples through the cloth. He bent to take first one and then the other in his mouth, lace and all. Valerie sighed in satisfaction and the muscles of his back quivered under her hands. He tore away from her and stood up. Valerie stared at him blankly, her body protesting the loss, before she realized that he was unzipping his denim pants and whisking them off. He stood before her, naked and powerful, and Valerie studied him greedily, knowing it was immodest but not caring. His body was a sculpted flow of muscle and flesh, spare, hard and brown. A white scar hooked around one hipbone and down his abdomen, emphasizing his toughness.

Valerie started to rise and pull off her gown, but Ashe stopped her with one hand. "No," he muttered thickly. "I've been aching all day to do this." Gently he pressed her back until she lay stretched out beneath his gaze. He sat beside her on the bed and with calculated slowness drew down the narrow spaghetti straps of her gown until the lace pulled away from her skin, lightly scraping the tender peaks of her breasts. Ashe gazed at her before he covered the lush globes with his work-roughened hands. Gently he squeezed and stroked, his callused fingers eliciting every sensation possible from the friction of skin upon skin. Valerie went limp and closed her eyes, luxuriating in the delights of his touch.

Ashe slipped from the bed to kneel beside her. He cupped one breast with both hands as if it was infinitely precious and bent over her to touch the nipple with the tip of his tongue. Light and wet, his tongue circled the peak, barely grazing it, but rousing such shimmering, shivering feelings in her that Valerie moaned incoherently. His tongue flicked the turgid bud, teasing it to greater hardness, while his fingers massaged her breast. Valerie moved her legs aimlessly, aware of an aching emptiness in her, a confused longing for the fulfillment only Ashe could bring her. "Ashe, Ashe," she pleaded.

His answer was to settle his lips around her nipple, drawing the pink-brown circle into the warm, liquid suction of his mouth. As he sucked his tongue continued its delightful torment, lashing and licking the sensitive center until Valerie whimpered, almost mindless with the exquisite pleasure. Her hands fluttered over his head and shoulders, caressing him with the light touch of moth wings, then digging in as some new sensation shook her. Ashe shuddered, her untutored touch increasing the level of his desire. He yearned to take her, to sink into her feminine softness and grind out his passion, but equally he wanted to linger over each delight along the way, savoring them to their fullest and giving Valerie every pleasure he knew.

He feasted upon the other breast with the same thoroughness, flooding her with such desire that she scratched his back with her searching fingers and arched upward. Ashe lifted his head. His face was flushed and his eyes brilliant with desire. With trembling fingers he slid the skirt of her gown up, pulling it off over her head. He ran his hands lightly over her naked body, caressing the smooth skin of her abdomen and running a teasing finger up the insides of her thighs. Her legs moved apart, and his hand began a delicate exploration. She was embarrassed at the moistness between her legs, for it revealed how eager and aroused she was, but its effect on Ashe was far different. He stroked the slick satin folds, his breath loud and ragged. "Ah, Valerie," he murmured, bending to kiss her stomach, his tongue delving into the well of her navel. "Sweet, so sweet, to be ready for me. I'd like to—to—" He broke off with a muffled groan as she closed her legs around his hand. "I can't wait. I have to have you."

"Yes," she responded. "Oh, yes."

His long, hard body covered her, and he supported himself on his elbows as his flesh sought its home. Hot and throbbing, he probed her tender entrance, and she welcomed him. As he eased into her, her hands roamed down to the cool skin of his hips, squeezing, urging. Wild, incoherent words bubbled from his lips, and he moaned, burying his face in her neck. He strained to contain the strength of his thrusts. Murmuring her name, he nipped her skin and soothed it with his tongue as he drove them higher and higher. Valerie's head rolled on the pillow, every nerve alive, every inch of her body taut, expectant, striving. She arched, her fingers clutching at the sheets beneath her as her body convulsed with joy. Ashe felt the jolt of her body, and he cried out, joining her in the shattering pleasure.

Slowly Valerie relaxed as the rippling tide receded, leaving only a glow in the center of the explosion. Ashe went limp, his breath gusting hot against her shoulder. He remembered the burden of his weight on Valerie's seemingly fragile body and rose on his elbows. But Valerie's arms went around him, urging him back against her, and he gave in with a sigh of contentment, sliding his arms beneath her. "Ah, Val, Val," he murmured, kissing her cool, damp skin. He rolled onto his back, carrying her with him, and they slipped into exhausted sleep.

Slowly Valerie drifted back to consciousness, becoming more and more aware that it was hot. Fretfully she shoved at the covers, but they were as heavy as lead, and the frustration brought her fully awake. Then she knew why it was hot. A man's long arm and leg were thrown across her, pinning her to the bed, and she was cuddled to his side. Ashe's long body radiated heat like a stove. Ashe. She closed her eyes, smiling, no longer minding the warmth. She had never dreamed what it could be like. Neither Felipe nor her fiancé had brought her close to the zenith she had reached in the night.

Ashe Harlan wanted her. She remembered his heat, his searching kisses, and flushed at the thought. He had appeared indifferent to her since her rejection in the cave. What had made him want her again? Of course, she had looked a mess while they were escaping, but yesterday she had cleaned up. Had that rekindled his desire? Had it been modeling clothes for him? The sexy dance at La Gaviota? She tried to remember what had happened immediately before he kissed her. He had stood beside her bed and questioned her about the men in her past, and she had told him about David. Valerie remembered the sadness in his eyes when she had finished. He had told her that she knew the wrong kind of men. Was that it? Did he pity her enough to make love to her? To give her the pleasure other men hadn't? Had kindness overcome his disinterest in her? Oh, please, surely not. It couldn't be that. Don't let it be that, she prayed.

Ashe groaned lightly and turned, flopping over onto his back. Released, Valerie rose on her elbow to study him. He was so rawly masculine. What could a man like that see in her? She would think he'd want a woman as earthy and stirring as himself. Lightly she ran a finger down his nose and over his lips. He swallowed and stirred. She traced the scar above his hipbone, and he awakened, the pale blue eyes blank as he struggled to orient himself. Then he smiled, eyes warming. "Hello. You're cruel to wake a man up." He yawned widely and covered her exploring hand with his, rubbing it across his chest and stomach.

"Sorry." She tried to keep her tone as light as his, although she wanted to blather on about her love for him, question him regarding his feelings for her. But at least she was smart enough not to do *that*.

He patted her familiarly on the bottom. "Get my cigarettes, would you, baby?"

"Men!" She rolled off the bed and padded across the room to his abandoned clothes, digging for the cigarette pack and the lighter. "All you want is a slave."

He grinned. "What I wanted was to get you out of bed where I could look at you."

She glanced away. How did he feel about her? She couldn't hope he felt the overwhelming love she did. But had he enjoyed it enough to make love to her again? Would he stay with her awhile? If only she weren't such a dope about men. Valerie handed him the package and crawled into the other side of the bed, pulling the sheet up over her. Ashe tossed the cigarette package onto the nightstand and reached out with one arm to pull her close, his other hand shoving the sheet aside. "I want to see you."

Valerie couldn't relax. She was too anxious to do the correct thing, too concerned about his feelings for her to be comfortable. He ran a hand slowly up her body and down again, but she didn't melt. Ashe pulled away. Valerie bit her lip. Now he would think her cold.

"What's wrong, Val? Did I make a mistake last night?"

"What do you mean?" His tone frightened her, and she stared away from him, afraid of what she might see in his face.

"You're so stiff. Did I imagine you wanted me last night? Do you regret it?"

"No! Oh, no, of course not." She turned, her expression anxious. "I'm sorry I'm so bad at this. I don't know how to act."

He grinned. "Is there an Emily Post edict on the subject? 'Polite behavior the morning after'?"

Valerie had to giggle. "No. At least, I hope not. But you'd think Pamela Stanton's daughter would know what to do."

"I don't think it's the kind of knowledge usually handed down from mother to daughter."

She grimaced. "But why didn't I pick it up from her—role modeling and all that?"

"Maybe I don't want you to act like your mother in my bed."

In my bed. The words set up a primitive warmth inside her. "How do you want me to act?"

"Try being yourself," he suggested, a smile playing at the corners of his mouth.

"Maybe you wouldn't like the things I'd say."

"How will I know unless you say them?"

She hesitated. "Why did you make love to me last night? I mean . . . well, you started right after I told you about David."

"Who?"

"My ex-fiancé. I—I don't want you sleeping with me because you're sorry for me." She was met with an astounded silence and hurried on. "I saw your face after I told you, and you looked sad, pitying."

"It made me sad. And angry. I don't like your being hurt."

"But that's not what I want. Not pity."

"Lady, you must think pity's a powerful aphrodisiac. What's the matter with you? I've wanted you from the first. You know that. I nearly went out of my mind yesterday seeing you in my robe, then in that dress with nothing underneath. I couldn't think about anything else. Next you drove me even crazier choosing lingerie and trying on clothes for me, like I was your sugar daddy. And dancing with you at that club . . . I was a wreck. I couldn't sleep for thinking about you lying in bed so near me. That's why I got up. I hoped a cigarette would calm me down. But I had to look at you sleeping. Your nightgown clung to your breasts the way my hands ached to, and I got more and more excited."

Valerie sat up, staring at him, her eyes almost hungry. "Really?"

"Yes, really. I'm not an actor—nor am I in the habit of bedding every woman I feel sorry for. You asked me last night why I was moody yesterday. That's the reason. I wanted you so much it hurt."

Valerie was flooded with warmth. She giggled, pulling her knees up to wrap her arms around them. Resting her chin on her knees, she prodded, "But you'd been so indifferent the past few days. You acted as if you couldn't care less. I thought I was a burden to you."

"Indifferent!" His brows soared upward. "Are you crazy?"

"Well, it's true! You haven't kissed me or even acted like you wanted to. That night in the jungle, you were lying about that far from me, and you didn't make a move."

"Val, I swear, if I didn't love you, I'd strangle you. When I started making love to you in the cave you pushed me away! You didn't want any part of me. What was I supposed to do, keep attacking you until you gave in? I wanted you. I could hardly sleep, knowing how close you were. But after what I'd said and done, I figured you hated me. I felt like a sanctimonious fool. I'd wronged you, hurt you—how could I imagine you'd have anything to do with me?"

Valerie hardly heard him, stunned by his first words. He had said he loved her. Could he have meant it? He'd said it so casually. She must have misunderstood. Or was it an expression, a meaningless countryism? But her heart swelled with a joy her brain couldn't suppress. He loved her! It was too incredible. She longed to ask if he meant it, but she didn't dare. He might deny it or scoff at her for believing an obvious exaggeration. She clasped her hands together tightly and concentrated on what he was saying, storing her joy away in her heart. Later would be soon enough to find out the truth. For now she would simply enjoy it.

His statement was almost as much a shock to Ashe as it was to Valerie. The words had slipped out. He hadn't intended to say it, although it was true, of course. Love was what he had been fighting since he had found out she was married. But he shouldn't have blurted it out. The last thing he wanted was to rush her. He hurried on. "Valerie, I'm sorry if I did the wrong thing. I was trying to be *good*. I didn't want to make another misstep. Hell, Val, I don't know how to act around women like you."

"Women like me?" she repeated, knitting her brows in mock anger. "Honestly, Ashe, you talk as if I were from outer space or something. I'm not made of porcelain or wrapped in tissue paper or silver-plated, just because I was born a Stanton. I'm a flesh-and-blood woman, like anybody else!"

He smiled. "Oh, no, Valerie, there you're wrong. You aren't like anybody else. You are quite unique."

His grin turned decidedly wicked, and Valerie's heart picked up its cadence. "What does that mean?" she countered breathlessly.

"I'll show you." He slid across the bed until his body was barely a fraction of an inch away from hers. Propped on one elbow, he slowly studied her naked body. Valerie flushed, embarrassed yet curiously eager as well. He bent to nuzzle her neck, his velvet lips an erotic contrast to the rasp of his morning stubble. "Your body is beautiful, did you know that?" She shook her head, too full of trembling to speak. "Well, it is. You're lovely. Sexy." He drew his hand over her body as he murmured against her skin, and his trailing fingers left fire behind them. "You're unique; I never wanted another woman as much as I want you."

He kissed her, his silent mouth revealing as much as his words. His tongue filled her mouth, slow and caressing, luxuriating in the sweetness. He pulled away and gazed down into her face. Her eyes were luminous and soft, trusting, loving. Ashe groaned. "Oh, baby, baby, I can't describe what you do to me." He bent again to take her lips in a deep, soul-wrenching kiss, and Valerie wrapped her arms around him, straining to be even closer.

This time he loved her with incredible slowness, delighting in the sweet torture of endless kisses and delicate stroking. His hands roamed her body, his lips following their path, seeking out each secret pleasure point, every sensitive area, finding places and bringing forth sensations Valerie hadn't known existed. His rough-tipped fingers brought her to quivering expectancy, then took her beyond the boundaries of anything she had experienced, until she was moaning, almost sobbing, crying out to him for fulfillment. Then, at last, he filled her and began the final, throbbing dance of love, sweeping them both to the glorious plateau of feeling and awareness that existed only there, in each other's arms.

Chapter 15

Señor Gutierrez's secretary was a thin young man with a perpetually pained expression. He cast Ashe and Valerie an accusing glance as they entered the attorney's office almost ten minutes late. Valerie had to bite her lip to keep from laughing. The guy would have fainted if he'd known what had detained them. She met Ashe's amused, knowing gaze. Valerie wasn't sure whether she wanted to giggle or to melt into his arms. Since neither was appropriate, she resolutely moved to a chair.

Sated and lightly dozing after lovemaking, they had almost forgotten their morning appointment with Felipe's attorney. When Ashe had recalled it with a startled oath they had jumped out of bed and hurried to shower and dress. There had been no time for the slow, dreamy breakfast Valerie would have liked to have had, full of hugs, lingering kisses and shared laughter. But as they moved about the bathroom getting ready, there had been a warming familiarity and intimacy. After a joint shower, which threatened to get out of hand, Ashe had shaved while she applied makeup. She had watched him out of the corner of her eye, admiring his naked form and the tilt of his head as he shaved, the way he stretched his upper lip to scrape the razor over it or looked askance in the mirror to see the side of his

face. There was nothing about Ashe that was less than
perfect, she decided. The only peculiar thing was the
fact that he wanted her, and she was quite happy for
him to have that oddity. Everything else—the curling
gold chest hairs converging in a V to his waistline, the
tousled wet hair, the sinewy feet, the shifting muscles
across his back—was so intensely, beautifully masculine that it made her ache simply to look at him.

Even now, seated sedately in the attorney's waiting
room, his hard body concealed in a conservative blue
suit and his thick hair tamed and dry, there was a raw,
restless quality to him that set up a fluttering in her
stomach. He glanced over and caught her watching
him. His face changed subtly, taking on the small
hallmarks of desire. There was a certain widening of his
lips, a glow in his eyes, a new translucence to his skin.
Valerie swallowed and studied her hands. Her heart
must have been in her face. She wondered if he saw it.
She wondered how long it would be before they could
return to the hotel.

Mr. Gutierrez bustled out, interrupting her reverie.
"Ah, Señora de la Portilla, I am so pleased to meet
you, though sorry for the circumstances." He was a
short, dark man, slightly rotund but brimming with
energy, as though his small frame were not enough to
contain it. He took one of Valerie's hands between his
and raised it for a polite, formal kiss. Then he swiveled
to Ashe. "Mr. Harlan, it's good to see you again. Won't
you please step inside my office?"

He ushered them into a large, darkly paneled room
furnished somberly in heavy mahogany and forest
green velvet. The result was imposing and dignified,
but cheerless. Valerie settled into one of the high-
backed wing chairs, as uncomfortable as when she used
to pay the annual courtesy call on her two maiden
great-aunts in their museum of a mansion on Long
Island. Mr. Gutierrez studied Valerie for a moment, his
hands together to form a steeple, the apex at his lips.
"Felipe often spoke of your beauty and charm, Señora

de la Portilla," he began at last. "I see now what he meant."

"Thank you."

"It is a most sorrowful time, most sorrowful."

"Yes." Valerie was used to the slow social graces preceding any business discussion in San Cristóbal, but Ashe twitched irritably.

"Mr. Gutierrez." Ashe leaned forward, elbows on his knees. "I'd like you to explain the terms of her husband's will to Mrs. de la Portilla. She knows nothing about it."

"I am sorry to hear it. There were times when Felipe indicated a certain—how shall I say it?—reservation where his brother and son were concerned, but I never dreamed they would conceal the terms of the will from you. I don't know what purpose it would serve. Felipe left several annuities to trusted employees and servants. He also made comfortable bequests to the church and to various other charities, chief among them the National Museum. He bequeathed the house in town to his brother for life, then to his son upon Alfonso's death. The remainder of his estate, which is to say the vast majority of his wealth and property, was placed into a trust."

Valerie nodded. "I see."

"You are the beneficiary of the trust."

"Me?" Valerie stared. "But before we married, we signed a premarital contract keeping our properties separate. Why—"

Gutierrez waved one hand as if to clear away her protests. "Felipe was a generous man and loved you greatly. The premarital contract was primarily to insure there would be no question of your property belonging to him, should you by some chance predecease him. But he didn't mean to exclude you from his property. I drew up this will shortly after your marriage."

"But I don't understand—what about Alfonso and Esteban?"

"They are not mentioned in the will, except for the provisions concerning the house and to say that he made substantial gifts to them during his lifetime and for that reason gave them nothing but minor bequests under the will. I believe there was some"—he paused delicately—"shall we say ill feeling between Felipe and his relatives for several years. It was Felipe's opinion that Alfonso would squander any money he received. Esteban received an ample sum at his mother's death."

"Well." Valerie stared at the lawyer. "I'm startled."

"There's your answer, Val," Ashe told her. "I knew there must be a bigger reason for Alfonso's behavior. That's why he wants you to marry Carlos."

"Marry Carlos?" Gutierrez repeated, aghast. "Oh, no, my dear lady, that would never do. Carlos is . . . well, he is not the man for you. Felipe wouldn't have wished such a thing. He tolerated Carlos only because of the blood tie."

"I know. *I* don't wish to marry him. But Alfonso tried to force me into it. Mr. Gutierrez, isn't there a way I can give the money to the family? I don't want it or need it, but they want it so much that they've shot at Ashe and kidnapped me. Frankly, I'd like to be rid of it."

Gutierrez gaped at her, his mouth opening and closing like a fish. He began to exclaim and question in rapid, excited Spanish that Valerie could barely follow. After Valerie and Ashe had related their story, interrupted frequently by his expressions of astonishment and dismay, he slumped back in his chair. "It seems to be a matter for the police."

"No," Valerie replied firmly. "I don't want to get mixed up with the police. You know that the de la Portillas are in disfavor. The government would welcome any excuse to put them away. I can't do it to Felipe's family. He would have hated to have his name shamed. Besides, I don't want to stay here for an investigation and trial. I just want to be safe." And lift the threat to Ashe, she added mentally. That was the most important thing.

"Well, you can disclaim the money, but it wouldn't return to Esteban and Alfonso. Under the terms of the trust, should you die or disclaim the money, the entire fund would pass to the National Museum. Felipe didn't want his family to have it."

Valerie sighed and closed her eyes, thinking out loud. "But if I disclaim the money and it goes to the museum, I would have nothing else to do with it, right? And Alfonso wouldn't benefit from my marrying Carlos." She smiled at the attorney. "Isn't that true, Mr. Gutierrez?"

"Yes. Yes, it is. You would have no control over it whatsoever."

"Good. I want you to draw up some kind of document saying I disclaim all the money Felipe left me."

"Well, of course I can," Gutierrez agreed, baffled. "But, Señora de la Portilla, are you certain you wish to do it? You are giving up a great sum of money."

"I'm positive. When can you have the document ready?"

He shrugged. "It is not complex. I could be finished by tomorrow afternoon."

They made an appointment for the following day and thanked the lawyer for his time and trouble. Then they left the puzzled man and walked toward the hotel. Ashe was quiet, his head lowered thoughtfully. Valerie glanced at him. "What's the matter?"

He grimaced. "Val, I can protect you. I promise. Alfonso won't get his hands on you. You don't need to throw away all that money."

"But what would I do with it? As it is, I have more money than I can spend. Why not give it to a charity Felipe and I believed in and at the same time insure our safety?"

"You weren't kidding when you said you were wealthy, were you?"

Fear encircled her heart. "Ashe, does it bother you? Do you still dislike people with money? Or think I'm different and untrustworthy because I have it?"

He stared off into the distance, then smiled at her. "No, I don't think so. I've cleared my head of a lot of that." He raised a hand to touch her cheek. "You helped me do it. In the past I've taken out my anger at Alec on a whole class of people. When I met Alec and his family my opinion began to change. I realized they were human beings, like me. I even liked them. When you came along it scared me to find out that you had money. I was afraid I'd do the wrong thing. But I had to have you. That's still the way I feel—only now it doesn't scare me." They stopped walking and turned to each other, their gazes locking. Unconsciously Valerie leaned toward him, seeking his hard, warm body, and his arms folded around her. His lips were hot and smooth on hers, a mute promise. She clung to him, oblivious of the people who passed them, staring. When at last they broke their kiss he whispered, "I love you, Valerie."

Her heart exploded in a pinwheel of joy. "Oh, Ashe, I love you, too. I love you."

It was several minutes before they became aware of the world again. Finally Valerie giggled and pulled out of his embrace. "We're probably shocking all of San Cristóbal."

"Just La Luz," he responded with a smile. "Come on, I want to get you back to our hotel room."

"Sex fiend," she teased.

"Very funny. Actually, I don't have ravishment in mind. Well, perhaps it's in my mind, but I'm not going to carry it out. I have a conference at the Ministry of the Interior."

"How dull. You're going to leave me all alone?"

"Yes, and don't try your wiles on me, young woman. I do have business to conduct while I'm here, you know. I need to finish it so we can leave as soon as your passport's ready. I intend to take you home, where we won't have to worry about nasty brothers-in-law firing at us or trying to steal you away or the national police deciding to imprison us because we kissed on the street. Then I can concentrate on the important things in life—like making love to you."

"Is that all we're going to do when we get home?"

"Yes," he answered decisively. "At least for a while. I have several weeks of hunger to make up for."

They ate lunch in a nearly deserted open-air café before returning to the hotel room. When they reached the room Ashe checked the closets and bathroom for intruders. "Would you like to look under the beds?" Valerie suggested lightly.

"It's no joking matter." He pointed his forefinger at her. "Don't let anyone in here under any circumstances, do you hear?"

"Yes, sir." She saluted smartly.

He seized her by the arms, lifting her onto her tiptoes, and kissed her resoundingly. "And don't look so damned enticing, or I'll forget about my business and spend the afternoon in bed with you."

Valerie glowed. He dropped another, lighter kiss on her lips, then turned and left the room. Valerie flung herself onto the bed and grinned at the ceiling. Ashe loved her! She could hardly believe it, didn't dare trust it. Yet it had happened. He had kissed her in plain view of everyone, right on the street, and whispered that he loved her. "Oh, Ashe, Ashe," she murmured, delighting in his name on her tongue. Please don't let it be that he was swayed by the time and place, caught up in the emotional excitement of their escape, she prayed. Please let it be real.

The phone rang late in the afternoon, and Valerie picked it up, thinking it was Ashe. When she answered there was silence on the other end, followed by the dead click of a receiver hanging up. Fear curled in her stomach. Alfonso. Was Alfonso trying Ashe's number to see if she was there? Valerie dropped the receiver hastily.

When a key scraped in the lock minutes later she jumped to her feet, still rattled by the phone call, almost expecting to see Alfonso's face peering around the door at her. But the door opened to reveal Ashe, his face lined with weariness from intense bargaining, his suit rumpled and his hair mussed by a careless hand. He smiled, the thread-thin lines around his eyes lifting when he saw her, and Valerie hurtled into his arms. "Oh, Ashe!"

"What's the matter?" His arms folded around her, and his voice was laced with concern. He recognized the anxiety and relief in her greeting. "What is it?"

"Someone just phoned the room and hung up. I'm sure it was Alfonso. Now he knows where we are!"

"Don't upset yourself over it," he reassured her, stroking her back. "We're leaving tomorrow. Even Alfonso wouldn't storm our room, so you'll stay here until then. Tomorrow I'll pick up your passport and finish my business with the government while I get it stamped; then we'll drop by the attorney's office on the way to the airport. Alfonso can't kidnap you if you don't go outside alone."

"Okay." Ashe's warmth and confidence seeped into her. He was right. Alfonso must realize he'd lost his chance in the jungle. He wouldn't attack them in the city, at least not smack in the middle of a popular hotel.

"We'll have room service send up supper." Ashe grinned. "I think we can find plenty to do here in the room, don't you?"

Valerie's eyes sparkled. Whatever doubts she had were smothered in a burst of love. "Mmmm, I don't know. San Cristobalian television isn't too good. Of course, we could buy a deck of cards."

He gave her a squeeze that left her breathless. "You're a heartless tease. Order dinner, would you, while I shower? A couple of hours in this city and I'm sweating like I've been in the fields all day."

"Okay. What do you want?" His answering chuckle was lewd. "For *dinner*," she explained with mock exasperation.

"Oh, that. A big steak, baked potato with butter, no sour cream, a salad with blue cheese dressing."

"I might have known you were a steak-and-potatoes man."

"Oh, I enjoy some spice now and then," he assured her, his long, lazy survey of her body making a double entendre of his words. Slowly, deliberately, he unfastened his tie and pulled it from around his neck. The tie slid across his shirt, clinging to the very end before it dropped away. He threw it onto a nearby chair and sat to remove his shoes and socks. Standing again, Ashe grasped the lapels of his suit jacket and shrugged it off his shoulders, the movement straining his chest against the thin shirt. He dropped the coat casually on the chair, and Valerie watched him, fascinated.

Ashe met her eyes levelly, pinning her with his pale blue gaze. His eyes were the color of a Western sky strewn with translucent wisps of white clouds. She wondered how such a frosty-cold color could carry such heat. His gaze was hypnotic. He wanted her to stay. She realized that he was stripping for her, and a thrill shot down her abdomen like a firework falling from its arc, bursting into fiery sparks at the end.

With the same deliberation Ashe unbuttoned first one cuff, then the other. His hand undid the collar button and moved lower, unfastening each button without haste until he reached the waistband of his trousers. He spread his long, agile fingers and grasped his shirt to drag the tail from his trousers. When it jerked free he unbuttoned the last button and it fell open, revealing a swath of brown chest lightly covered with golden hair. Ashe slipped the shirt back and let it drift down his arms. With a twist of the wrist that made his chest muscles ripple he caught it and tossed it onto the growing pile of clothes.

Hardly breathing, Valerie studied his chest: the firm

padding of muscles, the rigid framework of ribs visible in his lower chest, the pale V of hair tightening to a line, which disappeared invitingly into the waistband of his trousers. He was rock hard and thoroughly male. There was nothing narcissistic about his stripping, only a sensual invitation and a lover's excitement at revealing himself wholly to his beloved. Valerie swayed and leaned against the dresser to steady herself, not breaking the bond of their gaze. Passion swelled her chest and squeezed the breath from her lungs, but she knew there was no release for her except his touch.

Now he unbuckled his belt and pulled it from its loops. It slithered out and dropped, curling, onto the floor. The clasp of his trousers popped open beneath his fingers, and the zipper rasped downward, abnormally loud in the still room. The noise set up a thrumming within Valerie. The tailored trousers caressed Ashe's thighs as they glided to the floor. He stepped out, shoving them aside without regard for their immaculate creases. Lastly he slid his thumbs inside the band of his underwear, drawing it downward, the elastic expanding, then rolling over his flesh, dragging the soft cotton from his lean, compact hips. Valerie followed the movement down the length of his tautly muscled legs, unaware that her tongue stole between her lips. Her mouth was parched and everything else inside her liquid.

Ashe left the underwear where it lay and ambled toward the bathroom for his shower. Valerie stood for a stunned instant before she started after him. He was reaching for a towel when she came up behind him and spread her hands across his back, letting them float down to the pale, soft skin of his buttocks. "Ashe." Her voice conveyed all the meaning necessary.

He turned. The corners of his mouth drooped sensuously, and his nostrils were wide, the skin across his cheekbones tight with sexual hunger. "I was scared you wouldn't follow," he confessed huskily.

Valerie transferred her hands to his chest, twining

her fingers through the fine hairs, curling, tugging, teasing. A smile hovered on her lips. "You—uh—impaired my ability to walk."

His chuckle was deep and throaty as he bent to take her lips. This time Valerie moved up to meet him, returning his kiss with equal fervor, surprising him and shooting a new excitement into his veins. Ashe pulled her to him sharply, rubbing her clothed body against his naked skin and delighting in the exquisite sensations it produced. "Let me make love to you," Valerie whispered when their clinging lips parted.

He swallowed, shaken by her words, and released her. She drew away and quickly undressed. Then, shaking back her pale mane of hair, Valerie stared into his eyes as she reached up to touch his thick hair. She let it trickle through her fingers, then moved to his face, skimming over the skin and exploring each angle, hollow and curve. She learned the different textures: the slightly moist softness of his brow, the prickling of the day's-end stubble along his jaw, the weathered hardness of his cheekbones, and the fragile folds beside his eyes. His earlobes were pillowy soft, and she was struck with wonder to find such contrasts in this hard man.

Her hands roamed lower, examining the ridge of his collarbone and the thrust of muscle beneath his smooth skin. Her fingers played over his arms and chest, sometimes light, sometimes firm, now and then kneading the bulging pads of his muscles. Raising one of his arms, she nuzzled the inside of his elbow. At his faint hiss she glanced up. The thin skin of his lids covered his eyes, the lashes shadowing his cheeks, and his mouth was pulled almost into a grimace, the area above his lips damp. She hesitated, and his eyes fluttered open, a wild, fierce blue. His breath came out in a shuddering sigh and he wet his lips. "I thought you were supposed to be inexperienced."

She grinned. "I am. You're my guinea pig."

"Keep experimenting, Ms. Edison."

She returned to his elbow, amazed at his reaction, kissing it and drawing tiny circles with her tongue. The muscles in his arm corded beneath her. His skin was salty with sweat, and the taste excited her. She made crisscross patterns with her tongue up his arm and across his chest. Ashe sucked in his breath and dug his teeth into his lower lip. None of the sensations were entirely new to him; women had aroused him before. But no other woman had caressed him with Valerie's eager innocence, exploring him to satisfy her own curiosity and desires. Nor had any other been the woman he loved and desired more than everything else. The flicker of her questing tongue, the brush of her eyelashes like butterfly wings upon his skin, her silken hair trailing across him—all pierced him with a sweetly aching desire he'd never known before. He wanted it to last forever, but it electrified him so much that he wanted equally strongly to take her immediately.

Ashe's nipples were on a level tantalizingly close to Valerie's lips. Valerie touched them, watching the little buds tighten and lengthen beneath her fingers. Leaning forward and resting her hands at his waist, she tickled one nipple with her tongue. Ashe groaned and sank his hands into her hair, kneading the silky mass and encircling her head with his hands. Emboldened, Valerie pulled the nipple into her mouth, suckling the flat masculine breast and copying the delightful, tormenting things Ashe's tongue had done to her. His breath grew harsh and ragged, and whenever she brought him some particularly sharp new pleasure he gasped out an inarticulate word. Valerie's hands swept down his hips and thighs and back up the front, caressing the incredibly satiny flesh as her mouth went to work on the other turgid nipple.

"Ah, Valerie," he groaned softly. "Please. No more. I have . . . to have you."

She raised shining eyes to him, and he lifted her, his iron arms clasped beneath her buttocks. He took one breast in his mouth almost worshipfully, laving it with infinite care. Valerie dug her fingers into the shorter hair at the nape of his neck, curling her head down to stroke her cheek against the top of his head. Both burned with the need to meet at every point, to seal themselves together so absolutely that they could not be parted. Ashe walked to the bed, and one arm came up behind Valerie's back to ease her onto the sheets. His face was flushed, his eyes intense, his entire concentration on her. He lowered himself onto the bed, taking his weight on his forearms, and slowly came into her. As they lay joined he cupped her breasts and toyed with the engorged nipples as his lips and teeth nuzzled the soft flesh of her neck. The combination of sensations fizzed like champagne through her. When Valerie was awhirl in mindless pleasure, Ashe finally began to move, building slowly, inexorably to a final wild crescendo which caught them like a huge wave, tossing them into a far region of pleasure, indescribable and unforgettable.

Joy pierced her, so sweet it was almost an agony. She was utterly exposed, totally vulnerable, her walls of defense torn down. And the pain that the walls had held in poured out in huge, silent tears. They gushed out effortlessly, without sobbing, and for a moment Ashe, drained and sated to a blissful numbness, was unaware that she was crying. Then he felt liquid touch his jaw, and he raised his head, astounded to see rivulets of tears coursing down her cheeks.

"Valerie?" He scrambled to a sitting position, his voice raw with fear. "What is it? What's the matter? Did I hurt you? Sweetheart . . ."

She rolled her head on the pillow in mute negation, appalled at her wayward tears. She didn't really understand why she cried; she only knew that the fierce emotion inside her sought an outlet. "No! Oh, no. It was beautiful." Valerie brought trembling hands to her face to hide the drops as she struggled to stop. But inexplicably the tears burst forth harder than ever, and now sobs racked her chest. "Ashe, oh, God, I'm so awful!"

"Awful!" he repeated in astonishment. "What in the world are you talking about? You're not awful." Confused, helpless, Ashe stared at her, then did what his heart bade him, the only thing he knew to do. He gathered her into his arms and cradled her against his chest, soothing her with meaningless little words and kisses on her hair, as one would soothe a child.

Valerie cried and cried as though her heart were breaking, the loneliness and heartbreak of twenty-four years gushing forth. When her sobs finally quieted she began to explain, the words bursting forth in fits and starts punctuated by gulps, sobs and long shuddering sighs. Holding her tightly, Ashe frowned and tried to piece together what she said. "I'm no good. I'm not pretty. I don't know how to do things. Always. I've always been incompetent. Yesterday I could hardly manage to tip that guy. I don't know why. Mother's b-beautiful and I'm the ugly duckling. No personality. No poise." On and on her litany of self-debasement ran as she revealed the secret fears and anguishes of a lifetime.

Ashe listened in stunned silence, barely able to absorb what she said, so absurd did her statements seem to him. At last she quieted, and her breathing caught shakily, then turned normal. The tears dried, leaving her face splotched and her throat thick.

After she fell silent Ashe sat without saying anything for a time, attempting to marshal an argument that would convince her. "Valerie, honey, that's not true. None of it. How can you say you're not beautiful or lovable or competent? You're all of those. You . . ." He paused and shook his head in exasperation.

Valerie spoke in a low tone, staring across the room,

almost as if she were by herself. "When I was six my parents divorced. I was frightened by their fights, scared of my home dissolving right before my eyes. I kept thinking that somehow I had done it because I wasn't pretty or bright or good enough. One evening I got out of bed and crept downstairs to talk to them. I wanted to assure them that I could change, would make myself the child they wanted, if only they'd stay together. They were in the den. Mama was sitting on the couch, and Daddy was pacing up and down. They were arguing, but not as loudly or as violently as usual. You see, they'd just agreed to separate and file for divorce. They were working out the details." She stopped as tears clogged her throat.

"And?" Ashe prodded.

"And they were talking about me." Again her voice began to jerk with emotional upheaval. "Mama said, 'Valerie can remain with you, if you want.' And my father—*my father*—replied, 'My God, Pamela! What would I do with Valerie? You take her.' Neither one wanted me, you see. They were arguing over custody, and the *loser* had to take me."

"Oh, baby." He cuddled her closer, burying his lips in her hair, almost brought to tears himself at the thought of her childhood pain. Valerie's tears started again, but this time she cried more quietly. Ashe rocked her soothingly, chanting over and over how beautiful she was and how much he loved her. Her body relaxed against him, but he continued to hold her, rocking until the muscles of his arms began to cramp. Finally he shifted his position, easing Valerie onto the bed. She stared at him with huge smudged eyes, drained, too numb to speak or think. But curiously enough there was a strange feeling of peace mingled in with her lassitude.

Ashe brushed a damp wisp of hair from her cheek, caressing her with his knuckles. "I do love you, you know. And in a while we'll talk about this, okay?"

She nodded wearily, her lids drifting closed. He

watched as she slipped into the shallow breathing of slumber, then sighed and buried his head in his hands. He rubbed his face, shoving his hands into his hair. For a long moment he gazed at her sleeping face. Then he shook his head briefly in disbelief and rose from the bed. Leaving her to nap, he headed for the shower.

Chapter 16

A HAND GENTLY SHOOK VALERIE AWAKE. "BABY, WAKE up. Food's here."

"What?" She struggled to sit up, her voice hazy with sleep. Her head was pounding and her eyes ached. Her nose was stuffed up as if she had been crying. Crying. Valerie groaned and flopped back onto the bed. Oh, God. She had made a complete fool of herself by bursting into tears, then pouring out her whole poor-me story. She wondered if Ashe was thoroughly disgusted. She glanced at him tentatively. His face was a trifle drawn, but he was smiling.

"Our dinner's here. You've been asleep for an hour. I hated to wake you, but I'm starving." He cast her an impish grin. "And I didn't want to eat alone. Come on. Up."

Valerie rolled her head and slipped out of bed. Realizing that she was nude, she looked around hastily for her robe. Ashe chuckled, assuring her that she looked fine the way she was, but he politely handed her the robe from its hanger in the closet. Valerie put it on and sat down at the portable table, managing to avoid his eyes. "I didn't know what you wanted, so I ordered the same thing I got. Here." He uncovered the platter of meat before her. "Except the steak's a little smaller. I also decided that a little wine was in order."

He poured her a glass with a flourish and sat down across from her. Ashe dug into his food, but Valerie could only pick at hers. Everything tasted like cardboard, spoiled by the memory of the scene she'd thrown earlier. And right after making love, too! That was a wonderful thing to do to the man who had just become your lover, she thought savagely, burst into tears and trot out all your neuroses. She'd be lucky if Ashe hung around long enough to take her out of San Cristóbal. Ashe urged her to eat and poured himself a second glass of wine. Valerie swallowed a few bites of the potato and all her wine. She wondered if she could turn into a lush overnight.

Ashe laid down his fork and stretched, then relaxed in his chair as he took a leisurely sip of wine. Valerie glanced over at him and gave an awkward little smile when she found him regarding her. He didn't return the smile, only frowned into his wineglass and swirled the contents. Valerie's heart sank. When he began to speak she tensed to accept the rejection she sensed was coming. "Valerie, I've been thinking about what you said earlier."

"I'm sorry, Ashe," she broke in. "I really am. I don't know why I went crazy. I don't, usually. Maybe it's the tension of escaping Alfonso."

"Maybe," he agreed, undeterred by her apology. "And the emotional stimulus of making love. At first it shocked me, your crying like that. I thought I'd done something horrible. Then I realized how relaxed and soft our loving had left me. I guess it gives the locked-up stuff a chance to escape."

"I suppose so," Valerie agreed. At least he wasn't scorning or berating her.

"I'm glad you trusted me enough to tell me," he went on. "I gathered it isn't something you talk about freely."

Valerie blushed. "No. Never. Ashe—"

He held up a hand. "No. I can see what you're about to say, and I don't want to hear an apology. There's no reason for it. I'm proud I was the person you showed your soul to."

"Oh, Ashe!" Tears welled in her eyes, love swelling in her chest.

He smiled and reached across the table to take her hands. "Don't ever apologize for telling me how you feel. Valerie, I want to know you. Inside out." He squeezed her hands and she smiled tremulously at him, her love shining out of her gray-green eyes. "I love you. Remember?"

She nodded mutely. Ashe rose, pulling her to her feet, and led her to a comfortable chair. He sat down in it and tugged her into his lap. Sighing contentedly, Valerie snuggled against him. "But I want to talk to you about what you said," he continued.

"Oh, dear."

"No 'oh, dear' about it. What's the matter with you? I'm not going to scold you. But I am going to tell you a few home truths. Somewhere you've gotten a weird picture of yourself. Who told you you weren't pretty? Have you looked in a mirror?"

"Felipe taught me to dress right and carry myself attractively. I learned how to put on makeup to emphasize my best features and play down my bad ones, but that's all artifice. It's not really me. It's a creation."

"And how much artifice did you employ in the jungle? I saw you in those baggy jeans, remember? The attractive little getup with the hiking boots to match?" A giggle burst from her throat. "Right. No makeup. Dirt all over you. River mud caked in your hair. And you know what? You were beautiful."

"Oh, Ashe."

"Why would I lie?"

"I don't know, but I'm not beautiful. Morgan Stone —I mean Fletcher—is beautiful."

"Yes, she is, but she'd scare most men to death. Valerie, when you're dressed up in Felipe's choice of clothes, makeup in place and all that, you could scare a guy, too. You're as icily perfect as the Snow Queen."

He grinned. "Fortunately, I'm not easily frightened. But even when you aren't dressed up, you're lovely. Your eyes are a color nobody else has. Your hair's like moonlight. You're soft and feminine, and there's a glow inside that lights up your face. You're kind, sweet, witty, warm—and all that adds to your beauty. Okay, so much for your false ideas about your looks. Now, on to the rest of your misconceptions."

"Please, no; I don't want to talk about it. I got carried away, okay? I exaggerated. I'm not ugly. I'm not bad. I'm not totally incompetent. But I'm not a success at anything, either."

Ashe sighed and gnawed at his lower lip. "Look, Val, I tried to figure out the right way to present it so you'd believe me. I have experience with how blind people can be to the truth if they want to think something else. That's the way I was about Alec for most of my life. I knew you'd be hard to convince. But, Val, you have to face the truth sometime if you're going to have a decent life. You can't cling to this twisted vision of yourself. Maybe your parents didn't want you. Or maybe you heard part of a conversation and interpreted it in a kid's crazy way. I don't know. But whether or not Pamela and Darryl Stanton wanted you to live with them when you were a child doesn't change your worth. It only signifies something about *them*. Can you see that?"

"Oh, yes, I see." Valerie jumped to her feet and strode away from him, wrapping her arms tightly around herself. "I realize how wrong I could have been, how little it might have meant. But I'm still not competent, not smart, not good at anything. I'm a timid, bungling person. Think of the mess I've gotten myself into here. And I dragged you into it, too!"

"This mess is hardly your fault. Alfonso's greedy and wicked. Is that your responsibility?" Ashe stood up, taut with anger and frustration. "Damn it, Valerie! What did you do when Alfonso told you you had to marry Carlos? Did you wail and bemoan your fate? Did you meekly give in? No! You escaped from his house and came to me for help. *I'm* the one who failed *you*. Then, when I finally got around to helping you, you swam a wide, dangerous river. You led us to the Mayan cave. You uncomplainingly trekked through the jungle for two days, suffering thirst, hunger, aching muscles and God knows what else. To top it off you got into an airplane that looked like it could hardly fly and toughed out a bumpy, scary flight. If someone described that behavior to you, would you classify the person as timid? Good Lord, I think you've been exceptionally brave and resourceful! You are competent. You are able to handle things. You're more than capable of running your own life."

Valerie turned slowly and stared at him. "Do you really think so?"

"Yes, and so would you, if you looked at the situation rationally. Valerie, I love you. Tell me, do you think I'd fall in love with a jerk?"

She smiled. "No."

"Well, there's your answer."

Valerie ran to him, her arms stretching out to encircle his neck. "Oh, Ashe, I love you."

Ashe kissed Valerie awake. Her eyes fluttered, and she smiled sleepily, her arms automatically stealing around him. "Good morning, sleepyhead," he teased.

"Good morning." They kissed again and Ashe broke away.

"I brought you coffee and a Danish from the restaurant in the lobby." He pointed toward the low table where he had set them. "You won't be able to get room service. Things are a madhouse. Three-fourths of the hotel employees didn't show up today. The manager of the restaurant was cooking."

Valerie sat up, frowning. "That doesn't sound good."

"Especially for the hotel."

"No, seriously. It sounds as if something's up. People are going into hiding."

"Are you serious?"

"Yes. You don't know what it's like living here. Haven't you noticed how empty the streets have been lately?"

"I've never been here before."

"Well, normally La Luz is a teeming city. Flower vendors, open-air markets, lots of shoppers and people going about on business. It's the financial, cultural and social center of San Cristóbal. But everyone's pulling out. There's a noticeable lack of tourists. After they hear the rumors of revolution, no one wants to visit San Cristóbal. Suddenly the wealthy families are retiring for the season to their vacation homes in the hills or to their plantation houses. The poor visit relatives in the farming regions. If the revolution comes, there will be fighting everywhere, but especially in La Luz. A person would have more chance of surviving in the country, so the population has been trickling out. And you see more and more soldiers everywhere, watching."

"The signs of an approaching revolution, huh?"

"Yeah. But employees deserting in droves in one day means it's reaching a crisis."

"Well, I did have a difficult time getting plane reservations," he admitted. "It's a good thing we're leaving this afternoon."

Valerie nodded. "In another day or two we might not be able to get out."

"Oh, we'd get out," he assured her. "I have an ace up my sleeve."

"What?"

He winked. "You'll see, if it comes to that. Let's hope it doesn't. Now, listen. I'm running over to the embassy to pick up your passport, then to the government buildings to have it stamped and to sign the oil lease. I should be back about eleven. We'll eat, drop by Gutierrez's office and head for the airport. Our plane leaves at two o'clock."

"Okay. I'll be ready by eleven."

"Good." He planted a light kiss on her forehead. A

longer, deeper kiss on her lips followed. "You feeling better this morning?" he murmured, and she nodded.

"Thanks to you. Ashe, I appreciate what you said last night."

"It was nothing but the truth."

"I hope so. Anyway, I'm going to start acting like it is. You know, I feel happier, as if I've dumped something I'd carried for years."

Ashe kissed her again, one hand cupping her neck. Their lips clung, and his tongue flickered through her mouth. He pulled away with a sigh. "I better go, or I won't finish in time for us to make our plane. See you."

"Bye." Valerie watched him leave and continued to sit staring blindly at the door, her face lit by a grin. It was true. She did feel as if a weight had been lifted from her, as though a deep sorrow from her past had oozed out with her tears. Was she really the way Ashe saw her? Brave? Resourceful? Pretty? It seemed amazing, but why else would a man like Ashe love her? She felt sure he could have any number of women—gorgeous, sophisticated, witty women. Yet he had chosen her. Surely that meant that she had some winning qualities, despite her low opinion of herself.

Valerie slid out of bed and picked up the quick breakfast Ashe had brought her. She ate it as she walked around the room, choosing the clothes she would wear, brushing her hair, starting her morning tasks. All the while her mind was on Ashe and his perception of her. One thing she was sure of—even if she didn't possess the admirable traits Ashe believed she did, she was going to acquire them. She wasn't about to lose Ashe from some sick need to bolster her inferiority complex.

Valerie finished her meal, showered and dressed. Then she folded the clothes she had bought and squeezed them into Ashe's suitcase. By ten-thirty she was ready and sat down to wait for Ashe. She flipped on the television, but there was nothing worth watching. Finally she resorted to reading the English-language brochure about lovely La Luz and the country of San Cristóbal, which the hotel placed in every room. By eleven she was utterly bored and eager for Ashe to return.

She tried not to worry when Ashe didn't appear at eleven o'clock. He had several things to do, and he couldn't pinpoint his arrival to the minute. Valerie switched on the TV and settled down to watch an old western serial dubbed into Spanish, counseling herself to be patient. After another thirty minutes passed and her nerves began to twitch all over, she reminded herself that Ashe was unused to the San Cristóbal government. He had probably underestimated the time it would take to have her passport stamped. Or he could have been held up at the embassy. No doubt it was jam-packed with Americans anxious to go home, since San Cristóbal was edging closer to revolt.

Valerie began to pace, stopping by the television set and snapping it off with such frustrated force that the knob cracked and came off in her hand. Grimacing, she tossed the knob onto the dresser and went to the window to stare out. The street below was almost empty. Only one man hurried along, clearly anxious to reach his destination. Even from that height Valerie could see that the man wasn't Ashe. As she watched an army Jeep puttered around the corner and crawled down the block. There were three soldiers in it besides the driver, and they all held guns at the ready. Their heads swiveled from side to side alertly. There was trouble brewing.

The thought was no comfort. Valerie brought a chair to the window and continued her observation of the street. It was the only thing she could do at the moment. She dared not leave the hotel room. Ashe might call her with instructions or a cry for help. Besides, she had no idea where to start looking for him. She bit her thumb. She stood up. She sat down. She glanced at her watch.

Twelve noon. Ashe was an hour late. What if Alfonso had seized him? What if he'd been insolent to a soldier and they had hauled him unceremoniously to the Presidio? Or simply beaten him unconscious and left him lying on the street? There was always the possibility that he had been kidnapped by a guerrilla band, like other American executives in other Latin American countries. She couldn't bear thinking of it, yet she couldn't keep her mind off it. By twelve-thirty she was frantic.

The shrill ringing of the phone slammed against her raw nerves and she shot up from the chair, almost running to the telephone.

"*Sí?*"

Alfonso's voice sounded like the cat that got into the cream. "Hello, little sister."

"Alfonso!" Her stomach curled with fear. "What do you want?"

"What a question from my future daughter-in-law! You must learn to speak with more respect."

"Why do you insist on continuing this idiocy? I'm not marrying Carlos."

"No? I have something here that I think will change your mind."

"What?"

"Not what. Who." He paused significantly, letting her fear build. "It is your charming friend Mr. Harlan."

Valerie began to tremble, but she struggled to stay calm and think. She couldn't give way to her fear. She had to get Ashe out. For a few minutes she had to be the kind of woman Ashe believed her to be. Infusing her voice with scorn, she spat, "Don't be stupid. Ashe Harlan is Alec Stone's son, and Alec is an unforgiving man. You harm his son and he'll have your hide. He'll ruin you financially and every other way."

"I'm not a complete fool. Why would Stone's son be named Harlan?"

"He's illegitimate, but he's Alec's only son and Alec loves him dearly. He plans to leave Stone Oil to Ashe."

Valerie invented freely. "I wouldn't put it past Alec to hire assassins to kill you."

"I'll risk it. Anyway, Stone will have Harlan back unharmed if you cooperate."

"What makes you think I will?"

"You love him," Alfonso replied simply. "I've had you followed, you know. As soon as you two jumped off the boat I put a man in Harlan's hotel. He saw you kissing like lovers on the street yesterday. I know the way you looked at him when we were at the plantation house. You can't let him die."

"What do you want me to do?"

"I'm waiting for you on the boat. You know where it's docked. Be here in thirty minutes. When you're on board I'll release your lover and we'll cast off for the plantation. You'll marry Carlos as soon as we arrive."

Valerie's knees shook, and she had to sit on the floor to keep from falling. She couldn't. She couldn't. But how else could she save Ashe? "Let me talk to Ashe," she stalled.

"I'm afraid that's impossible. He's unconscious at the moment."

"Unconscious!" Her pulse began to hammer so loudly in her ears that she could hardly hear Alfonso's answer.

"Yes. Something was added to his coffee this morning in the confusion."

"All right. But give me forty-five minutes. I have to dress."

He agreed and hung up the phone. Valerie set the receiver on its cradle and slowly drew herself to her feet. She stood for a moment in thought before she picked up the receiver to ask for an outside line. It took ten minutes to get the operator. She asked to be connected with the police, but the operator could rouse no one at their number. Next she asked for Carraboza, the official with whom Ashe had been negotiating, but his office didn't answer either. Valerie set down the receiver and chewed at her lip. Finally she placed a long-distance call to Alec Stone in Dallas. If she was unsuccessful in getting Ashe released, she wanted Alec to know what had happened. He would make sure that she and Ashe were found. However, a somber voice on the other end of the line informed her that no international calls were being placed at that time. When Valerie began to argue the man hung up on her.

She slammed down the phone and skinned out of the peasant dress she had been wearing, changing to jeans and a blouse, which would give her more freedom for physical action. Grabbing her purse, she started toward the door, paused and cast a glance around the room. A weapon. It would be better not to go to Alfonso with her hands empty. But what could she use? Her eyes fell on a heavy glass ashtray, and she dropped it into her bag. It would have to do.

She hurried from the room and down to the lobby. It was almost deserted, but she paid little attention to that. No taxis were waiting in front of the hotel as they usually did, so Valerie began to walk. She'd be late, but what could Alfonso do except wait for her? The streets were virtually deserted. Once Valerie spotted a police patrol as she rounded a corner and she ducked back hastily. When she peered around the edge of the building again it had gone, and she scurried on.

By the time she arrived at the river she was breathless and her feet ached. She located pier 7, where the de la Portilla boat was moored, and started down the long wooden jetty. She could see the boat in its slot, second from the end. For a second she stopped, panic filling her throat; then she forced her leaden feet to move again. She couldn't let Ashe down. As she neared the boat she spotted Alfonso on the deck, arms crossed and his brow knitted into a frown. He jumped onto the pier and grabbed her arm, hustling her toward the gangplank. "You're late!" he accused.

"I had to walk. There were no cabs out. I think the revolution's starting."

"We'll be safe at the plantation. The peasants are loyal." He steered her toward the shallow steps leading to the cabin.

"Where's Ashe? I want to see you take him off the boat, or I'm not going anywhere."

"We'll release him," he assured her. "He's no use to me now."

"That's the only reason why I believe that you'll let him go," Valerie retorted bitterly. "Now, where is he?"

"In the cabin." He shoved her toward the steps. Valerie ran down and flung open the cabin door.

"Ashe?" She stepped inside and glanced around the room. It was empty. She whirled as Alfonso entered and shut the door. His mouth curled into a sly grin. "Where is he?" Alfonso shrugged. "You don't have him!" Valerie burst out. "You never did, did you? What's happened to him?"

"I imagine that our dear Mr. Harlan is trying to catch up to a car speeding to San Mateo. He thinks you're in it, because I sent him a message at the Ministry of the Interior two hours ago."

Valerie's face paled with shock and anger. How could she have been so foolish? But she knew the answer. Her love and concern for Ashe had overwhelmed her common sense. She should have insisted on talking to him, but she had been afraid to take the chance. And, she had to admit, she had been thinking like Valerie Stanton, assuming the worst, taking the weakest position because she didn't believe she would win. She had expected Alfonso to stop her from leaving the country, and his lie about Ashe had confirmed her doubts. Ashe wouldn't have allowed himself to be taken. It was her lack of confidence that had made her accept the falsehood.

She slumped onto the edge of the bed in dejection. Tears burned at the corners of her eyes. Useless. Useless. She had failed again. Then she thought of Ashe and her new resolutions. If she could escape

Alfonso, she wouldn't have failed. She recalled the heavy ashtray inside her purse. Did she have the nerve to hit Alfonso with it? Yes. Oh, yes. She would have the nerve. In fact, she thought it would be a pleasure.

Valerie sneaked a glance at him from the corner of her eye. Alfonso was smirking as he leaned against the door, enjoying her despair. He was so certain that she would give up hopelessly that he hadn't even locked the door. If she let him continue to believe it, his guard would drop even more and she could get close enough to hit him. Valerie let the dammed-up tears flow, forcing out her sobs. She watched him from beneath her lashes as he moved toward her, smiling. "No, please, Alfonso," she sobbed aloud. "Don't make me marry Carlos. Please!" She began to babble that she would do anything, including signing over the money to him. He rocked up and down on his heels, pleased at her capitulation, and turned away, seeming to study the nautical picture on the wall.

Valerie knew that he was prolonging his moment of triumph, ignoring her pleas so she would continue to beg. She also knew that this was her best chance. Surreptitiously she opened the clasp of her bag and slipped her right hand into it. Her fingers closed around the thick glass ashtray. Valerie rose and started toward him, still pleading tearfully. Stubbornly he kept his back to her. Valerie smiled, her expression incongruous when compared with her broken voice. When she was directly behind him she whipped out the ashtray and brought it down as hard as she could on the back of Alfonso's head. He staggered forward, pitching onto the desk and bouncing off to land on the floor with a loud thump.

Valerie raced for the door and fairly flew up the steps and across the deck. Behind her she heard Alfonso shout, "Stop her! Don't let her leave!" She hadn't hit him hard enough.

One crewman stood at the opposite end of the boat, pushing the boat away from the pier. The crewman had already thrown off the mooring ropes, and the vessel floated from its slip. He heard the shout and stared at Valerie, frozen in a moment of indecision. Valerie took advantage of it to haul herself onto the top of the railing. She teetered for a moment, her breath swept away by the view of the water widening between the boat and the wooden pier. She closed her eyes and jumped with all her strength.

She landed hard on one foot and fell forward. A pain shot through her ankle, but she didn't have time to worry about it. Leaping to her feet, she cast a glance back at the boat. It was still bobbing away from her. The crewman gaped at her, and she saw Alfonso stagger to the top of the stairs.

Valerie sprinted away. Alfonso might be conscious, but he was swaying and unsteady. Besides, he was an aging, pudgy man. She ought to be able to outrun him . . . if the crewman didn't chase her. She pounded along the pier, but her ankle gave way suddenly and she pitched forward, rolling to the edge of the pier and crashing into one of the beams that supported it. The blow stunned her, but Valerie heard running footsteps and she pushed herself up. The pain in her ankle was fierce. She could do no more than limp along. Behind her the feet were gaining. Sobbing, Valerie hobbled forward. Her lungs were filled with fire and her ankle nearly buckled with every step. She reached the end of the pier and stumbled onto the rough dirt street. Ahead of her a long black limousine blasted onto the street and ground to a halt, dust billowing from beneath its tires. It must be Esteban. Valerie sank to the ground, defeated.

But it was a familiar lanky form that vaulted out of the back of the limousine and raced toward her. "Ashe!" Valerie struggled to rise. The crewman was almost upon her. But he, too, stopped, staring at the shouting madman hurtling toward them. He glanced toward the boat, where Alfonso stood screaming at him to grab Valerie. He looked back at Ashe, then broke and ran past Valerie down the street in the opposite direction from Ashe.

"Valerie!" Ashe knelt beside her. "Are you okay? Can you stand?"

Valerie nodded, gasping for air. Ashe dragged her to her feet and bent to scoop her up in his arms. He carried her to the car and settled her tenderly in the back seat. He slid in beside her, his face a mask, tight and pale. His eyes were so icy that they frightened Valerie. "If I had more time I'd go back and beat the living—" He bit off the words and continued in a softer tone. "Are you okay?"

"My ankle hurts, but other than that I'm all right."

Ashe nodded at the driver. "Hit it." They swooped away from the curb and turned in the middle of the street, heading toward the center of the city. They bumped over the rough pavement, and it seemed to Valerie that their driver was taking every narrow back street in La Luz.

"Ashe, where are we going? This isn't the way to the hotel."

"No. Our luggage is in the trunk. All hell's broken loose. The revolt's started. When I went to have your passport stamped I could hardly find anyone to approve it. Señor Carraboza was long gone, so the oil deal's still not signed. I cooled my jets in the Ministry of the Interior for a while and went to half a dozen different offices. Finally I persuaded a guy to stamp it by threatening to throw him out the third-floor window."

"Oh, Ashe!" Valerie suppressed a giggle.

"It's a madhouse. I realized there'd be no hope of flying out from the airport today, so I put my second plan into effect. That's where we're going now. We're taking the back streets to avoid the mobs, the revolutionaries and the army."

They rounded a corner and the car bounced to a stop. At the opposite end of the block was a swarm of people. The driver screeched backward, sending Valerie and Ashe sliding across the slick leather seat and crashing into the far door. Then the driver peeled out, taking a side street. Valerie struggled upright and peered out the back window of the car at the mob pelting after them. A rock bounced off the fender just as the car rocked around another corner, taking them out of sight of the mob. Valerie slipped down to a sitting position and turned to Ashe, her eyes wide with fear. "Are we going to get out of this?"

"Sure. Don't worry."

"How? Do you plan to drive across the border?" Valerie asked in disbelief. "There'll be fighting all over the country."

"Nope. We're flying out. Remember our friend Geraldo?"

"The stunt pilot?"

"The same. Cavaldos's Flying Service. I contacted him yesterday. He's my ace in the hole."

"I'm not sure which is worse." Another question popped into her mind. "Didn't you get Alfonso's message? He said he sent you a note to take you off on a wild-goose chase toward San Mateo."

Ashe raised his eyebrows. "No. We can thank the chaos in the ministry building for that. I was delayed getting the passport stamped. When I returned to the hotel you were gone. I was afraid you'd done something crazy like run out to find me because I was late. But I figured that if Alfonso had taken you, he would have gone to the docks to sail upriver to the plantation. I decided to check there before I started searching all over the city. Why did you leave the hotel? Did you go to look for me?"

Valerie shook her head. "No. I realized that we were both better off if I stayed in the room. But Alfonso called me and said he had you. He said he would release you if I went with him to the plantation and married Carlos."

Ashe's face softened and he brushed her cheek lightly with his knuckles. "You would have married Carlos to save me?"

"Yes." She paused and grinned impishly. "Of course, I was pretty sure you'd rescue me before the actual ceremony."

He pulled her close, resting his cheek against her hair. "Don't ever let me hear you say you aren't brave again. Understand?"

Valerie smiled. "Yes, sir."

"Oh, Val, if anything had happened to you, I don't know what I would have done."

They drove through rows of sagging tenement houses and emerged on a major thoroughfare. The driver blasted along the wide paved street for a few miles before he wheeled onto a narrow dirt road. Through the rear window Valerie could see the high buildings of La Luz behind them. "We're out of the city."

"Yeah." Ashe leaned forward to speak to the driver. "How long now?"

"Not far," the young man assured them, grinning.

"This guy must be Geraldo's first cousin, the way he drives," Valerie murmured to Ashe in a quiet aside.

He smiled. "That's just what I was thinking."

A light optimism flooded her. No matter what happened, Ashe could handle it. Her ankle was beginning to throb, but she was too happy to pay it any attention. The car bowled down the rutted dirt road, dust rising around it and blocking off any view except to the front. They swerved onto what seemed little more than a track. Within minutes the ramshackle tin barn of the flying service came into sight and they jounced across a field toward it. Valerie was sure that any vestige of a road had long since disappeared. Ashe and Valerie were bounced against the roof of the car and tossed from side to side. Once Valerie even found herself sitting on the floor. But eventually they arrived on the smooth asphalt of the flying service's parking lot.

Valerie caught sight of the fragile four-seater plane in which they had flown from San Mateo. Leaning against its side was their grinning pilot, Geraldo Munez. He waved to them merrily. After he greeted the driver of the car he turned to Ashe, and together they stowed the luggage in the plane. Then Ashe carried Valerie to the plane, ignoring her protests that she could walk. She buckled herself into the seat, closed her eyes and hoped they'd take off without crashing.

As before, Munez chattered nonstop while he taxied and took off. When they were in the air he reached back to pat Valerie's hand reassuringly. "Don't worry. We can't get lost. All we have to do is follow the mountains." He pointed to the left at the distant spine of the Sierra Azul mountains, which ran the length of San Cristóbal. It seemed a rather vague flight plan to Valerie, but she shrugged. They'd made it before. She'd have to trust Munez to do it again.

Several hours later they landed at a private airport close to Mexico City. Customs officials deferentially scanned their passports and luggage in a small private office in the airport and let them go. Valerie suspected that that was the hand of Alec Stone at work. A conservative brown Mercedes with a driver waited to speed them into Mexico City. Valerie fell asleep in the back of the car, and when she awoke they had pulled into the circular drive of a large, elegant hotel. The hotel doorman opened the car door, bending solicitously to help her out.

It took a good deal of time to check in, request a doctor's services and locate a wheelchair for Valerie, whose ankle was swollen and throbbing. She refused to let Ashe carry her through the lobby, but she had to admit that she was unable to walk. A porter whisked her chair into the elevator and up to the top floor, where he opened the door to a plush suite. Ashe lifted Valerie out of the wheelchair and set her on the couch, then tipped the porter. As the man left Valerie glanced around the spacious sitting room. "Well, well, Mr. Harlan; you must be a wealthy man."

He grinned. "Nope, just planning to marry a wealthy lady."

Valerie stared, her heart pounding, hardly daring to

believe what he was hinting at. Finally, through blood-less lips she whispered, "Who?"

"Oh, one of the Stantons." She could think of nothing to say, and finally he burst out, "Well, Valerie? End my misery. Is it yes or no?"

"That wasn't exactly a proposal," she hedged.

"All right." He went down on one knee, a hand placed melodramatically over his heart. "Miss Stanton, er, that is, Mrs. de la Portilla, would you do me the infinite honor of giving me your hand in marriage? I have admired you from afar for some time. If I cannot marry you, I will never marry. You have every quality admirable in a wife. You move with grace, speak with charm . . . and have the sexiest legs I ever saw."

Valerie burst into laughter. "What a charming pro-posal. How can I refuse? Oh, Ashe, yes, yes, of course I'll marry you. That is, if you're sure. We haven't known each other very long."

"It doesn't take me long to make up my mind." His face sobered and he caught her hands between his, raising them to his lips. "Val, I mean it. I love you. Forever and ever. I'm a one-woman man."

"I love *you*," she whispered in return, her eyes shining with proof.

Behind them someone loudly cleared his throat. They jumped and whirled to see a portly gentleman in a rumpled suit standing in the doorway, black bag in hand. "I'm Dr. Mendoza," he explained. "I under-stand that you sent for the house doctor."

"What? Oh. Oh, yes."

Valerie had to smile at Ashe's discomfiture. The doctor entered placidly, as if he hadn't walked in on Ashe kneeling before Valerie like a nineteenth-century swain. While the doctor probed her ankle Ashe placed a telephone call to Dallas. As he spoke in low tones into the receiver Dr. Mendoza poked and prodded at the sore ankle until Valerie cried out. Then he wrapped it carefully and handed her a small bottle of pills. "It's not broken, merely sprained," he assured her. "Take these for the pain. You should heal in a few days. If not, send for me."

Valerie nodded, thanking him, and the doctor left, discreetly closing the door after him. Valerie glanced at Ashe, who was seated by the window, still cradling the receiver against his shoulder. He smiled at her and winked, then covered the receiver. "Just giving Alec and Laraine the good news," he stage-whispered.

"Ask about Cara's baby," Valerie urged. "Has she had it?"

Ashe rolled his eyes as if to say "Women!" but obliged her. When at last he hung up the phone she burst out impatiently, "Well, was it a boy or a girl?"

"What a thing to think about at a time like this. You just escaped from a kidnapping and a revolution and received a marriage proposal. And all you can say is, 'What was Cara's baby?'"

Valerie lifted her chin. "Well, I want to know. Laraine would understand."

Ashe chuckled. "I'm sure she would. She'd already told me about it, right after she asked if you and I were both alive."

"Then quit keeping me in suspense, you monster!"

"It was a girl. A big, healthy girl, and they named her Anna."

"Really? How nice." She smiled, her eyes sparkling. There was something warming about the news of a baby's arrival, even when she didn't know the mother well. But this baby would be part of her family, and the thought flooded her with sentimental pleasure.

"I told Alec that since your ankle was bad, we intended to spend another week here. A honeymoon in advance, so to speak."

"I don't know. We might as well go home," Valerie mused. "With this ankle, we can't do any sight-seeing."

Hands on his hips, he growled, "Lady, sight-seeing isn't exactly what I had in mind."

"Oh?" she questioned innocently. "And what is?"

"This." He strode forward and knelt beside her.

Taking her face between his hands, he kissed her thoroughly. When at last he drew back Valerie was flushed and her breathing irregular.

"Good," she whispered, "because that's what I had in mind, too." She twined her arms around his neck and pulled him to her for another kiss.

Silhouette
Intimate Moments

more romance, more excitement

$2.25 each

SILHOUETTE INTIMATE MOMENTS, Department IM/5
1230 Avenue of the Americas
New York, NY 10020

Please send me the books I have checked above. I am enclosing
$_____ (please add 50¢ to cover postage and handling. NYS
and NYC residents please add appropriate sales tax.) Send check or
money order—no cash or C.O.D.'s please. Allow six weeks for delivery.

NAME _____

ADDRESS _____

CITY _____ STATE/ZIP _____

Silhouette Intimate Moments

Coming Next Month

Raven's Prey by Stephanie James

Honor Knight had to convince Judd Raven the two men who
had hired him to find her weren't her father and brother.
Only Honor hadn't realized Judd was holding her prisoner
for his own reason: he was in love.

Against The Rules by Linda Howard

At seventeen Cathryn Ashe had fought Rule Jackson and lost.
Now, more sure of herself and her new-found independence,
she was ready to challenge him again—only this time,
her heart was at stake.

The Fires Of Winter by Beverly Bird

As editor of a small paper, Heather Cavelle tried to write only
of the good in the world. Then David Sullivan took over and
plunged the paper into a search for crime and hidden truths,
and what they discovered was their love for each other.

Fantasies by Pamela Wallace

When Spencer Tait met the new studio president
Devon O'Neill they clashed immediately. Tensions were high
and the future at stake as the cameras rolled—because this
time, the real story was taking place behind the scenes.

Dear Reader:

Please take a few moments to fill out this questionnaire. It will help us give you more of the Silhouette Intimate Moments you'd like best.

Mail to: **Karen Solem**
Silhouette Books
1230 Ave. of the Americas, New York, N.Y. 10020

1. How did you obtain **THE AMBER SKY?** `9-17`

10-1 ☐ **Bookstore**   -6 ☐ **Newsstand**
  -2 ☐ **Supermarket**   -7 ☐ **Airport**
  -3 ☐ **Variety/discount store**   -8 ☐ **Book Club**
  -4 ☐ **Department store**   -9 ☐ **From a friend**
  -5 ☐ **Drug store**   -0 ☐ **Other:**_____
                                              (write in)

2. How many Silhouette Intimate Moments have you read including this one?
(circle one number) 11- **1 2 3 4 5 6 7 8 9 10 11 12 13 14 15 16**

3. Overall how would you rate this book?
12-1 ☐ **Excellent** -2 ☐ **Very good**
  -3 ☐ **Good** -4 ☐ **Fair** -5 ☐ **Poor**

4. Which elements did you like best about this book?
13-1 ☐ **Heroine** -2 ☐ **Hero** -3 ☐ **Setting** -4 ☐ **Story line**
  -5 ☐ **Love scenes** -6 ☐ **Ending** -7 ☐ **Other Characters**

5. Do you prefer love scenes that are
14-1 ☐ **Less explicit than**   -2 ☐ **More explicit than**
      in this book   **in this book**
      -3 ☐ **About as explicit as in this book**

6. What influenced you most in deciding to buy this book?
15-1 ☐ **Cover** -2 ☐ **Title** -3 ☐ **Back cover copy**
  -4 ☐ **Recommendations** -5 ☐ **You buy all Silhouette Books**

7. How likely would you be to purchase other Silhouette Intimate Moments in the future?
16-1 ☐ **Extremely likely**   -3 ☐ **Not very likely**
  -2 ☐ **Somewhat likely**   -4 ☐ **Not at all likely**

8. Do you prefer books at (check one)
17-1 ☐ **A longer length of 256 pages?** **-3 Other:** _____
  -2 ☐ **A shorter length of 192 pages?**   (write in)

9. Will INTIMATE MOMENTS affect your purchasing SILHOUETTE DESIRES? 18-1 ☐ yes -2 ☐ no

10. Please check the box next to your age group.
19-1 ☐ **Under 18**   -3 ☐ **25-34**   -5 ☐ **50-54**
  -2 ☐ **18-24**   -4 ☐ **35-49**   -6 ☐ **55 +**

11. Would you be interested in receiving a romance newsletter? If so please fill in your name and address.

Name_____

Address_____

City_____ State_____ Zip_____

                          19___20___21___22___23___